Web of

– KATHLEEN STEELE –

FASTPRINT PUBLISHING
PETERBOROUGH, ENGLAND

FastPrint

www.fast-print.net/store.php

WEB OF TORMENT

All characters are fictional. Any similarity to any action person is purely coincidental

ISBN 978-184426-874-0

First published 2010 by
FASTPRINT PUBLISHING
Peterborough, England.

An environmentally friendly book printed and bound in England by
www.printondemand-worldwide.com

Mixed Sources
Product group from well-managed forests, and other controlled sources
www.fsc.org Cert no. TT-COC-002641
© 1996 Forest Stewardship Council
FSC

PEFC Certified
This product is from sustainably managed forests and controlled sources
www.pefc.org
PEFC
PEFC/16-33-415

This book is made entirely of chain-of-custody materials

Chapter One

The Arrivals Hall in the International Airport at Fuerteventura was thronged with folk all of whom were desperate to hear news of their loved ones. Folk who were here because their loved ones should have already have arrived on a flight that for some unknown reason had never landed! Still showing abject disbelief at the sign that indicated that this flight had been delayed they were thus forced to watch as other passengers from off different flights to this area made their way out of the Customs area. Some of those who were waiting spoke only in sombre whispers; others paced the tiled floor as if by doing this the delayed flight would miraculously re-appear amongst the listings, whilst still others held the agonising fear of what could have happened to the plane that had left its home base supposedly on schedule, whilst all the while the time ticked monotonously by and the mechanism moved the fingers around the face of the clock that was set high above their heads.

Perhaps because she was unable to bear the agonising expression in the faces of those waiting relatives, Rachel turned away. It was not that she was being a coward for after all she wasn't even sure that he would be on that flight and even if he was then there would be a decision for her to make that so far she had avoided, for in truth she had not reached a decision about it. In fact she had come to the airport today more in anticipation than anything else for she knew that one way or another she had to try to seek amends for the past.

In all truth Rachel had to admit that Brad had been good for her for it was through his efforts that she had been launched upon her literary career. It was Brad who had been the one to support her through that long period of rehabilitation and yet, despite his many kindness she had spurned the feelings he professed that he felt about her, claiming that the time was not yet ripe for her to make any such decisions. But now after this lengthy time lapse the time of decision had finally arrived and yet she was still not clear about her future.

It was as she turned whilst still in that Arrivals Hall that she almost collided with yet another figure. She recognised the person immediately for she was positive that this was a man that she had been watching on the beach earlier the same morning, for she had been quite fascinated with the fellow's exploits on the surfboard as he appeared to be taking some lesson in how to perfect further skills!

"Sorry!" The fault, she realised, was her own and she began her apology in a somewhat flustered manner.

Much to her surprise he gave her a crooked grin. "Surely there is no need for apologies at a time like this-------Lance Turner!" He extended a hand to introduce himself. "Were you expecting someone on the flight then?"

"Yes ----Well actually I'm not absolutely sure!" It was little wonder that he now showed an element of surprise at her answer. "Well that is I thought that my employer could possibly have been on that flight. I already know that he intends flying out here, I understood that it was today, and I felt it imperative that I should meet him!"

Upon that the stranger opened his eyes wide. She knew full well that such rhetoric sounded feeble in anybody's tongue and yet she was almost certain that she now saw a spark of interest flash into the brown eyes that were regarding her own. "It seems to be a very bad business Miss –err------?" Her companion now appeared to have drifted off into thought.

"Rachel ----Rachel Aldred!"

"Correct me if I am wrong but I believe you were on the promenade at El Castillo earlier this morning?" His look of puzzlement had now turned to one of recognition. How on earth he could remember seeing someone who was just sat gazing out to sea whilst he himself had been in the throes of attempting difficult windsurfing turns she had no idea. She remembered that at the time it had been quiet and peaceful on the beach nestling around the cove with only the lapping of the tide to furnish the sound effects to the silent world before the visitors arrived who came after partaking of their breakfasts. She had in fact just picked up her book with her mind now firmly fixed in the process of creation when she had spotted his feet in the sand as he made to cross over the beach to that windsurfing school and at the time she had found herself quite fascinated in watching the two men, one of whom was obviously the teacher whilst the student himself had appeared to be no novice at this sport

"Guess I was attempting to chill out a little before I came here!" Her answer seemed to satisfy him but on the other hand he never attempted to explain why he himself was currently at this airport.

Further conversation however appeared to be none forthcoming for it was just then that a voice calling out over the Tannoy system required all those persons waiting for the arrival of flight E 7197 to go to a place that had been set aside from the main gate area. She supposed she instinctively knew before she went that it would be bad news and she was not to be disappointed for it now appeared that the flight had disappeared from off the radar screens and although there had been no May Day alert as such, the signs now looked rather ominous. There were a bevy of councillors there to assist and many of the folk who were waiting and in obvious distress appeared only too glad to take advantage of their presence but feeling she had heard enough Rachel turned away perhaps even looking for the stranger whom she had met briefly in the Arrivals Hall Maybe she would have asked him if he had any idea what all this meant. But of that man there was now no sign. It was almost as if he had disappeared into thin air!

-----------The next time that Rachel indeed clapped her eyes on Lance Turner was when he came up out of the sea close to where the rocky pools lay just off the shore in Tenerife. Of course a great deal had happened in the intervening period. The fact that Brad had never made it and was now presumed dead along with many others was one thing. The fact that she had never been subjected to give him the answer that he wanted was another and something she felt distinctly disturbed about.

She supposed that he had been egoistic when she had first answered his advert for a Girl Friday on the web. At the time her sister had strongly disapproved and had informed her in no uncertain terms that she was wasting her time toying with that thing instead of facing reality and finding herself a proper job. But after the collapse of her old firm not to mention the fact that she had discovered the one person she believed she had loved was already married and was simply looking for some outside attraction Rachel had lapsed into a form of escapism and the web had been the highway in leading her forward to accomplish this. Employed primarily as his secretary Brad had soon discovered her flair for the written word and had encouraged her to write, meticulously reading through her work in this field and helping her to develop her unique style. Thrown together in this way she supposed it was inevitable that Brad would soon want to further their relationship. In fact the man had finally asked her to marry him. Yet the question even then had raised its ugly head. Did she in fact really love him? That was when her mind in something of a turmoil she had begged for time to think upon the matter and consequently had found the holiday to Fuerteventura to do just that. Yet for his part, Brad, had decided after a suitable lapse of time, that he had some sort of a business deal to cement in the area and therefore he had decided to come himself for her answer!

--------She remembered returning back to England still without experiencing any remorse at what had happened for in truth this accident had possibly saved her from making the inevitable choice and that in itself was something of a relief!

Of course her sister and family had been very supportive of her when she had finally returned and they had rapidly decided that the girl must be suffering from trauma after such an event, not to mention this all happening on top of the previous upset in her life. Nothing however could have been further from the truth. For although she was sorry that Brad had been taken from them in this way, in some senses for her it had been a happy release. But this was the secret she had been determined to keep to herself, and therefore it had been easier all round to let them think that she was after all, mourning for the man that her family had been determined she was about to marry!

Still she had to admit that she was surprised when Mandy had come up with this notion. She had known of course that her sister and her husband had booked a holiday but when they had suggested that she should come with them to Tenerife she had in the first instance refused. But then her brother in law was not in the habit of taking no for an answer and she supposed that after he went to the trouble of obtaining additional accommodation and a seat on the flight for her she could do no other than accept with the proviso that she would be prepared to look after little Jake should the need arise, a stipulation that they had reluctantly accepted!

At this time however her eyes were focussed on the Island that was currently shrouded in mist giving an almost eerie scenario to the picture in front of her. Now with the breeze plying upon the windbreaks the sea itself had become a little choppy in the last hour or so. At least she assumed that was the reason why she had not spotted the swimmer before. As it was, with the hotel built after the manner of a ship giving the appearance it could weather any storm that the Atlantic dare throw up at it, the ocean had become a fascinating medium to watch from off her balcony, confined as she was that day through no reason of her own.

It was merely idle supposition that led her to believe that the man must have been snorkelling, for there were others also clinging with such apparatus in those rocky inlets that provided them with a temporary shelter from the tide, a place where they could catch their breath before venturing out again into the ocean currents. But strangely enough this individual appeared to be on his own for he certainly did not stop to exchange pleasantries with any of the other sun worshippers. Instead he made to make his way off the beach wrapped only in the towel that he had clutched from off one of those rocks and now she actually believed that he was making in the direction of the hotel.

Her attention was diverted at that point by the sound of a child's fretful whimper and she turned away to attend to her nephew.

"Too much sun!" The doctor at the hotel had peered at her over his spectacles as he had given his verdict earlier on that day, at the same time obviously blaming her for lack of attention and insinuating that with all the recent adverse publicity she should have known better than allow a child to subject himself to this. Not that it was her child, but she had promised that she would care for little Jake whilst Mandy and her husband went on that long awaited boat trip to see the whales and dolphins in their natural habitat, basically she believed so that she could ease her conscience, and therefore she had not enlightened the medic that the boy was not her own.

After soothing the child with a cooling drink and wiping his fevered brow, Rachel returned once again to her balcony position. The man she had spotted earlier had now completely disappeared and therefore she idly fixed her eyes on the small town she could just about make out from her present position. She supposed in some ways the old town had few redeeming features perched as it was on the side of those rocks that surrounded a quiet bay whilst it stubbornly chose to ignore the erosion that the sea had already caused in pounding the shore year after year. Indeed in acts of down right defiance against this element man had sculptured steps leading down onto those rocks that had once been part of the shoreline in order to brag of his own close proximity to the ocean. But the Atlantic, schooled in years of wisdom, had merely laughed at man's endeavours for it well understood the need to bide its time, for hadn't it been doing exactly this since well before man had first inhabited the earth?

. Watching the fishermen in that quarter now busy with their nets Rachel turned her attention to where one particular boat had recently been recently hauled out of the water. A working vessel, it seemed obvious that it had been bought there for some minor repairs before it was due to commence work again later that night. But now it was the figure of the diver who caught her eye, still wearing that towel slung loosely around him to soak up the surplus water, something that easily identified him as he spoke to a member of the crew,

She pulled herself sharply back to reality. Really none of this was any of her business; indeed she was only watching the scene because she was at a loss for something else to do as she awaited her sister's return. Not that she had any notion of staking herself out on any sun-bed even when they returned for she had already eyed the toasted lumps that the sun had left in its wake. No her idea when the family finally came back was to obtain a nice cooling swim but after what she had observed around the hotel pool it did little to titillate her palate. Instead she imagined now the waves of the ocean riding on her back!

Thus whilst she accepted the thanks that was proffered to her upon her sister's return, she didn't really want to hear those tones of enthusiasm upon their own day's sailing nor even the number of dolphins and whales that they had spotted. And in turn she supposed that they accepted the fact that Rachel herself felt the need to now chill out. Still she supposed when she muted the idea of going for a swim they had in their wisdom visualised that she intended to go to use the hotel pool and therefore she couldn't help but wonder whether their enthusiasm would have lasted if they had realised that she had little intention of heading in that pool's direction.

Finally reaching the shore she realised that the wind itself had change direction during the afternoon thus provoking the sea to act out its part with a thundering crashing motion along the coast, leaving those small boats that were still anchored off the port to bob around in a somewhat unregulated manner whilst the nearby bore holes sounded out a tympani as they expelled the sea that had invaded their terrain, with spurts of froth. Today with the water level still being high it was not the perfect condition for the natural inhabitants of the place even though the human kind relished the breeze that had now served to regulate the previous high temperature. But even though the bajas had all but disappeared under the mass of water man still appeared to be keen to sample this mass and Rachel, after waiting for so long was no exception to this rule. Besides she was a strong swimmer this at least was one of her attributes although after the recent past she doubted whether she had many others left and therefore she thought little about entering that mass. No more that was until she felt a pair of strong arms holding her back and an angry voice now in the midst of some tirade.

"Have you not read the warning signs woman? Don't you realise that it is dangerous to attempt to swim in conditions like these especially for the inexperienced?" The voice almost snapped as he issued forth his challenge. Of course she supposed he wasn't to know that she was a strong swimmer and not so inexperienced as what he wanted to make out. In fairness she supposed she had momentarily allowed her mind to languish in the pulsating motion that would invigorate her very being but she could not have described herself as being in any immediate danger.

Turning to face her would be rescuer and anxious to deliver a short clip back for his angry tirade Rachel was forced to pause under the gaze of those luminous brown eyes that appeared capable of piercing through the portals of her head. But it was not her voice that sounded out now in the afternoon air. "You? But what are you doing here? I thought I left you in Fuerteventura!"

She felt tempted to make a rejoinder by telling him that she was in the process of Island hopping but quickly realised that this man would hardly share the same sense of humour. "Me, oh I am here with my family!"

Perhaps he looked a little crestfallen at these words although why he should feel that way she had no idea. "Your employer, the person you went to meet at the airport that day, what eventually happened?" So he had remembered her.

"I'm afraid he was eventually presumed dead, although there was never any confirmation by the recovery of a body. But from what I was later told he did actually leave England on that plane!"

"Then I am indeed very sorry to hear about it!" There was still no explanation forthcoming as to his own role at the airport on that fateful day. Still she wasn't all that interested, or so she told herself, or was she? "So what made you decide to enter the sea in conditions like these?" He had now returned to his initial subject matter.

"Believe it or not but I am a strong swimmer!" She wondered now whether she was defending herself against some sort of poetic injustice.

"But not I deem strong enough for conditions like these that can blow up almost instantaneously!"

"Such conditions did not appear to stop yourself!" The words had been issued before she realised it.

"So you have been watching me again have you Miss Aldred?" He seemed in addition to remembering her name to be ready for her retort.

"Not intentionally I can assure you!" She tried to give the impression that it had been a mere coincidence,

"Well to save you from craning your eyes any further I'll tell you my next move for nothing. I was actually in the process of returning to the hotel when I spotted you. Therefore maybe I ought to suggest that you accompany me. I presume that is where you are presently staying?"

She nodded for there was little else she could do under the circumstances even though a goodly part of her still wanted to defy the man, to refuse to let him have the last word on this issue. Even so perhaps the added bonus was to be able to walk alongside of him back through the gardens of the place. "You haven't been away long?" It was Mandy who queried her presence at being back so soon.

"The day has changed it sort of put me off!" She crossed her fingers behind her back as she spoke the words. She had never been known to lie to Mandy, but then conditions had not warranted it except perhaps in one or two isolated cases and strangely enough one of these cases appeared to be the man with those brown eyes that were even now haunting her.

Still it was never planned that they would be in the Restaurant at the same time that evening for it was there that the salad buffet table began to take on a new meaning. But any anticipated pleasantries were to be short lived once a small pair of hands belonging to a child who now felt much better started to tug on her skirt and Lance looking down at the small boy for some obscure reason immediately presumed that Jake was her own. That was when he turned away and Rachel was left with a strong feeling of disbelief at his action!

She later remembered that the craft was there when she woke the next morning. In fact it appeared to have been there all night anchored approximately some fifty metres or so off the shore with its spotlights blazing and lighting up the night sky. Even before she had left the confines of her bed she had heard the humming noise of a generator powering the vessel and because she had simultaneously roused she had ventured outside onto the balcony to try to see what it was after first dismissing the idea that the noise could be a new dance craze that had seeded its sound through the night air! Noticing the craft at first she had presumed that it was some sort of fishing vessel that had put out from the tiny port, after all there were others present in that bay with their lights shining in the night sky. Not that these were in the same position as the other vessel that seemed to be anchored quite close to the hotel and by the first sign of dawn these other fishing vessels had returned to the shore with their night time haul, ready to make the markets with their wares. But this one had not returned with them and as it became lighter it was now possible to discern that this was not the single vessel she had first envisaged but rather two vessels that were anchored together almost as if they were Siamese twins!

Now able to discern its features more clearly in the morning light neither could she describe it as appearing to be anything like a fishing vessel. Intrigued as she might have been it was then that she heard her sister about in the next room and therefore she called out to her to come and take a look, but by the time that Mandy had finally stumbled over to the window, grumbling at being disturbed at this ungodly hour, the boats, if that is what one could call them, had also taken it upon themselves to disappear, and neither could Rachel spot any sign of them approaching the tiny port itself!

Yet even as she still watched possibly mesmerised with the scene she was convinced that she spotted a small rowing tender from the vessel approaching the shore with two men on board. What appeared to be more significant was that one of the two happened to be someone she had seen before!

“Probably some sort of a survey vessel sampling the waters off the coast!” Douglas Ogden looked up from his morning newspaper in an attempt to answer his sister in law’s bleating at breakfast later on that morning for in truth she was still confused as to what the vessel could have been. Yet her brother in law apparently did not care to be disturbed when in the midst of one of his morning rituals but nevertheless he had decided that perhaps the lesser of two evils was to attempt to shut his sister in law up on the matter. Well she supposed that was typical of Dougie, completely down to earth about such matters. Still Rachel was the first to admit that he and Mandy appeared to have a nigh on perfect relationship. At least she could say that her sister did not appear to have made the same mistake in life as what she had done although perhaps Mandy's choosing of a mate had at first surprised her!

Still call it her creative spirit or whatever you will but the subject of that vessel was still on her mind when the family decided to cross the bridge onto the Island later on that same morning mainly because young Jake, now feeling much better after his enforced rest, was demanding to go on the beach and after due consideration Mandy had declared that there might possibly be some shade still in evidence in that direction at this time of the day!

They had mastered the first set of steps necessary to climb up from the hotel where they were staying in order to cross the bridge to the Island before they then dropped down into the neighbouring resort when Rachel was convinced she spotted that vessel again but this time it appeared to be making towards the port where they were heading themselves. She knew full well it was the same craft because of the distinguishing markings she had noticed on it earlier and her mouth must have sagged open in surprise at the sight for the next thing she knew she was being treated to a load of verbal abuse from Doug who had by this time managed to climb to a higher position than what she was herself.

"Now what's the matter? Don't tell me that you are having trouble keeping up with us older ones now!" He eyed her rather critically.

"It's the same boat, the one I saw before just off the hotel!" Ignoring his comments she made some effort to point but in response her brother in law let out a throaty chuckle.

"You've got a damned fixation on boats Rachel but before you get any more ideas that is merely a large fishing vessel!"

Rachel said no more. She was only puzzled as to why she had seen that rowing boat leaving this craft earlier on that morning, and possibly, what was even more to the point what her male encounter of the previous day had been doing on board it!

Perhaps she decided that she had a better chance of finding the answer to this conundrum when she spotted him yet again in the Restaurant that evening for he looked across the bar range and for a brief moment his eyes met her own. Possibly realising that she was watching him he left his own things to make his way across to her.

"Guess we'll really have to stop meeting like this!" His tone was jocular yet she got little further with her answer when she was to be disturbed once more by Jake, this time demanding to know what was taking his Aunt all this time. Misconstruing the situation Lance hastened to make his excuses.

"Damn and blast it!" Rachel gave a voice to her feelings as she returned to their own table.

"I beg your pardon, what's the matter now?" It was her sister who spoke. Mandy, who objected most voluminously to any such disturbance at the dinner table, more especially in front of Jake.

"Oh nothing sorry it was just a thought!" Well she supposed that she could hardly bleat out the fact that the child was to blame for spoiling an opportunity she had spied.

In return her sister gave her a nod of understanding. She knew full well that Rachel was still in the process of recovering from a traumatic experience, and that in addition to the previous one she had experienced in her short life, and therefore she had good reason to suppose that such occasional outbursts were only to be expected.

"Tell me, how do you fancy a bus ride tomorrow Rachel? Jake has been belly aching that it is time he visited the water park and I suppose now that he is better we might as well go along with the idea!"

"Not if I can plead to be excused!" Rachel pulled a face at the very idea. "Besides I really think that you three ought to spend some time as a family together. As it is you have been more than good to me already. But don't worry I can assure you that I can find plenty of things for me to occupy myself with around here whilst you are away!"

"Such as? We are certainly not going to leave you here simply to mope all on your own?" The girl obviously still had something of a guilt complex over leaving her sister determined as the woman was that Rachel was still reacting to the trauma in her life.

"I can promise you that I most certainly will not be moping! For starters I'll probably want to catch up on my beauty sleep if we stay up for that show tonight because in point of fact I'm not really a nighthawk. After that I'll probably find a nice quiet spot either around the pool or on the promenade and catch up with some of the reading matter I brought with me. One thing that is dependable round these parts is the weather is simply ideal for doing things like that!"

Matters were left very much like that until the following morning when the usual rigmarole commenced, so much so that Rachel felt she would be glad when that bus arrived to carry them off. As usual Doug seemed to be oblivious to all the fervour whilst he was immersed in his morning newspaper.

"I see that they are opening up a further route to Miami from here --- well from Tenerife North as a matter of fact. Anyway you know what that will mean. American tourists here and we'll soon see the prices rising even further as if things aren't dear enough already!" He grumbled as he picked upon one particular article amongst many.

Rachel herself peered across the table to ascertain whether this was his usual Times he was prevaricating off. Make no mistake her brother in law was a lovely person and someone she was very fond of. Yet although the man had a good brain on his shoulders there was little room for any creativity within it! Indeed she had often wondered what had motivated him to work as a steel constructor rather than choosing a more academic career. In fact she had been quite surprised when Mandy and he had taken up together for they were two whose paths, one would have thought, would have never crossed.

"I hope there's no trouble!" Now all eyes were fixed in Amanda's direction. Occasionally it had been known for the girl to come out with some well-chosen pearls of wisdom for despite her earlier academic qualifications she appeared to be now overshadowed by her husband.

"What do you mean?" It was the man who spoke indicating that he thoroughly hated anyone to interrupt when he was in full flow and that included even his wife!

"Jake will you put that down immediately!" The child was quite obviously back on form this morning. "No, I'm sorry but you will have to just sit and wait for us to finish. You are not to leave do you understand or there will be no water park for you my boy! No Doug, I was just referring to that article you read out the other day when you said that it was rumoured that Al Queda was regrouping in the Sahara!"

"Paper talk only!" Obviously Dougie had forgotten his previous outburst.

"If you two will excuse me whilst you continue playing happy families!" It was Rachel's turn this time knowing where this conversation was likely to lead. "Come on Jake you can come with me whilst your Mum and Dad finish their breakfast!"

The child trustingly placed in hand in her own happy to seize the opportunity to get out of this stuffy dining room now that he had eaten his fill! They had in fact almost reached the door to the place when they ran into Lance who was currently coming in the opposite direction. The man glanced down instantaneously in Jake's direction.

"I trust your child is feeling better this morning?"

"My child! What on earth do you mean?" Rachel suddenly let out a laugh. "Jake happens to be my sister's child, my nephew for want of a better word!" She could have sworn that the expression on his face that had initially looked rather foreboding changed upon her words. He even appeared to be a little more approachable.

"I'm sorry but I thought -----!"

"You thought that Jake was mine! Well I'm sorry to disappoint you Mr Turner but I have no such entanglements!" And with that she left him standing there as she grasped the child by the arm, determined that this little imp would not make for the children's playground especially as that place happened to be in full view of the dining room!

He was out there again in that rowing boat, of that she was now quite convinced. At the time she had been glancing down at the Bajas that the corporation had adopted for use by the local folk as a safe sea washed place where they could bathe. Having finally got rid of the family she supposed she had gone there initially to see if it captured her imagination and set her creative vibes alight for she was determined that these would not perish alongside of Brad, but now in the light of her current observations that was all forgotten.

Yet the man she saw was not fishing from that boat. Indeed he appeared to be waiting for someone, and possibly sensing a good plot Rachel's nose began to twitch in anticipation. Well after all that was what she had set herself out to do today! It was when the larger vessel appeared around the corner heading from the port she realised that this must surely be what he had been waiting for and consequently her curiosity grew even stronger in anticipation of what might happen next!

Strangely enough before the man she had been watching finally rowed across to the larger vessel he chose to look up towards the promontory upon which she was stood. He could hardly mistake the fact that she was there for at the time she was on her own for the place was not crowded with other tourists choosing to take the short cut across the Island. Not only that but the sun had seized upon that particular moment to pause behind some waiting clouds therefore she could not hope that the sunlight had served to detract him. Even so after pausing for a full minute and looking up in her direction he finally carried on and Rachel in turn now felt glad to scamper away like some wilful schoolgirl who had disobeyed the house rules. The whole thing was ridiculous really especially when she felt the need to scurry like some frightened rat back to the hotel pool area, which was not the place she had intended to make towards in the first place.

By the time she arrived back however Rachel found that she had something to pout about. For here she had been determined to spend the day in becoming creative but the next thing that seemed to happen was that the sun now decided to take a longer break than was absolutely necessary and therefore the Island she was basing her supposed tale upon was nowhere to be seen that day of all days! She sat back at least meaning to relax and possibly waiting for the mist to finally clear. The next thing she remembered was that she became conscious of a shadow that had fallen across the page she was attempting to scribble upon and she inadvertently jumped up presuming that she must have dozed off.

"Sand in the atmosphere blowing from the Sahara, it tends to obscure the place sometimes!" She heard a voice informing her, not that she felt that was much consolation to her creative muse, but the voice she definitely recognised. The words had been issued in a casual fashion and yet even as they were uttered Rachel felt that this man had still more to say, She waited and he didn't disappoint her. "Tell me, have you ever been there?"

"Me go to the Sahara? That's a funny question. No I haven't been there nor am I in any hurry to fill in my lack of experience. In fact I've never had any inclination to venture further than these Islands. I guess they are my ultimate goal as far as destinations go. But why do you ask?"

"Oh simple curiosity that's all!" He now seemed keen to change the subject and he appeared to do that rather quickly to her mind. "Well at least one ought to be glad that you are not trying to drown yourself today. That I suppose can be said to be one mercy!"

"I notice that you are not playing about with your boats either!" The well-deserved retort flipped off her tongue in a typical Rachel fashion. Indeed her family had often warned her in the past that her tongue would probably toll the death knolls for her!

"Boats?" He responded almost quizzically. How could anyone put on an innocent expression in that manner especially when she knew the truth? Mind you she was sure that with this mist it must provide the fodder she could develop in one of her future characters. "Oh I suppose you spotted me helping out at the boatyard when they needed a hand. I guess I have a particular yen for intricate machinery and the fellows who were there didn't seem to mind me interfering too much!" He laughed at what he considered to be a pun against himself but Rachel found she was dying to question him about the other times she had seen him with a boat that day!

"No swimming is for later I think!" Deliberately she reverted back to his original question whilst she invented a new strategy. "First I need to catch up with my novel!"

"And the family have left you alone to do that?"

What damned business was it of his? Still she nodded almost complacently now in her response.

"Then how are you at scuba diving?" Well this was something that she certainly had not expected.

"I haven't a clue. I've never tried it so I don't pretend to know!" Well at least she supposed that was the truth.

"In that case I will teach you if you wish. I believe you said that you were a strong swimmer. Well believe me when I say that whilst you are swimming on the surface you are also missing out on an awful lot on what goes on under the water!"

She was mesmerised by his words. Why on earth, she asked herself, should this man offer to teach her? Yet it was her emotions that appeared to settle before common sense prevailed. "Well put like that I suppose it would be churlish of me not to have a go. Still what with scuba diving and wind surfing you must be able to claim the honour of being an all round sportsman!"

"I thought I told you I went to Fuerteventura to perfect my skills with the experts there, something that I had always had a yearning to do but seldom got the opportunity. Have you never felt that way about something? But I can assure you that it is merely a hobby even though it does have serious overtones in that the attributes I have acquired I can also use back home to help disabled children!"

She had been ready with a retort but his words now served to halt her tongue. Instead she now asked him almost humbly, "So is that your work then are you a carer back home?"

He shook his head, "That is my charitable work brought about through a friend who is now disabled through no fault of his own! No, I guess you could say that my daytime profession, or what keeps the wolves away from the door is simply that of being a pen pusher with the Ministry! But tell me what about yourself? You spoke of your employer but never what you actually do when you are not enjoying yourself and driving me to distraction?"

"Amongst other things I attempt to write. Brad is or rather was my publisher ---he is the one who used to make me write it all out again when I thought that I had finished!" She smiled a little whimsically as she thought back to those times.

"So I take it that you write full time?"

"I would love to be able to do that but unfortunately that would be quite unlikely to provide enough sustenance for me to exist upon. Therefore in between writing I work or rather I did work for Brad as a secretary!"

"In that case he must have trusted you with all that business empire at his feet!"

She glanced at him hard for a moment. She had never mentioned anything about Brad's many interests. If this one knew so much the next thing he would be asking about was her own relationship with her boss. Well she supposed that would have been something of a laugh for after all she had never been afforded the opportunity to find that out for herself!

Even so she had later to admit that she found the experience of scuba diving quite exhilarating for Lance was nothing if he was not a good teacher. In fact the only thing that stopped her from rushing to tell Mandy and Doug about it on their return was the thought that perhaps they would have read more into her little venture than was completely necessary. Still one good thing that had come out of that afternoon was that she had acquired a date for herself that evening so she couldn't imagine what they would have had to say about that! But for once in her life Rachel couldn't have cared less what they thought!

-----------Possibly Rachel would have been more than a little surprised if she had witnessed exactly what Lance Turner's next move was after he left her however. For once back in his room he produced a tiny camera from out of his pocket and connected the card to a computer before opening up the web.

The answer he was waiting for was not long in forthcoming, printed out under the condensed photograph he had recently dispatched.

Name ------Rachel Aldred ------Occupation ----- freelance secretary and author ----- associate ---Bradley Stevens, financial magnate involved in publishing as well as diplomatic activities. Current whereabouts------Morocco Africa! ------ Suggested Category -----2.

Lance was very thoughtful as he turned off the machine. In truth the boys didn't get their facts wrong very often. So if this man was not dead after all but presently residing in Morocco, then what the girl doing here acting out a part: Unless of course someone had tipped them off and they were on to him? Consequently did this mean that the woman was some sort of decoy who had been ordered to follow him, in which case they were probably already aware of his own current interest in the Sahara!

⋆ ⋆ ⋆ ⋆

Chapter Two

"Now they are saying that they anticipate that it was a bomb that caused it!" As usual Doug was giving his oration from the headlines of the morning newspaper at the breakfast table the next day.

For her part Amanda looked around quickly to make sure that Rachel was not within earshot of this verbal entourage. "Be careful what you are saying Doug especially with Rachel about!"

Her husband responded by glancing at his wife as if she had stated something that was quite unrelated to the present time. "Well she'll have to learn the truth sooner or later, won't she woman?"

"There are other ways and means once we are sure that it is not all paper talk!" The retort sounded determined enough.

As for Rachel herself she was at the time in a bit of a quandary. She had decided that in all fairness it would appear rather pointed if she went back to scuba diving again today much as she would have loved to have gone back to that diving school for further lessons even if she did have a yen to see more of the fascinating world of the deep as well as its inhabitants. The place where the tide no longer frothed and exerted its turbulent self but instead moved with a gentle motion to caress these creatures and where because of the rocky surface the water was abundantly clear to reflect the spectrum of the sun's rays as they were deflected by the surface of the water giving rise to a variety of different colours in this natural world that was so often ignored by man!

Her thoughts mused back onto the previous evening. They had not gone very far, merely in point of fact to one of the small bars that were situated in the resort. Even so one could have termed the locale as being both cosy and intimate. She supposed in all truth she had learnt little more about this enigmatic male however except for the way his lips curled at the side when he was amused, a stance that appeared to suit him far more than the stern inapproachable face, and also his impatience when a certain strand of his hair deliberately set out to provoke him. Yet the vibes that had floated across the airways between them had spoken far more than actual words and in turn Rachel felt at least relieved that he had finally stopped questioning her.

They had not been late returning back to the hotel for Lance had claimed that he had to be up early the following morning even though he never condescended to explain the reason for this. Yet before they had parted when the lift reached her floor his lips had briefly touched her hair and the gentle wisp of this action had been enough to set her pulses racing!

Perhaps the decision of what she should do that morning was taken away from her when once back at the table she suddenly felt two hands placed upon her shoulders with their warmth defusing into the muscles at the top of her back. The very touch left her in no doubt as to whom this was even before she turned to greet him.

"I was sat there wondering how you would like to visit the dolphins this morning?" He posed his question as if this was the most natural thing in the world for him to say. Yesterday they had been strangers but after all that had been yesterday!

For a moment she did not know what to say in reply for in spite of her heart egging her forward she also knew full well that Both Dog and Mandy were currently straining their ears like dogs on a leash at this surprise manifestation. But then of course they had already made that sea trip when she herself had stayed behind to look after young Jake.

Speaking of this young rascal, the boy appeared on cue for he was naturally not far away from them. But for once Jake was silent as he stared agog at the stranger who had approached his aunt in that manner whilst his own back was turned.

"Afterwards if you wish we can probably take a swim off Masca. It is really quite beautiful there, the perfect place in fact for a picnic lunch!" His eyes begged an answer and Rachel realised that so far she had not introduced him to other members of the family.

"Oh this is Lance Turner by the way. Lance; meet my sister and brother in law. I think that you have already met their offspring here!" It now seemed to be far easier to perform the introductions than to deal with her confusion. Doug nodded and Mandy, though still surprised, gave a half smile in his direction. A smile that if Rachel had possessed the wit to question may have left her feeling rather puzzled.

"I've seen you speaking to Rachel before!" Perhaps the accusation came because the youngster believed he had been left out of such formalities, but at least it certainly appeared to break the ice.

"Of course we wouldn't forget you. This by the way is my nephew Jake if you haven't already realised that!"

"Ah yes, the young man who actually believed he could master the sun! But I see that you have thankfully now recovered young man!"

"Yes thank you!" Jake was certainly not used to being addressed in this more formal of manners.

"Well then Rachel, how about it? Are you game enough to encounter the big fish?"

The man was possessive there was little doubt about that but even so Rachel found herself nodding. Possessive he might be but after the previous evening she found Lance Turner to be completely fascinating!

Doug grunted and immediately went back to searching through his paper. In truth he didn't like anyone to spoil his morning read, Mandy often said he was stereotyped but if that involved glancing through the morning headlines to keep abreast with the news at home then so be it. Immediately noticing an opportunity to escape she felt Lance take hold of one of her hands as he gently persuaded her away from that table. Perhaps it was only the keen eyes of the child who noticed them depart but then if these two were involved in that grown up stuff then the lad had decided that he was no longer interested!

In the event there was to be no sailing for them that day for quite unexpectedly and without any prior warning the wind suddenly woke up and raised the sea to the frothy mass in a manner that one might expect the Atlantic to behave.

Undeterred by this action however Lance appeared to have an alternative plan to fall back upon and in a sense Rachel felt the situation almost surreal as she sat on the small beach watching those rollers and wondering where the next one would choose to descend as the tide now gave the sense of miniature tsunamis. He looked up from what he was doing and suddenly warned her to move her feet as one of the waves he had spotted now threatened to engulf her.

"Why not take your sandals off!" He urged her thoughtfully. "Never trust the tide especially when it is like this and on the turn. Sometimes the sea can behave as if it was a docile lamb but today I guess it is more like a roaring giant, one that is also in a very bad mood!"

She smiled at his words of explanation for they seemed to be so fitting to the current conditions but in actual fact she found the effect of being able to dig her bare feet into the newly washed sand and to allow the occasional wave to wash the discolouration from the beach away quite soothing with the medium in effect intent at that time to smooth away any footprints that had been left by man upon its own hallowed surface!

Because of the unpredictability of that day there appeared few who chose to share this area with them all of which gave the place, hidden well way from the port a certain feeling of serenity.

"The Calima I believe has now past its worst!" He sounded almost like an authority on the subject as he gazed up into the sky. "And if that is the truth then I will be able to keep the promise I made to you tomorrow. Still as I believe the water is far too cold yet to suggest a swim I think perhaps we will settle for lunch instead!"

There seemed to be no arguing with this man once he had made up his mind and Rachel herself felt completely mesmerised. For the action man out of action still appeared far too damned attractive to her eyes. She shook herself reproachfully for such thoughts; whatever had got into her? And the tide for its part seemed almost to echo her thoughts with its resounding roar as it sought for one more time to take its chosen victim if only to remind them who was the rightful master by pulsating its water into the bag that they had previously placed on the rocks and which at the time they had believed to be ostensibly out of the way!

Still the warmth of the day appeared ready to return again when they made their way back to where Lance had parked his vehicle and today the humidity was not as intense and conditions were much more pleasant so that the warmth of the sun was made to feel welcome as it hastened to still the cooling breeze that had gone before. In actual fact Rachel did not know where they were supposed to be heading at the time but Lance had pointed the vehicle out of the metropolis itself and up towards the hills and into the countryside. The place where they were now heading for, her companion obviously knew quite well for the owner greeted him upon their arrival as if he was a valued customer whom he was familiar with, and after the customary greeting they were ushered to a table that offered fantastic views of the whole of the coastline in one direction whilst Teide itself stood as a stark reminder of the Island's origins in the other.

Neither the Canarian meal that was subsequently served nor the wine accompanying it that was also from that region could give anybody any reason to fault. Indeed at one stage closing her eyes Rachel could almost imagine the troupadors arriving at such a locale playing their haunting music. Perhaps indeed she was daydreaming in this newfound sense of peace and tranquillity when Lance chose his moment to speak and bring her back into reality from her somnolent state.

"I have heard that a bomb is now suspected as being the cause of that air disaster!" His voice remained serious but the tone he adopted was gentle in the way he broke the news to her almost as if he did not wish to shock her too much but at the same time felt he had a need to inform her. And not for the first time Rachel remembered that he also had been at that airport awaiting the same plane's arrival. Had he himself gone there to meet someone then? If that was the case then it had been very remiss of her not to question this earlier even if he had been non-committal at the time.

"I heard my brother in law speaking about it during breakfast. Not that he realised that I was listening at the time of course!"

In his own mind Lance was more than a little surprised that she had taken this news so calmly. "Oh don't look so surprised I wasn't supposed to hear it of course. Mandy, that's my sister, made him shut up and close his blasted newspaper when I came back to the table with my breakfast. But speaking of the accident I guess there is a something that is very remiss of me not to have asked before. You were also at the airport on the day the plane went missing. Does that mean that there was someone on board that you knew as well?"

Much to her surprise Lance shook his head. "No one that was known to me personally!" He did not appear willing to go any further in the explanation of his presence there, but now possibly because she had posed the question he sought to change the subject.

"On most days it is possible to get a clear view of Gomera from here, but not I am afraid in the last week or so. But then as I told you before it is because of the sand storm that had emanated in the Sahara. Who knows, perhaps people are right about this global warming for I believe that this year, more than any other, the weather has proved to be quite unpredictable!"

"The way that you are speaking leads me to believe that you know these Islands well------so you are not on holiday then?"

He shook his head. Really she fumed within her, she knew nothing at all about this man either where he came from or how he earned his keep, for simply saying that he worked for the Ministry meant nothing at all to her. Perhaps Lance could read into her thoughts for he smiled as he attempted to put things to rights.

"Before you ask the question that is obviously uppermost in your mind at the moment I am a representative for a real estate firm here in the Islands. Not quite such a lucrative position as what it was a few years ago I am afraid. Not now we have the global recession!" He cast her a smile as if this had explained everything to her.

"And to think that I had you decked out as being at least a physical training instructor with all your outdoor activities!" Somehow Rachel did not feel totally convinced with his real estate story, but then the ones that she had previously met had usually been time-share touts. Besides she could hardly equate this activity with what he had previously told her for it hardly made sense that a pen pusher from the Ministry should be involved in real estate. Now she felt his words had served to destroy the image of him she had much preferred, seeing him in the action man role!

Unfortunately as far as she was concerned anyway the leisurely lunch was also drawing to its conclusion. In truth she admitted that she knew it couldn't last forever and by this time Pepe was now busily rearranging his tables giving them a further clue that it was now time for them to depart.

"But you will come back again Senor and I think that maybe you will bring the beautiful Senorita with you!" No doubt some of these sentiments came from the handsome tip that Lance gave to him upon departing, but this was not all the story for the Canarian had obviously been genuinely pleased to see Lance, which obviously meant that he was a regular customer there.

After paying their respects Lance then carried on to Masca. "Now Senorita you will have the chance to walk some of your lunch off!" He smiled at his own flippancy. "Well I did tell you that the place was beautiful and therefore I wanted you to see it for yourself!"

She remembered once viewing the valley on a television documentary and of the commentators remarks at the time that this surely must be the most beautiful natural place left on the earth and now she was able to view the place for herself she tended to agree with him. Not however that it was to prove easy going under foot and Lance moreover had the appearance of being a hard taskmaster, which was probably one of the reasons why she never made the trek as far as the beach!

"That is no matter!" He responded to her sheepish pleas for a respite. "For even if we had managed to walk all the way to the beach we would have only had to walk all the way back again in order to collect the car. The idea is to actually be dropped off at the village at the top and then eventually catch the boat back from off the beach, which obviously we could never do today!"

Even so it was Lance who stopped the car at the point above Crab Island and as Rachel ventured to look down into the deep clear water with something that approached fascination, Lance was at the time pointing further out to sea. The sight that he was now indicating served to veer her mind away from the predominant intention to get him to tell her how a man from the Ministry could be involved with real estate.

"Take a look in the distance out there where the waves are breaking on what appears to look like rocks off the shore. Well I did promise you would see either whales or dolphins today but you will have to look carefully to see their shape as they playfully rise above the tide. I guess that they must have come closer in shore today because of the weather conditions but the afternoon is traditionally the time that they like to catch the feel of the sun on their backs!"

Looking carefully now Rachel was just about able to discern those dark shapes that momentarily appeared as if engrossed in their own form of surf riding. Shapes that so easily could have been confused with off shore rocks by the uninitiated. This was certainly something that young Jake would have given his right arm to be able to see.

"So what can I claim as my just reward for keeping my promise?" His eyes were twinkling but Rachel discerned that he was currently standing far too close for comfort and her mind flickered onto the memory of Brad. In truth she had never felt this way about that man. Possibly that was the reason why she had decided to go to the airport that day. To tell him and to finally get it off her chest if he was on board that plane, for things could not possibly work out between them in that way. It promised to be a daunting task she knew for Brad had always been the one to bulldoze his way into anything and not only that but to also claim that he was right every time. She had realised that and at the time she had been searching for the right words by which she could convince him. But then the whole of the task had been taken out of her hands, she could hardly say thankfully for the man in question was now dead and surely she would not have wished that terrible accident on anybody!

"I'm still patiently waiting for your reply!" The voice from behind her stirred her thoughts to chide her a little. "All right then if the lady won't talk then I demand the right to have dinner with her tonight and after that she can reveal the plot of her latest novel to me. Well how does that suit you?"

The guilt complex that was still within her rose even further for since meeting this man here on Tenerife she had not completed a single stroke in her writing. Yet there were other plots now completed that filed systematically back into her memory. One in particular seemed to predominate as a small lizard type creature chose that moment to run across their path to claim his quota of afternoon sun.

"All right then I accept!" She turned now to face him with a smile. "Perhaps with the recent change in the weather conditions it would be apt to relate the story of Christopher's dragon, for the creature back there just reminded me of it!" She referred now to one of her characters in a past work that had included a small boy who had a penchant for such creatures that he assumed were dragons!

"And has your story got a name to it yet?"

"Yes, perhaps a most apt one under these weather conditions for I have called it In the Shadow of the Storm!"

He made a slight motion of surprise but said nothing more about it as they motored back. He left her at the hotel entrance after exacting a promise from her that she would be ready for seven o'clock.

-------------She half expected the family to be waiting for her, to have even posted look out guards to spy her approach in their eagerness to learn about her day. But in all truth Rachel did not feel in the mood for telling them or enduring a never-ending barrage of questions, such as – what did he say then------ or where did you go next? For her mind was still in something of a whirl, half of it still left in the company of that enigmatic male. Moreover even though she realised that she still really knew nothing about him she still desired his company more than most other things!

Consequently with a little bit of luck not to mention sheer connivance she managed to sneak back to her room whilst Jake was still enthralled in that game of deck quoits arranged by the animation team and currently cheered on by a couple of proud parents. Thus she was washed, changed and was ready long before her family decided it was time to return to their own room to prepare for the evening meal. Cautiously Rachel herself then made towards the area that was set aside for reading and quiet table games that were expected to be played in a mode of silence, and taking her notebook and pen with her, even before members of her family could think of knocking upon her door, she made in this direction.

Strangely enough however the more that she tried to get back into the writing of the new story she had started, and back to the original story line she had decided upon, the more she found she was supplanting her original ideas and now relating the day's happenings through the eyes of her two principal characters. Finally she laid aside her pen in an attempt to think some more about her original plot. But this time it was Brad who came to mind, she remembered now the first time she had met him after he had agreed to publish her story. In fact Brad's own profession was something of an enigma to her even though she worked as his secretary, for publishing only appeared to be part of that man's pursued career.

"Although having said that I feel that I must warn you that there is little market for any new novelists nowadays!" His words had come some time after his initial perusal of the script. "All right in the first instance I quite like the plot but I think it will be better once you have made one or two changes to it! I am now thinking particularly in terms of Chapter one and in addition I feel that Chapter seven also requires a little more emphasis, it may have to be altered quite dramatically if you want to hold your reader's attention for all that period of time!" She had later to admit that Brad had been right but then wasn't that Brad's forte to always be right on everything? In truth he hadn't liked the tale of her dragon either, claiming it to be childlike and too far fetched to attract more than a mediocre interest amongst the reading public although in truth, once it had been published that book had sold better than any other. Not that any of her books were sufficient enough to make her decide to give up the day job however!

Glancing again at her watch she realised that the time had flown past. By this time the family no doubt would be back at the dining table for Doug had a thing about being all inclusive, he considered that he should glutton as much and as often as time allowed. Instead and feeling rather glad to be away from the expected onslaught that usually accompanied meal times she now eased herself away from the hotel and hired a waiting taxi to take her to the venue that they had agreed upon earlier that afternoon after Rachel at the time had suggested that for them to go in his own car was an act that could be easily misconstrued particularly if her family managed to get hold of such a fact! Such explanations if they were necessary, she determined, could be left until a later stage. She paused quite suddenly as the thought hit her for surely this was what she had been doing with Lance, putting off the explanations she felt she deserved until a later stage.

"You appear to be very quiet tonight. It's not because you are finding that you have still to rehearse the plot of that story you promised me by any chance?" Her appearance had obviously taken him by surprise and although throughout the meal he had proved to be most courteous even though at the time he himself had appeared to have other matters on his mind.

In fact returning to his own room earlier on he had switched on his computer for the express purpose of seeing if there were any E-mails waiting in cipher space for him. He noted that there were several, most he could immediately disregard but one of these letters of convenience had however stood out above all the rest. Realising who it was from he opened it up only to read the message that referred to the recent caption in the local paper that had mentioned the apprehension of those illegal immigrants on the Cayucos that had been spotted six miles off the coast of La Gomera the previous week. Two of the seventy-one people on board had apparently been arrested as suspects and what was more his own orders were now to go to La Gomera himself to try to establish exactly what was going on!

The idea of having to carry on with this job upon which he had initially been so keen hardly served to please him at the present time. Whilst he accepted that the Island was only eighteen kilometres away and was linked by a regular boat service, the idea of spending the day at that place from where Columbus had initially set sail from, did not please him at all at this time, for in his terms the time spent there would only serve to take him away from the girl he had recently become fascinated with and what was more to the point, the way in which she had begun to pluck at his own heart strings!

Nevertheless in spite of his emotions on the matter he found that he was still able to listen and show interest in the story she related which was about the couple who from initially setting out to destroy one other had allowed this same Island to cement a relationship that had served to bring them back together again. Initially his first comment was that although he found it to be a nice sort of story it also seemed to be totally divorced from the current attitude of the have now pay later brigade, folk who wanted the goods now and often in fact pocketed the money instead of paying their dues after deciding that it would be of more use in their own pocket!

"Perhaps that is being rather cynical of you!" She responded quickly to his argument and Lance fell silent for the thing that was still bugging him the most was actually the next day. She must have waited a good ten minutes before she finally spoke again.

"What is the matter with you tonight Lance. I know that something is troubling you. I finished relating my plot some time ago and all I have had up until now is to witness your disapproval!"

"No, I didn't disapprove and you were quite right it was churlish of me to come out with that comment. Unfortunately the reason for it is quite simple. I have had an E mail to go to that damned bird sanctuary over there on that Island tomorrow, which in effect means that we will have to cancel our own plans. Now that is something that really doesn't please me!"

"Our own plans?"

"Yes I have still to keep my promise to take you sailing remember!"

"But there will be another day for that!"

"Maybe, we'll see!"

Matters appeared to be left at that yet the silence still prevailed as he took her back to the hotel. If Rachel had expected anything any different from a polite good night after the day they had spent together then she was to be disappointed. Indeed the girl was left to ponder as to why a man who was supposedly involved in real estate as well as the Ministry had suddenly received an E mail to go to a bird sanctuary on La Gomera!

----------It seemed to be so much fresher the following morning after the unexpected shower during the night for the day had dawned fair with already the promise of the sun's reflection up in the sky and Rachel felt content to pause on her balcony for a few moments to breathe in the new day's promise and listen as the sea sounded far more content with its lot as it gathered one more time to edge its way towards the rocks almost as if it was trying to soothe them and apologise for its previous show of temper. Of course at this stage she still had the family to come to terms with and she didn't doubt that there would be questions waiting for her when she arrived down in the dining room some even of a pertinent nature. She sighed as she took one last lingering breath before she made her way to join them.

"So what happened to you yesterday?" Mandy agog to hear her news did not disappoint her. Doug however seemed to be far more concerned at the time with the rain that had fallen unexpectedly in the early hours of the morning wetting the towels that he had left out.

"It's not right you know. It's not supposed to rain between May and September or so we were informed. I call it false pretences I do advertising that in their brochures. We ought to be able to claim compensation!"

"Perhaps it had something to do with the tropical storm that they had off Brazil!" Now his wife tried to be helpful.

"Tropical storm be damned, anyway that was weeks ago now!"

"Well sometimes it takes it a long time to cross over the Atlantic!"

"A long time when you can fly across that damned pond in under twelve hours. Show some sense woman!"

"Then maybe it's because of global warming Doug, you know you are always being told about it!" By this time Mandy had obviously forgotten her initial reaction to Rachel.

"Fat lot they know the ones who do all the spouting that's my opinion. Anyway is lover boy not around this morning then?" Doug approached the subject in his usual brusque manner now turning his attention onto his sister in law, as he appeared to be getting little credence from his immediate family.

"He has a business appointment today!" Rachel kept her lips tightly closed after revealing this much and stubbornly refused to relate anything else about the previous day and where she had been with the man. As far as she was concerned they could think what they liked!

"Then you will have to come to Loro Parque with us, won't she Doug? Jake is looking forward to seeing all those parrots, aren't you Jake?" Mandy was trying her best to smooth over any troubled waters but Rachel quickly declined the offer shaking her head to emphasise the point.

"I am thinking more in terms of the peace and quiet of the beach actually. I have some writing that I need to catch up on!"

"But the tide is on the turn this morning. How can you sit on the beach if the sea is in?"

"Oh I am sure that I will find some isolated rock that is free from the water!"

"If you ask me what I think I would tell you that I consider it is high time you got on with your own life and forgot all about that chap!" It was Doug who now decided he didn't want to be left out of this conversation anymore and therefore chose to make the profound statement out of the blue! "Can't you get it into your head that the man is dead and he isn't coming back?"

"Doug!" Mandy tried her best to stem the flow.

"Anyway if you ask my opinion I'll tell you something for nothing, I never did like the fellow. His eyes were too close together for one thing! Oh I know he was your boss and all that. But the thought of you marrying him did nothing for me!"

"There was never any suggestion of you marrying Brad, was there Rachel?"

"Then what the bloody hell was she doing at that airport with a load of grieving relatives if there was nothing between them? Use your brains woman and stop forever trying to shield the girl, she's all grown up now!"

"Oh excuse me the pair of you!" Rachel made a desperate effort to move. Perhaps after all it had been a mistake to come on holiday with them. It was then that young Jake seeing that his Aunt now appeared upset slid his little hand into her own.

"Dad doesn't really mean it Rachel 'cause he shouts at everybody even me! So if he shouts at you as well that must mean that he also loves you!"

Doug may now have scowled in his child's direction for his interference but Rachel smiled gently at the boy for making such an effort. Still even for Jake's sake she didn't want to become involved. At least not today at any rate!

Finally taking her leave of the family once the coach arrived and after wishing them a great day out at Loro Parque that she felt sure they would surely have, Rachel made her own way slowly towards the beach determined that today at least she would get to grips with the characters that had so far been evading her in revealing their innermost selves. The thought of being able to tread on the virgin sand and to feel it moulding to the shape of her foot, as the sun had not yet been offered the chance of baking it after the tide receded filled her with splendid anticipation.

Yet as she made to sit upon those rocks in contemplative mood the waves that initially had appeared to be so docile had apparently decided to now adopt a more sinister mood as they edged their way ever closer to her own position with the sound of threatening, which signified that at any moment they were ready to act and cut her off from the mainstream of civilisation. For in truth it was not the waves that roared and made the most noise that posed the main danger but rather those that approached silently in their wake to claim more and more territory for themselves by frivolously piling the beach sand first into dunes as they sought to reclaim their territory on the shore and then upon their return sadistically collapsing these dunes in the vain hope that man in his innocence would be standing upon them!

It almost added to this ominous threat when she also heard the helicopter now overhead almost as if it in its turn was looking for lost souls that had been stranded so that it might haul them back to safety. But Rachel wanted none of man's so called safety. This was the place where she had chosen to be so that the very ides of the elements could inspire her with their talents.

"Hey what do you think you are doing down there. Are you fancying your chance of taking a dip or something?" She suddenly heard the voice calling her from the top of the cliff path and recognised whom it belonged to immediately and in return her heart pounded as it almost missed a beat. She still firmly believed that the man had already left to catch the early ferry to La Gomera and therefore to her mind by this time he should have already have departed. She looked up at him questioningly and in response he shrugged his shoulders. "Well I did promise you a boat ride today, remember?" He grinned at her look of indecision. "Well this morning after the rain the conditions are not too bad and La Gomera is after all only eighteen kilometres away. So how do you fancy your chances or is it a question that you cannot trust me to sail that far?"

"But what of your meeting?" She remembered how serious he had appeared when he had finally told her about it the previous evening.

"That isn't until twelve o'clock which will give us plenty of time to get across. Also I don't expect that it will last all day. Therefore I reasoned with myself as to why I should waste my time catching the ferry when we can easily sail across and utilise the time for ourselves. Oh you needn't look so worried. I do have a permit to dock there and I'm not suggesting that we try to go across in a rowing boat either! But you haven't answered my question, do you trust me?"

She thought of what she had already seen him doing on board a boat there was little doubt that she had already realised that the man was a keen yachtsman amongst his other attributes But more than that she was in effect so glad to see him and to realise that he had thought about her at the time that she wouldn't have cared if it had been a rowing boat he was suggesting they should use after all.

"Well we do have a motor on board as well as sails if you are still wondering. Also I can personally vouch for the seaworthiness of the vessel!" Perhaps he believed she still needed some reassurance

Rachel however was in for quite a surprise after he had helped her from off those rocks whilst watching her every move with a certain look in his eye especially when she decided to don her tee short and shorts again; for the boat that was currently moored in the harbour resembled more of an ocean going yacht than any small fishing boat. She looked at him in surprise and he understood her meaning.

"It belongs to a friend of mine who allows me the use of it when I require!"

"But won't it take more than one person to handle such a craft?" She queried as her hand automatically stroked the slim port side.

"It is actually all automatic. But you needn't worry for Jose over there will be coming with us to give us a hand!" He nodded towards a Canarian who was currently tending another vessel. "In actual fact Jose likes sailing this vessel because I know that he is always willing to leave his own vessel to have a go when I require his services simply for the hell of it!"

As if on cue this dark skinned and weathered beaten individual thereupon fixed a beaming smile in Rachel' s direction that revealed the missing teeth at the bottom of his mouth. To the man's mind this must be the Senorita, the Senor's new wench and a fine sight the girl made for the Englishman certainly appeared to have taste.

Still once aboard the craft Rachel was able to experience afresh the motion of the sea as Tenerife began to gradually fade in the background and the Island of La Gomera loomed ever larger in front of them now.

"Actually if the weather conditions happen to be right you can get a view of Tenerife from the Island that surpasses any picture that you can buy! For you are able to see all of Teide complete in all its finery with pockets of cloud which act like a garment around her, halfway up the mountain all of which appears to be in line with the lady's strict sense of dress code!"

To Rachel however the prospect of visiting the unknown held even more appeal for now her creative juices were already beginning to tingle in anticipation of being able to do the Island justice in those newly composed words.

"We will be landing of course at San Sebastian, that is the capital of this small Island and the only place that one can reasonably anticipate will have the facilities to land a vessel such as this. It is also the place where my meeting is currently due to take place. But as I previously stated I do not anticipate that the meeting will last for long. Therefore whilst I am in attendance perhaps you can explore the town to your heart's content. I doubt if it will be possible for you to lose yourself in the place anyway!"

His words told her that he was already familiar with this Island even before he pointed out the arrival of the fast speed ferry that crossed on a regular basis from Los Christianos thus linking the two Islands

"Many of the locals living on the Island actually work in Tenerife for outside of farming there is little work for them over here. Probably that is also why they pressed for their own airport that lies in the South of this place, although for years it was always sworn that they would never be able to get a plane to land on this rock!"

They walked together towards some official looking buildings situated in a square just off the promenade and it was there that he pointed her in the direction of Christopher Columbus' house.

"Of course I'm not saying that it will be open, but synchronise your watch and I'll meet you by the statue over there in abut half an hour's time, say round about half twelve!"

She watched him leave as her mind was already beginning to fix itself on a new plot. This time however it was centred upon the fact that he had previously told her he was to visit a bird sanctuary there, something that she could not easily equate with the stone building in the centre of the town. This was yet another contradiction in addition to him first saying he was a pen pusher for the Ministry not to mention his later admission that he was involved in real estate. In her mind she tried hard to reconcile these three synopses yet even her creativity could not provide an acceptable answer to this puzzle.

Still she had to accept that Lance was true to his word in one aspect for he was back with her within the allotted half hour yet even as he joined her she began to sense that something had changed. Indeed his previous boyish good humour and teasing appearance seemed to have now all disappeared and instead his mood had been replaced with one of more serious overtones, almost indeed as if he had suddenly matured from the boy into a serious young man, a motion that had not been of his own choosing!

"I guess it's time we considered getting back!" He nodded in the direction of the quay thus destroying the current notion she had of the two of them spending some time together at this place. "Anyway no doubt Jose will be wanting his lunch by this time!" He tried to put on a smile and to sound light hearted about the matter using words that had been carefully chosen for the occasion. She knew full well that something was now upsetting him, something that he had learnt at that meeting but he had completely closed up by this time, closer indeed than any clam and she managed to obtain no detail as to why from him!

Consequently Rachel was left to watch those small fishing boats moored just on the periphery of the harbour bob around like mad as they made the approach on their return for once again it appeared that the afternoon breeze had been aroused from its slumbers to stir the ocean into bouncing backwards and forwards upon those rocks, blowing out belches of spray from the blow holes prevalent along that part of the coast and consequently wet through any individual who dared to venture out onto that promenade. Despite this the weather itself appeared to be more settled, a fact mirrored in the deep blue coloration of the mass that lay away from those rocks, a colour that made it the more inviting to those whom it sought out as its prey by luring them with a hypnotic power to dare to venture into their midst! Now finally nearing the shore with the magical Island of Gomera fading away back into the myths of time, she watched the crabs through the glasses that Lance had handed to her as they in their turn pulled themselves from out of the watery depth for their afternoon sojourn!

* * * *

Chapter Three

In retrospect she supposed that she had sensed that there was something wrong even before he left her at Gigantes, for he merely guided her ashore and then claimed that he had something that he needed to see to. At the time Jose for his part had merely sighed and shrugged his shoulders at this action that suggested that if the two of them had now had some sort of a tiff then he wanted to be no part of it!

Her sister however was not to be so easily satisfied when the family returned from their outing to Loro Parque a little later in the afternoon.

"Yes, we had a great time!" Mandy pointedly reminded her that she had never asked about their day. "So what is the matter with you then. I can tell by your face that your own day has not exactly lived up to your expectations!"

"I suppose you could put it like that!"

"You mean to say that your characters didn't behave in the manner you expected from them?"

"One could say that is a truth yes I suppose so!"

"You appear to be supposing rather a lot sister. So where exactly did you get to? Just remember child I can always tell a fib from the truth when I hear one!"

"If you must know I went on a rather lush motor yacht to La Gomera!" Rachel didn't particularly want to go into details about her day but she knew full well that Amanda had her own method of extracting things.

"And----?" Why was it, she wondered at a later stage, that her sister never showed any element of surprise in her eyes at this revelation?

"That was it in total! We went there and then we came back!"

"I believe you said we ----Am I correct in presuming you are now referring to Sir Galahad?"

"I am referring to Lance yes. Apparently he had some business matter to attend to on the Island and so I was persuaded to go along for the ride!"

"So where is he now then? Don't tell me that the two of you have had an argument!"

"Nothing like that. I think that perhaps he heard something on the Island that wasn't exactly to his liking!"

"You mean that they are not in the market for selling plots of land for real estate over there?" Damn it, she had forgotten she had already told Mandy that Lance was involved in real estate. At the time it had sounded a little more forceful than merely saying that he was a pen pusher for the Ministry. Well there was one thing for certain she certainly wasn't going to speak of any bird sanctuary to her sister now!

"He didn't actually say what the meeting was about. Nevertheless whatever it was it certainly appeared to give him food for thought!"

"By that I presume you mean that he excluded you in his thoughts afterwards?"

"I have to admit it was something like that!"

"Rachel I am aware that you are still distraught over losing Brad but please don't be tempted to jump into something with both feet on the rebound as it were. Maybe this Lance appears to be a nice guy and all that but really you haven't known him for very long at all and consequently you know very little about him as yet!"

"Strange as it may sound I did know him before meeting him again here. Actually he was at the airport at Fueteventura when it happened!"

"You mean he was selling real estate on that Island too?" Maybe Amanda's tone did sound a little cynical.

"No he was actually there to try to perfect his surf board skills so that he could endeavour to raise funds for a disabled friend of his!" She deliberately omitted to mention his occupation whatever that might be amongst the string of responses he had already given her to that question.

"Is that what he said? Sometimes I wonder if you are after all far too gullible our Rachel!"

Although Mandy appeared willing to leave matters after she had given vent to her own opinions and had voiced some measure of disapproval, her brother in law on the other hand was certainly not once he had cleaved his allotted time over the breakfast table the following morning. By this time his wife had already filled him in with many of the details therefore once he had partaken of his victuals he was ready to voice his considered opinion quite voluminously.

Although to the outsider Doug Ogden may have appeared to be both coarse and bullish by nature, there was however one thing that the man did appear to care about and that was his family. Moreover he also considered that his wife's sister was part of this family and therefore as such he did not like to see the girl hurt. In fact the man was quite capable of defending through fist power any member of his family should the need arise and anyone who tried to upset them was moreover quite likely to feel the full weight of that fist!

To his mind what he now witnessed in Rachel was not right. He had managed to conjure his wife into letting one or two things slip and the rest, well he was no mug he could come to his own conclusions! Good Lord hadn't the girl suffered enough as it was through that damned tragedy that appeared to have been of nobody's making without being subjected to another upset quite so soon. And upset he now deemed that girl currently was. Moreover when he posed himself the question as to why she should be like this the answer came back quite simply with the name of the recent rat bag who to his mind now appeared to be taking the girl for a ride. What else was one supposed to think when the devil had gone and dropped her and offered little reason to do so at the first hurdle they had come across?

His spleen thus geared into taking an active role Doug decided that it must surely be left to him as the head of the family to try to do something about this. He couldn't be having the girl upset, not even if she was Mandy's sister! A look outside informed him that she was currently out on the promenade watching those boats bob up and down yet again whilst wearing an almost inscrutable expression on her face! On the other hand the devil that appeared to have upset her was still right here in the hotel. Doug waited his chance savouring the moment when the man would have his mouth full of cereal or something equally obnoxious before he made his approach, congratulating himself at the time that he had forgotten none of the tactical manoeuvres he had learnt in the army, even though he had only joined the Territorials for a bit of ready cash!

"Look here Mister, I for one don't like to see my sister in law looking for all the world as if she's dropped a dollar down some grid hole! Believe you me if that girl is upset it has an effect on the whole family and we are supposed to be here to enjoy ourselves mate. Therefore I see no reason why the likes of you should be allowed to spoil our holiday. The question is as you are the one responsible for the girl's dire mood, what the hell are you going to do about it?" He ended his tirade by slamming his fist down on the table making the young man's tea slop over into his saucer.

For his part Lance stared at the speaker with an element of surprise. As far as he knew he had done nothing to warrant this angry attack by a complete idiot. And then his mind focussed upon the fact that this was Rachel's brother in law! Well he had heard that the man was often on a short fuse but to his mind he had done nothing to hurt Rachel if that was what this idiot was on about. True he had been a little perplexed at the news he had received concerning the girl back in La Gomera for as far as he had been informed the girl he had coveted had actually been involved right up to her pretty little neck with lover boy prior to his so called demise. In truth he had never envisaged Rachel as being some sort of gangster's moll but the authorities on the Island had been adamant that this girl, had in all likelihood, been currently employed by those who she worked for, the one's who were in all probability in league with the disappearing Brad, to seek him out and then to follow him and report back to them what he himself was up to! This opinion had moreover been further highlighted by the fact that she had just happened to be present on both of these Islands at the same time as he was himself!

Lance looked again at the person issuing forth this petty speech. "Guess you have got me wrong Mister. I meant your sister in law no harm but in truth our interests do not always coincide with the other person's and consequently we often find that we need a little space to sort our own thoughts out. Besides I believe your sister in law is currently in the throes of this new book she is writing which is something that I am afraid I cannot share. But if it will ease your spleen a little you might just like to know that I was already in the process of attempting to seek the girl out, that is once I have finished my breakfast!"

"Then if that is the truth you will find her on the promenade looking for all the world like a wet lettuce at this moment in time! All I say is that if the two of you have had some sort of lover's tiff then you had better get busy and sort matters out or I will be back pronto Mister!"

At this point Lance felt he could surely have hit the man but not even realising his intention Doug had turned away considering that he had said his piece anyway and that should be a good enough retort to give to shut his wife up from keeping on moaning about the girl.

Lance found Rachel as Doug had intimated, gazing yet again out to sea taking in the whole of the vista and attempting to turn her mind's eye almost like one would use a camera to record the scene with a sense of purpose. Watching her he could not help but think how attractive she looked framed as she was against the backdrop of those cliffs and without even thinking he sat himself down on some rocks besides her. Above their heads the sun terrace on the sixth floor of the hotel almost gave one the impression that they were currently out on some ocean liner but on a vessel in calm waters for today in contrast to what had occurred previously that ocean could almost be aligned to a mill pond. Even so those boats were out there again as if to remind Rachel of a previous occasion when one of them had appeared to be shining a light into her room all night not forgetting the enigmatic figure who appeared to have some knowledge of them!

Upon hearing the man who was currently in her thoughts approach, Rachel fumbled for her top to fasten it securely for after the manifestations the previous day when they had returned from the Island she hadn't really anticipated seeing him, for hadn't he himself intimated that today he had something else on; and yet when he opened his mouth he appeared now to be back again in the adoption of his suave self.

"Pretty impressive don't you agree?" He nodded towards the view. Even so, after the excuses he had made the previous night that he needed some time to himself she still wondered why he had come. Why indeed he had intruded upon her thought pattern when she had once again been attempting to make some effort with her creativity actually in a vain attempt to dismiss this man out of her mind?

Standing there in contemplation it had somehow appeared to be the most natural thing in the world to have dived from this place into those alluring depths below. But that of course was the trickery that had been adopted by that aqueous mass that fermented there, to have the effrontery to tempt man to hurl himself into its depths that twinkled as the sun shining down on them made them act like some hypnotic charm. This, she claimed must surely be a place where one could feel at one with nature, a place that soothed the soul out of the reach of man. Yet it was also a place that belied its own secret torments. For indeed it appeared that the ocean still resented man's continuing prosperity on the earth, for after generating millions of years before from out of the sea itself, this mass still regarded itself as the true home of its prodigal children and awaited upon their return. The battle that was to come, it deemed, must be raged between the elements and man was unfortunately the one who always stood in the way of this final battle being waged.

She had in fact remained so still that at first she had been unaware that he had spoke that was until she realised that his hand had now chose to rest upon her shoulders in spite of the fact that at first she had determined to flick it away perhaps symbolised something in this change of attitude towards her. Yet even as that humble fly attempted to land she realised that something must have been said at the meeting he had attended that had included her, for the gathering itself had lasted no longer than the promised thirty minutes and yet had resulted in this change of mannerisms.

"I guess I didn't think you were up and about yet!" Well that was a lie for starters for he knew full well that she rose early for she had already confessed how she appreciated being able to complete a little of her writing before other's stirred.

"I was simply attempting to use my mind's eye like a camera in order to record something of this scene for posterity!"

"Then why did you not settle for a simple photo shot instead? I suspect that would have been far easier!"

She shook her head in response pouting her lips just a little and unaware of how desirable this made her appear. "That I do not consider to be the same for after all such images can be destroyed or even conveniently misplaced when you require them and then the image is lost forever! This way however I can easily conjure up any picture when

I need it!" She looked at him in the face that still appeared unclear as to what she was doing here at this time.

"Perhaps I ought to start by offering an apology for my attitude as we were coming back yesterday!" He had obviously read her thoughts even more clearly than what she could herself. "My only excuse is that something was said at that meeting I attended that gave me some food for thought!"

"I would have thought that the real estate business would be quiet at this time with the recession and all that!" She immediately wondered after issuing this challenge whether such a declaration had been really necessary and then dismissed the thought after deciding that it most probably was!

"In that case I did upset you, for which I am truly sorry!" She wondered if it was a look of true contrition that passed across his face although she still had it mind that his declaration could always be some part of a bizarre act, but then as she analysed this idea further she decided that perhaps her reaction had been strictly uncharitable. After all she supposed that everyone was entitled to have mood swings, more especially in Lance's case if it was something to do with that so called meeting he had been involved in. Chiding herself therefore she decided that perhaps it was far better to act out the role of living in the present, not on something that had once happened in the past and after all this was already something she ought to have appreciated. "I was wondering whether you fancied trying some snorkelling again?" Again he seemed to be able to read her thoughts and yet something of her previous enthusiasm for this activity now appeared to have evaporated.

"Actually I was contemplating whether I should catch a bus!" In truth there was nothing on the girl's mind at the time excepting this man who for some obscure reason she now found she wanted to kick out against because of his attitude towards her, and this to her mind had suddenly manifest itself to be a good idea! She glanced towards the small sail boat now plying the harbour as it did with monotonous regularity ready to sally forth on its way forward with the folk on board who in turn were now forced to listen to a dichotomy of sound, with words spoken in many different languages aboard the vessel

"A bus? But where on earth do you want to catch a bus to?" For a brief moment it did cross his mind that perhaps there was something that he ought to know, especially as he had been told to keep a sharp eye on this girl's movements.

"Oh just somewhere out of this place, that's all. Maybe I'll try to get to Santa Cruz!"

"But why there, is there any particular reason?"

"Well for starters I have heard that there are some decent shops in the city simply waiting to be perused!"

"Then why do you want to take the bus when we have the car at our disposal?"

"Perhaps I believed that you currently had other things on your mind!" Lance bit his lip. His mood from the previous afternoon must have got through to her. If that was the case it was no way for a member of Special Branch to act.

"Would you believe me if I said that I have nothing on my mind that doesn't concern you Rachel? Therefore if you want to go and let your hair down in Santa Cruz then that is the way we will head towards!" He wondered to himself if the girl would attempt to hedge now and attempt to put him off. Indeed perhaps she already had it in mind to meet with someone else there, but now to undermine such thoughts she smiled a little warily in his direction.

"Well I suppose that if you are sure that you don't mind, although I must confess that I'm not completely innocent in the manner man often portrays because he hates the activity of trailing around shops!"

Still somehow Lance regarded that perhaps he had made something of a conquest as he finally helped her into his car. By this time she had also confessed that one reason for her decision was because she didn't really relish having to spend the day with her family on that occasion and the beach was exactly the place one would be likely to find them at the present time. "Well I all can say is that if you feel this way about disliking their company so much then why did you actually choose to come away with them?"

"I guess that Mandy, that's my sister used her art of persuasion on that one! Don't get me wrong however I love them all very much, in small doses that is! I am afraid that over a prolonged period they can acquire the habit of starting to destroy me or at least destroy any yearnings I might feel towards my writing!"

"What will you do for a publisher now that Brad is no longer with us?"

"To be perfectly honest I have not yet fathomed that one out yet. Still the fact that I have now no publisher will not deter me from writing. As for any monetary employ well I guess there is always a need for a secretary somewhere!"

He supposed that he was surprised that she had apparently come to terms so quickly concerning Brad's death all of which served to leave him with the strangest suspicion in his mind that perhaps after all the girl did know more than what she was admitting. To add to his annoyance the mobile decided to choose that precise moment to start to warble its melody in his pocket and Lance was forced to pull off the road in order to answer it.

"Tell me, why is it that someone always wants to speak to you at the most inconvenient of times?" He pulled a face as he flipped the O.K. button on the machine as if indicating that this nuisance factor was not of his choosing. Still it did cross Rachel's mind that if this was indeed true, why he had not let the message go through to the answering service. Nevertheless she saw his face change as he heard what the caller had to say.

"--------What you mean you are coming here? ------------At this moment we are heading in the Santa Cruz direction. My ---err----the person I am with felt an urge to visit the place -------Then I suppose I will have to say that I will see you there!" He closed the line almost with a thump. "Why can't they let folk be?" He did not explain who the call was from but now his voice sounded almost ugly almost as if he was being forced into doing something he didn't want to do.

"Who was that then, your real estate?" The expression she issued was largely tongue in cheek she had to admit. In fact she didn't know why she had felt the need to utter the phrase in the first place for after all it was really no business of hers who Lance had been on the telephone to.

"No, it's not damned real estate!" For the first time since they had met Lance sounded quite vicious as he slammed the car back into gear. "As a point of fact I only bloody well wish it was!"

The rest of the journey was completed in practically total silence and Rachel was not surprised when he found some excuse not to trail around the shops with her after all but instead arranged to meet her later outside of the Corte de Anglais. It was therefore when she finally left this place, a store where she could easily have spent a lot more time in that she spotted Lance talking to another person. Yet even as she made her appearance through the doors of the place she could almost feel their eyes upon her from across the road. In her estimation the other man looked European, but then in these days it is sometimes difficult to discern from what part of the world most subjects came from. Still that didn't answer the question as to why the two of them had suddenly focussed their interest onto her. After all, she reasoned with herself, she wasn't late back; she hadn't been in that store for all that long. To make matters even more complicated the stranger moved once he saw Rachel's approach thus leaving Lance to force a false smile on his face in greeting but not before Rachel noticed something vaguely familiar about the stance of this stranger..

"You haven't been gone all that long, couldn't you find what you were searching for then?"

"There is plenty within that store that I could have found but I imagined that you would be waiting rather impatiently for me. I didn't realise of course that you had found someone to talk to in the interim period!"

It could well have been her imagination but she thought that she witnessed his face flush a little upon her words. Yet whatever it was Lance got over it remarkably quickly for the next moment the frown he had sported was replaced with a gushing smile. The question when it came therefore took her completely by surprise even if she had noted his earlier broodiness.

"Where exactly did you meet him Rachel?"

She knew to whom he was referring almost instantaneously although at the same time a goodly half of her now wanted to rebel and tell him it was none of his damned business. But now he was waiting almost impatiently for her response and something in his eyes warned her that he had now no intention of moving until she answered this question. Not that she felt there was any need for secrecy concerning her actions but still feeling rather bloody minded over his tonality she decided she would reply but in as many monosyllable words and short phrases as was possible.

"On the Internet!" She attempted to make her voice sound as feeble as the response she gave.

"The Internet? Tell me did you never heed the warnings about picking folk up on that contraption?"

"Brad was no child molester if that is what you are inferring!"

"There are other kinds!"

"If you must know although I still fail to see what it has to do with you, Brad was both understanding and kind as well as helping me a great deal at the time I needed it! Indeed it was Brad who actively encouraged me with my writing and made me snap my thoughts out of the past!"

"So that was your reason for going to Fuerteventura then, because this fellow was kind to you?" Disbelief now echoed in Lance's voice.

"No I went there because I needed a holiday and I also needed to think certain things through!" Damn it! There was no way she was going to admit that she had gone there in the first place because she was running away from having to make a decision.

"So you chose Fuerteventura a place that is situated so close to the Sahara Desert for that?"

"If you must know I chose the place for peace and quiet!"

"So was that the reason why Brad was coming out that day for a little peace and quiet as well?"

"No he was coming because he said that it just happened to be convenient for him. Apparently he had some business matters to attend to in the area but he was coming to the Island primarily for the answer to a question he had posed." Damn it she was repeating herself. Surely she had told him all this before and she did not anticipate that Lance was the sort of person who would forget her uttering.

"Which was?"

"If you must know Brad had asked me to marry him!" Now she almost rejoiced at being able to shout out this response if only to watch the reaction in those still probing eyes. Strangely enough she was not disappointed because for a single second it almost seemed as if a fierce blow had stung the other. Yet in truth the man recovered quickly.

"And if Brad had made it what would your answer have been?"

"That is none of your damned business!"

"I'm afraid that I disagree Rachel. You see much as I would like to believe your story at this moment I still have very few facts to go on!"

"Then if you must know at the time I was almost relieved he didn't make it because that way I didn't have to provide him with any answers!" Her response now bordered on the vicious and Lance gazed at her almost as if he did not believe what he was hearing.

"What if I suggested that it is possible that Brad was not on that plane after all?"

"What if I now say that I believe I will make my own way and catch the next bus back?" She felt her senses reeling; she wanted to be away from this pointless conversation.

"Get in the car Rachel and please stop acting so foolishly!" His lips were held taut and for a moment she determined to defy him, yet at that time she could not know the thoughts which were currently running through the man's head as he pondered as to why he had suddenly broke his oath of silence on matters he had no right to have told her. Still the hand that grasped her arm to make sure she got back in the car was firm although the entire journey back to Santiago was to be spent in an uncomfortable silence and once he stopped the car outside of the hotel Rachel was more than anxious to get out without casting a backward glance in his direction.

--------------It was Jake who happened to be the first person she spotted as she passed through the foyer still in a state of mournful indecision and as if realising something was wrong the child slipped his hand into her own. In truth there seemed to be something that was strangely comforting to her in this action and Rachel felt forced to smile down in the boy's direction.

"I thought that you would have still been on the beach!" She realised that she needed to say something to the child who was now regarding her with wide-open eyes.

"I was but then Mum decided that we'd been out for long enough!"

"So where are your Mum and Dad now?"

"Oh I guess that they're probably doing grown up things! I was with the kids' stuff when I saw you coming in and I noticed that you looked upset Rachel. Are you upset? What has happened to upset you?"

"Oh nothing!" She began and then realising the child did not appear convinced. "Oh grown up things I suppose!"

In return the boy now nodded his head somewhat wisely. In truth he had really no idea why grown ups had to always do things that upset them. In fact the grown up world was really a very silly place and he made up his mind that he certainly wouldn't behave in that manner when he was grown up. Not that he particularly wanted to be grown up mind for to his mind it was bad enough getting to be a year older for even though he knew he would be moving into the big school it would mean that one was expected to do much harder sums and so forth. "Has Lance not come back with you then?"

"No!" She shook her head. "In actual fact I came back because I felt it was time I spent more time with you!"

The child's face suddenly brightened. "Then will you come with me to the bajas tomorrow? I went swimming there today and it is so much fun especially when the tide is coming in and washing over the walls. I think that you will like it Rachel because I know that you are a good swimmer!"

"But what of your Mum and Dad? Won't they want to go there with you?"

"Shouldn't think so 'cause Mum claimed she was going to be kept busy 'cause it is coming to the end of the holiday and she says she has a lot of sorting out to do!" Remembering the truth of what Jake had just said Rachel opened her eyes wide in surprise. Somehow she had forgotten how close the holiday was in coming to an end. Well under the circumstances perhaps the sooner it was over the better. She forced herself to smile again in the boy's direction.

"If that is the case Jake I think I will allow you to take me to your magic pool tomorrow. I must admit I have been dying to take a dip in the ocean but things seem to have kept preventing me from doing that this time!"

The little face beamed at her. "I caught a crab in one of those rock pools when we were coming back!" For the first time Rachel noticed that the boy was holding a small bucket in his free hand. "Do you want to see my crab Rachel?" He brought the bucket closer to give her the opportunity to observe its contents in a somewhat excited manner.

Rachel pulled a face as she peered at the small obviously terrified creature within this small container. "But it's only a baby Jake, and it seems to be very frightened; do you really think you should have taken it away from its Mummy and Daddy?"

"I wanted to show it to my friends!" The boy, obviously proud of his prowess, for such an act had obviously made the boy go up in his peer group's estimation, looked surprised at her comment for he couldn't quite understand her attitude.

"And now you have shown it to them don't you think it is time to take it back then. I am sure its Mummy and Daddy will be pleased to see it!"

Jake nodded soberly the thought that he had separated this creature from its family now beginning to dawn on him. "Then will you come with me Rachel whilst I take it back then?"

"But of course if that is what you want!" The hand now had a firm grip on her own. Therefore she reasoned to say otherwise would have been churlish of her.

Thus Lance still in a state of indecision as to whether he should follow her into the hotel was treated to the sight of the two of them carrying the bucket and heading in the direction of the steps that led to the rocky shoreline.

In all truth perhaps Lance wanted to say something but he decided that this was a scene that required no interruptions as the sanctimonious disposal of one small crab took place, a creature that immediately it sensed that it was free scurried quickly away to find some rock less its captors should change their mind. Yet Lance's eyes at the time were not focussed upon this creature but upon the girl and how damned attractive she looked. Now whilst he could have kicked himself for what had transpired earlier between them and especially the things that he had intimated on that occasion, which in turn had resulted in their separation, all he could do now was to watch these proceedings from a distance!

"Then if you are not going out with that Lance today perhaps you can help me to sort out all out things. We are leaving tomorrow you know!" Mandy faced her sister over breakfast the following morning with an almost belligerent look in her eye. In all truth the older woman felt relieved that Rachel hadn't agreed to go out with that man today for now at least it would give them the opportunity to act like sisters. Realising that this was woman's talk Doug had immersed himself in his morning paper after giving some sort of an indistinguishable grunt.

"Sorry but I'm afraid I can't help you for the whole of the day!" Rachel looked steadily in Jake's direction and was rewarded by the look of glee on the boy's face. "You see it just so happens that I have found myself another young man and I have already promised that I will go out with him this morning!"

"You have found yourself another man? Really Rachel!" For her part Mandy now looked quite perplexed.

"It's me!" The child could contain himself no longer and was currently jumping up and down in some sort of excited dance. "I've promised to take Rachel to the baja because I know that she likes to swim and she hasn't been able to do that yet! Besides I know that you wouldn't have let me go there on my own and if I asked you then you would say that you were too busy, although I really have no idea why grown ups make all this fuss about packing up to go home. I suppose that it is all right when we are coming on holiday, but then you always have to wash everything when we get back home so I can't see why it takes you so long!"

"So what has happened to your other friend then?" Now shrugging her shoulders at the child's outburst, to which she had basically no reply, Mandy endeavoured to change the subject by allowing her eyes to search the dining room for sight of Lance's figure. Unfortunately this character appeared to be conspicuous by his absence that morning.

"They've quarrelled of course like all grown ups do!" The voice of wisdom piped up now determined that having made his stance he would not be ignored.

"Well perhaps under the circumstances with us returning back home tomorrow it is just as well. Anyway I wouldn't have thought you would have wanted to have got yourself involved with anyone at this stage Rachel?"

"Who said that I was involved? I can tell you quite categorically that I am not nor have I been involved with Lance Turner!" Rachel crossed her fingers behind her back. In all truth she was disappointed that she hadn't been able to spot Lance in the dining room in spite of all that she had said to the contrary. But quite obviously the man had now, for reasons better known to himself, little time for her.

She had slept fitfully the previous night toying with matters that had passed and consequently she had woke early that morning and ventured out onto her balcony in time to spot that strange looking boat once again close by the hotel. At the time she had felt her heart lurch because she had even imagined that there was a chance she would have caught a glimpse of him out in that small boat again, but today there had been no sign of the man!

"Have you got your swimming costume with you then Rachel. I have already got my trunks on under my shorts?" The boy it appeared was now beginning to get impatient for to his mind the grown ups were at it again and once they started anything could happen!

"Just give me five minutes will you?" The girl in question was forced to flash him a beaming smile.

"My Dad says you should always set your watch when a woman says anything like that. What does he mean by it?"

Rachel felt forced to smile but nevertheless this afforded her the chance to return to her room for no matter what Mandy had said at least it felt good to be able to escape in the boy's company today and preferably before Doug had seen enough of his paper at that.

She had to admit that what Jake had said about swimming in the bajas being good fun proved to be right as she relaxed in that pool and allowed the incoming tide to come over the wall and wash over her. Being mid-week the locals, who usually frequented this spot at the weekends and when it was holiday time were conspicuous by their absence as many of them were currently at work. In addition not many visitors chose to come to this spot possibly being put off by the ruggedness of the steps down which were followed by having to clamber over the rocks to reach it. But to Rachel's mind such efforts had been well worth the trek and once one had sampled it in truth it was understandable that folk would want to come back for more. She kept a wary eye on Jake and his antics of course but at the time he seemed to be acting rather like King Canute by parading up and down the stone jetty that lay to one side of the pool and thus appeared to be in no apparent danger and therefore in all truth she felt only too glad to be able to relax and wonder how she had managed to miss out on this place before.

In the throes of her relaxation she was completely unaware of the person who had been watching this scene for several minutes from the cliffs above before he finally began his descent down those steps and across the rocks to where she was. In fact she only finally saw this person when he was right up to their position yet now instead of speaking he appeared to be bending deep in thought as he traced his fingers through the water of the pool.

On the other hand however Jake had spotted the new arrival from his current position and it was typical of the child to race over to that side of the pool if only to ensure he was not going to miss out on anything. Recognising the new arrival as he drew closer he immediately made to slip his own hand into the other person's.

"I suppose you have come to see Rachel?" The boy eyed him with wide-open eyes.

Seldom could it be said that Lance Turner was taken off his guard but this was surely one exception. When he had first seen the girl from the top of the cliffs he had presumed that she was here on her own, that was when he had descended those steps as if some force outside of him had propelled him on. Now he was looking down into the face of one impatient young boy. He knew the child of course but his own speech now appeared to have frozen so surprised was he at seeing this child.

"Well, come on then!" Now the boy was impatiently tugging at his arm even as Rachel herself finally realised what was happening. "Right, are you two going to kiss and make up then?" The command that sounded in the boy's tonality brought them both up sharp and they stared at the child as if he had emanated from another planet. "Well that is what they always tell me that I have to do when I have had a quarrel!" Realising their sheer disbelief the boy now tried to justify his argument whilst the two concerned looked at each other and then regarded the child almost in suspicion. "Well go on then, get it over with!" Their silence had given the boy a sense of renewed vigour.

"Do you mean like this?" It was Lance who was the first to speak and then after giving the child a beaming smile of gratitude he moved forward to claim his reward.

"All right, that's enough!" It was then that the boy realised that this was no simple kiss, for the two, now wrapped in each other's arms seemed to be oblivious to all else.

"Oh grown ups! I really don't think that I ever want to grow up at all. I think I will remain as Peter Pan!"

Lance and Rachel however paid scant attention to anything the boy had to say for they appeared to be engrossed in each other to the exclusion of everything else and thus the would be modern day Cupid had to remain with a deflated ego as the two of them stayed confined in their own private world!

★ ★ ★ ★

Chapter Four

It was raining when they arrived back in the U.K. not a gentle infrequent shower that serves to aggravate only, but the more depressing deluge that left large puddles of lodged water along the roads that in turn awaited the passing motorist in a somewhat gleeful state as it attempted to flood their carburettors and promote the rust to start to form. They had been sheltered whilst inside the airport going through the formalities of immigration and customs as well as the tedious wait for their luggage to appear on the carousel; but once they left the confines of those buildings the worst of the elements met them. In addition as if that dark ominous cloud overhead that sought to lose weight by dispersing its water was not enough, a wind had also rose up that scotched at their person and now played havoc with any umbrella that they tried to raise.

For Rachel the very sight of this welcoming mass caused something of a deepening depression to flow over her and she now felt cruelly wrenched from the night she had spent with Lance. Was it really only this morning when she had awoke early and slipped out of that bed leaving the motionless figure of her lover still in the land of slumbers?

Deep in thought she had opened the balcony doors and slipped outside onto the tiled floor. It was then that she had spotted that boat yet again.

She remembered that at the time, obviously missing her, he had stirred and begged her to come back to bed. But to her mind the night was now over and she had much to think about. Perhaps it was with some degree of exasperation that he had finally joined her outside, his arms immediately encircling her figure as if he could not bear the thought of being separated from her.

"That's the survey vessel!" He answered her unspoken question even before she uttered it. The words had not been spoken simply because she had remembered that the last time she had spotted it there Lance himself had some part to play in its presence, for hadn't he been in that small craft that was approaching the vessel?

"But how can they possibly manage to survey the coastline in the dark?" The words were finally exacted for she was still curious about this vessel and such curiosity needed to find its voice!

"It isn't actually the coastline as such that those people happen to be studying but rather shall we say that they are watching out for illegal immigrants who just might feel inclined to try their luck at entering the place and thus gaining a foothold into Europe under the cover of darkness. Perhaps you read in the papers only last week how a boat load of these people were apprehended just off the coast of Gomera?"

"Poor souls! It seemed to be a great pity that after finally succeeding, at great risk to themselves, they never even got the chance to land and realise their dreams before they were deported back to where they had come from!" In truth she had forgotten that far from it being about a bird sanctuary, this was the same matter Lance had been summoned to Gomera about.

"Not all of them I am afraid for at least two of them managed to escape and as far as I can gather they are consequently still at large. I wonder if you would show the same quality of pity towards them if you discovered that these persons just so happened to be terrorists? Don't forget foreign nationals have already intimated that they will stop at nothing to infiltrate into our own country!"

Rachel pulled a face for she really had no answer to that, although what Lance had to do with it her thoughts could not conjure up any explanation. But those arms had never released their hold on her and now they grew more pressing as he tried to change the subject. "So now you have had your fill of strange looking vessels are you going to come back to bed Rachel for already it is almost morning?"

She snuggled down besides him feeling his arms still protectively holding her whilst at the same time she sensed the warmth of his body now on her own flesh and she now rapidly abandoned the thought of having spotted him in that boat on the previous occasion. But now all that was over. It was almost as if it was a closed book. He hadn't come to the airport with them, merely watched them leave in the taxi later on that day from the steps in front of the hotel and at that time Rachel had found his expression inscrutable!

She suddenly sensed that Mandy had been speaking to her, but then that was her sister who never wanted anyone to feel left out. "Why don't you come back to our place for the night? I'm sure you don't want to drive anywhere in such appalling conditions. What a difference a day can make to the weather!"

Rachel shook her head believing that at least her sister's words held some truth in them when she had stated what a difference a day could make! "No, honestly Mandy you have all been more than kind to me but I feel that I really need to get back to the flat!"

Knowing full well that once she had spoken her sister was unlikely to change her mind Mandy shrugged. "Oh all right then, but I will phone you tomorrow!"

"O.K." The respondent nodded in return. She knew full well that Mandy was only trying to be helpful as she always was, but there were times when Rachel coveted her own company and perhaps this was one of those times if only to reflect upon Lance and the way the relationship between them had developed. Even so he had never once suggested that they should meet up when they were both back in England. Was then all that this had been, a sort of holiday acquaintance after all?

The switching on of the central heating was the first thing of paramount importance to do upon her arrival for in truth the flat appeared forlorn, unlived in, not withstanding the fact that already she had begun to feel the cold due to the difference in temperature. Then after putting on the kettle to make herself a drink she decided that she had better check up on her E Mails. Here she found the usual pile of junk mail that had built up during her absence and she supposed it provided some degree of therapy to see all those envelopes quickly disappearing into the recycling bin. But there was one E Mail that had been waiting in cyber space until she switched her machine on that proved to be of some interest to her. It was from a Donald Jarvis, the solicitor who had been in charge of administering Brad's estate, informing her that he wanted to see her and therefore would she please get in contact with him at her first available opportunity.

Rachel frowned even as she read the message. With Brad's demise she had believed that the firm he had run had been all wound up and his estate settled, so why this person now wanted to see her appeared to be quite a mystery. She doubted very much that Donald Jarvis would require a girl Friday. But there was after all only one way by which she could find out and that was by contacting the man.

"I believe you wanted to see me ----I telephoned!" After waiting for what appeared to be an eternity Rachel finally put her own feelings to voice although for the life of her she still couldn't decide what it was that this man wanted to see her about. First however she had surmounted the difficulty of getting past the man's secretary who regarding Rachel with a somewhat disdainful look had inferred that her boss was far too engaged at that particular time to entertain any visitors. Well, at least she supposed the man had a secretary, he hadn't got her in mind for that job which made her muse on the fact as to whether she whilst she had been working as a secretary had appeared to be so unapproachable! Now however her response finally came when the person she had finally managed to see and now addressed, a man well past his years of maturity, glanced up over the top of his spectacles to ascertain who was speaking to him, almost indeed as if he had forgotten that she had an appointment for that day. Indeed it appeared to take this character several seconds before he finally recognised her, during which time Rachel became conscious of the ticking of the carriage clock perched high upon a shelf that had once boasted to be part of a mantelpiece that had been placed over an open fire.

"Ah Rachel isn't it ---good of you to come!" At last some sort of recognition as to what constituted her presence in the office seemed to register with him. He started then to fish into one of the drawers that adorned the antique piece of furniture that he termed as his desk. Still when he finally produced the envelope and handed it to her across the top of this item of furniture she was still surprised even though she knew full well that Don Jarvis had been left to tidy up Brad's estate. In truth she had never expected to receive anything at all for she knew full well that Brad had other relatives whom he had spoken about but whom she had never met and therefore the sight of this envelope now served to puzzle her.

"Brad left instructions that this envelope was to be given to you personally. Indeed it was left in my trust only a short time before his unfortunate demise following that dreadful accident. Although I must admit that I have no idea what is inside it, for as you can see it is stated on the flap that this envelope is only to be opened by you!"

Rachel's fingers curled thoughtfully around the article as she caught sight of her name scrawled on the front of it in Brad's familiar handwriting. Still puzzling as to what this was all about she immediately made to tear the envelope open. Inside of it there was a single sheet of paper and yet scanning her eyes across this Rachel could make little sense out of the contents at all for to her mind her initial perusal noted only numerous figured listed in well organised rows.

"This isn't some sort of sick joke is it?" She turned almost in a stroppy mood to face the solicitor and waving the contents in front of him.

"Sorry Rachel but I have no idea. I was merely instructed that the envelope should be passed onto you. I am afraid I have no idea as to its contents!"

"But the whole thing is totally absurd. What are these columns of numbers referring to and what on earth have they got to do with me?"

The other man shook his head peering now at the paper she still held aloft. "I really have no idea Rachel although I must say that knowing Brad I can hardly concede that it is something of a joke. Surely you must have some idea to what the numbers refer to otherwise why should he have been so insistent that they were to be passed on to you?"

"To me they resemble the machinations of someone who was sick in the mind. Well although I know Brad may have been said to be some things but he was most certainly not sick in the mind!"

"Then perhaps when you have had the time to peruse them more closely their meaning might possibly become clearer to you!"

"Maybe but I very much doubt it!" Still pondering she folded the slip of paper and returned it to its envelope. At least she supposed she had the satisfaction of seeing Don Jarvis exhibit some element of surprise when she subsequently returned the envelope back into her pocket.

"Then you do have some idea what these numbers are for after all?"

"In a word I have not a clue. But maybe I will just hang onto them for posterity!" She adopted a light-hearted tone. In truth the whole exercise in coming here had been quite pointless, but then there was something about Brad that had always remained a mystery to her, for whilst he openly ran a publishing business there had been another side to his character and she for one had never understood how deeply the man had been involved with the second string to his bow. Oh yes, as his secretary she had handled the mail appertaining to his pleasure yacht hire, although in truth she had never quite understood his involvement with this apart that was from supplementing his income when the recession had made the other part of his business appear to be a little unstable, and as far as she could gather this line had appeared to prove most profitable.

"Well it helps to keep the wolf from the door!" She remembered him saying those words whilst he had passed her a crooked grin once when she had questioned him, but never at any time had she seen anything at all that could be said to relate to these columns of numbers. Her first inclination had therefore been to lay the paper back down on the lawyer's table, but then she had decided that if Brad wanted her to have these things and had therefore left them in his lawyer's safe keeping then perhaps the least she could do was to keep the paper for a time before she despatched it to the recycling bin! Come to think of it there was quite a lot that she didn't know about Brad even though they had worked together, but then she had only been his secretary. Of course perhaps in fact Brad had expected more but to Rachel's mind there always had been a certain something that separated them. That of course was the reason why she was going to decline the man's proposal on that unfortunate day in Fuerteventura, why in fact she had made some excuse to go there on her own in the first place, although primarily to sort her own thoughts out she had accepted his proposed arrival as an opportunity to clear matters between them once and for all.

"So have you found another job yet?" The lawyer regarded her candidly across the table possibly realising that it was time to change the subject.

"Not yet!" She shook her head accepting the change of topic almost gladly now. "But there again I've haven't really had the time nor the opportunity up until the present to even think about it!"

Her companion grunted although Rachel almost aligned the sound he made to some sort of snort. "One must admit that there is some truth in your argument, but if you are interested I happen to know that a colleague of mine could no doubt afford you such an opportunity if you would like me to speak to him!"

"Thank you but no!" Something inside her made Rachel shiver at the thought of working in some dreary office such as the one she was currently in. "Actually although I must thank you for the offer I do feel that I must now try to stand on my own two feet in this matter!" To her mind Rachel felt she wanted to finish with anything that was remotely connected to Brad and now find a new beginning for herself. In this she desired no further memories of the past to confound her for now she only desired to be able to push them all to the back of her mind although she admitted it might be difficult to forget them completely.

"Well if you do change your mind once you have tested the market then you have only to contact me and I will see what I can come up with!" Don Jarvis attempted to fuse a smile upon his dour features but his efforts resulted only in giving her something of a grimace.

Consequently in her anxiety now to leave the place any thought of that envelope and its contents seemed to pale into insignificance. Indeed the envelope and it contents must have lain where she had placed it in her handbag for six weeks or more before she had reason to bring it to mind yet again. But by that time other things had impinged upon her that had served to impede any thought process on those nonsensical numbers!

Lance Turner read through the message he had just received for a second time. As one would expect the contents were precise but succinct and to the point, the man known of as Bradley Stevens had now apparently left Morocco and under the assumed name of Winston Devereaux had entered Tenerife with the express purpose of awaiting a certain pleasure cruiser that was at this time travelling from the U.K towards this destination. Apart from the fact that the man was supposedly deceased and was travelling under an assumed name, the one he had actually chosen was of little surprise to Lance. For the person in question had been associated with Devereaux hire boats on the Island for some time, yet although upon its arrival this craft called the Sea Witch was supposed to dock at Gigantes this item could by no means be taken to be the absolute truth for the manner in which this vessel was travelling by seemingly putting into ports at will on the journey led one to suspect that such a destination could be changed if so desired. All of which naturally served to place Lance in studious thought, for there were ample ports where such a pleasure cruiser could make a landing here on this Island and so the question was which way was he supposed to turn? As well as this his attention was now also been drawn to a second matter, one that intimated that Stevens had some sort of involvement with another person in the U.K. It was the name of this second person moreover that caused him to frown all the more.

He shrugged his shoulders as he glanced yet again at the likeness of Bradley Stevens before printing out a copy of the man's features. To his mind there appeared only one thing he could do about it and that was to inform the contacts he had in this place to be on the look out for a man answering this description and to let him know immediately if they were to spot him. He frowned again for no doubt these contacts would have been at a loss to know that at the time it was not so much the man their colleague wanted to apprehend but also the contents that this craft was carrying.

The first person therefore Lance was to contact was Jose, for the man already having a boat in Gigantes had a good eye for any strange vessel visiting that port and Jose also had friends and acquaintances in other ports on the Island omitting Santa Cruz itself where he deemed Stevens would never dare to have the boat to land bearing in mind the strict security around that major port.

His strategy appeared to be paying off for going down to the port in Gigantes several days later it was to find Jose in the state of some considerable excitement expressed in an attitude that spelt out the phrase that one could always rely upon Jose to meter out the most difficult of challenges.

"Your man has been spotted in the area!" Jose spoke with a sense of achievement almost as if he had accomplished this mission for himself. "Also I believe that a pleasure cruiser, the Sea Witch is due to arrive from the U.K. any day now. So what do you want me to do about it?"

"Nothing, precisely nothing at the moment. Just inform me when this boat arrives will you?"

"But what of this man you were enquiring about?" The fisherman was now definitely puzzled.

"We do nothing at the moment. Oh don't worry amigo for his time will come. First however I need to find out exactly what cargo that boat has on board!"

"But it is a pleasure craft Senor Lance. Such vessels do not normally carry cargo!"

"I am led to believe that this craft could be slightly different. But then I am only obeying my orders!"

"Then it has some connection with your real estate?"

"Perhaps Jose, perhaps!" Lance was not prepared to go into any more detail as he paid the fisherman for his trouble.

Still in the event the vessel did not land as was predicted for an unexpected storm sprung up to suddenly hit the coastline and both the ship and the man who was awaiting it appeared to vanish as a result of this storm that lashed the coastline over the next forty-eight hours.

----------------Bradley Stevens, for perhaps the first time in his life had appeared, at least on the surface, to be most benevolent towards Ned Dorkins, a part time yacht skipper, whom he had employed on several occasions to ferry his pleasure craft.

At the time he had posed his request in an almost beseeching manner to the seafarer. "Ned, the Sea Witch is now ready for hiring out next season and consequently I would like you to take her down to Tenerife for me!"

"And I presume that would be to join your other vessels in Gigantes?"

"Of course. If possible I would like her to be there in good time for the start of next season but after saying that it should leave you plenty of time to make the trip there. In fact if you want to I have no objections to you pulling in at Vigo on the way and even Cadiz if you wish. That should give you time to be able to stretch your legs and buy in fresh supplies. By the way who have you got crewing for you at the moment?"

In truth Ned could not believe his ears at the offer of such a leisurely trip with days off on route as well as all expenses being thrown in for good measure. "Old Tom. Say what you will about the chap's age but yon bastard is still a good seaman. Still when would you want us to leave?"

"I suppose I must say as soon as it is convenient. Have you got other work on at the moment?"

The other shook his head. "Nay, not with the recession methinks, folk seem to be too worried about their brass at the moment to be bothered about yachts, especially at this time of the year!"

"Then their reticence must I think, prove to be in my favour!"

With a casual look at the speaker Ned fished in his cabinet to produce the necessary charts and waited for Brad to furnish him with a few more details. "I suppose you have got the necessary papers for this voyage?"

"Why, don't you trust me?" In response the speaker dangled a substantial retainer in front of him and as he had anticipated the seaman's eyes were immediately fixed upon the bundle.

"But of course Mr Stevens, I am sure you will have attended to such detail!"

"Good then we can consider the matter settled. Oh by the way Ned, because of my profession I am finding it necessary at the moment to call myself by another name and therefore, for reasons I am not prepared to go into at the moment, you will be working for a certain Winston Devereaux if the question arises!"

"Then if that is the name you prefer to be known of then so be it!"

"Good man Dorkins. I think that when you finally arrive in Tenerife with the craft you will not find me ungrateful!" He left the seaman in a rather abrupt manner. Not that Ned considered that was anything to do with him. As far as he was concerned the man provided him with work and more than that he was always over generous when he had completed a task for him. Therefore to his mind it was quite irrelevant as to whether the owner was present when he arrived in Tenerife or otherwise. All that was left for him to do was to root out old Tom; he knew full well where he would find him, reminiscing in some seaman's hostelry and then the two of them had to prepare the Sea Witch for its voyage. It was said that the Bay of Biscay could be rough at this time of the year, but not to men of their experience. Besides with the time lapse they had been allotted it was perfectly feasible for them to cruise in shore and close to the coast.

Even so Tom was given to query the matter when Ned approached him. "What's he on about changing his name for anyway? Must say it all sounds a bit fishy to me if you want my opinion. What's he got on that craft then?"

"As far as I can understand his yacht hire company in Tenerife goes under the name of Devereaux. I once asked him about it and he said it was more expedient for him to have it that way, his mother's maiden name being that for she apparently had some French connection. Anyway for a thousand knicker for the tour not to mention all expenses paid perhaps it is best not to ask such questions. But in all probability it will be some sort of a tax dodge if I know that man and if it is then all I can say is good luck to the guy especially when the government is only too keen to relieve one of their hard earned brass!"

"You are saying that he is paying a thousand quid for this job?" To Tom's mind this amount seemed to put a different complexion on matters.

"Not only has he paid us a thousand quid but he has also given us a card to cover our expenses in Vigo!"

"Then I wonder what his cargo is worth if he is able to splash his money around like that?"

"That is not for us to question Tom. Not if we want to benefit out of this job. Anyway he says that his load has already been cleared by customs so I for one am not willing to question him. Why are you?"

"Suppose not!" The other man shrugged in something appertaining to resignation.

"Then just see that you don't go shouting your mouth off about all of this when you call for a pint tonight. Otherwise there are those who will be wanting to take on this job for themselves!"

"So when do we leave?"

"As soon as possible. Apparently the boss has already gone to the trouble of getting supplies on board for us. The man appears to be in something of a hurry for the Sea Witch to depart these shores but then I suppose if he wants to get it to his fleet before the season finishes --- Anyway I suggest we leave tomorrow before he changes his mind!"

The other grunted in a non-committal way. To Tom the whole idea stunk but then he wasn't going to forgo the proviso of the generous payment made for undertaking the trip!

-----------Rachel supposed she was lucky when she managed to find a job as a secretary in a manufacturing firm that was situated quite close to her flat this time around and life therefore began to settle into some form of normality as she tried to turn her mind now on her work during the weekday s and her family at the weekend.

She had in effect just closed her transactions for the day and was making to cross the road to catch the bus back home when she suddenly spied a certain figure she had never expected to set her eyes upon again. With a slight gasp she stood for a moment absolutely still, quite sure that her eyes must be deceiving her before she shouted out a name more out of shock than anything else, yet although she felt sure that her voice must have carried across the road the other figure did not turn, although she felt convinced at the time that he hesitated for a brief moment before she saw his shoulders flinch. She called out his name again but this time the stranger appeared to quicken his step and Rachel found that it was impossible to cross the road immediately because of the sudden surge of teatime traffic as the lights changed allowing them to proceed along the street, and by the time she eventually did reach the opposite pavement the figure she had once espied had completely vanished.

"What's the matter then? Have you got something on your mind? I must say that you appear to be very pensive tonight!" Mandy stopped her sisterly recital in mid flow as she now eyed her sister's face. Being her sister and because the girls had always been close, Mandy could usually decipher if something happened to be troubling the girl.

"Oh it's nothing! I think I must have been having some sort of illusions that's all!"

"Why, what happened, what makes you say that?"

"If you must know I was convinced for a moment that I actually saw Brad in the town just after I had finished work. So now perhaps you will be convinced that your sister is in the midst of some traumatic condition!"

"Who was it that you saw then, have you any idea?" Mandy looked puzzled.

"I've no idea!" Rachel shook her head. "I shouted out but whoever it was never responded and by the time I managed to cross the street this person, whether a ghost or otherwise, had completely disappeared!"

Mandy adopted an air of concern. "Well I suppose that after all you have been through it's not really surprising. In all probability your mind has not yet fully adjusted to the fact that Brad is no longer with us. It is not as if they ever found any remains of anyone who was on that flight and therefore I expect your brain is still finding it difficult to accept the fact that the man is dead. Still I did presume you might be getting him out of your system after you met Lance whilst we were out in Tenerife. Have you not heard form him since we got back by the way?"

"No but there again Lance Turner was a law unto himself!"

"And I actually thought the two of you had something going out there. At least that is how it appeared to me. You disappoint me sister. So it was Brad you cared about all of the time?"

"Nothing could be further from the truth Mandy. If Lance did nothing else he did convince me that marrying Brad would have been the biggest blunder of my life! Anyway for reasons we need not dwell upon, the question of marrying Brad never arose and for that I am truly thankful!"

"Yet now you are claiming that you have seen a man who no longer exists? To change the subject however what did the lawyer have to say when you were summoned to his holy grail the other week?"

"Not a great deal except for informing me that Brad's estate had now been finalised!" Rachel frowned for to her mind the fact that she had been asked to attend that dreary lawyer's office still just didn't make sense! Surely that envelope containing the paper was not all that important, and if the man had been determined she should have it then he could always have posted it to her. "Apparently for some reason unknown to me Brad had left this envelope with my name on it!" She obligingly fished in her bag to produce it. After all there was no secret about its contents, she only wished she knew herself what it was all about. Still in truth up until this time she had thought little about it since discarding it to her handbag having decided that she could make neither head nor tail of its contents.

"But what does it mean?" Mandy eyed the paper containing those numbers with the same abhorrent horror as she would have eyed a school maths examination paper and of course mathematics was one subject that Mandy had not relished when she was at school.

"Guess I really have no idea!" Her sister glanced at her frankly as she made to pick the paper up again. "That's part of the trouble!"

"Maybe Doug will have some idea. He is actually useful for some things you know and puzzles like this usually intrigue him!" Mandy smiled benignly as she took the paper again this time to hand over to her husband who had just appeared on the scene.

"What makes you think I should know what it is?" The big man turned the paper over thoughtfully eyeing it like some Sudako puzzle and then making a series of grunts as if this was a clue to set the machinations of his brain into action. "Well I could be wrong but to my mind it almost looks as if it has something to do with a shipping chart!"

Having issued his profound statement Doug put on the appearance that he was glad that he had been asked!

"A shipping chart, now why on earth would Brad be wanting to leave Rachel a shipping chart? For goodness sake the man was in the publishing business!"

"He did have another interest, I know that from acting as his secretary. Apparently he had something to do with yacht hire for holidaymakers in the Canaries. He seemed to be the major shareholder in some organisation that went under the name of Devereaux, he told me once that was his mother's maiden name and therefore he had adopted that name so as to keep the two businesses separate!"

For a moment Mandy regarded her as though she had been withholding some vital information. "That still doesn't explain why he left you with a shipping chart if that is what it is! Anyway I tend to disagree if the matter was so important to him although why he should have recorded lines of latitude, if that is what they are, that have no bearing whatsoever on those Islands is I suppose another matter. You are saying that you know nothing of this? Then to my mind the chap must have been something of a joker!"

The very idea of Brad ever having the wit to joke about anything was not something that Rachel could accept however. For in truth she had never experienced the man in a jovial mood at all. Maybe that had something to do with her final decision concerning their relationship. "Somehow I don't think it is a joke although the answer to the puzzle completely evades me!" Doug shrugged. As he did not appear to be getting much farther in this argument he decidedly began to lose interest for he had far more interesting things to occupy himself with. Perhaps his wife also took the hint from him as well.

"If we don't know the answers perhaps you ought to try to forget about it Rachel. After all even if we knew what it was it would still mean little to us!"

Rachel supposed her sister did have a point and without another word she retrieved the paper and returned it to her bag.

-----------The fact that the Sea Witch pulled into Gigantes harbour several days late was one thing, the fact that the customs searching the vessel could find nothing untoward stowed away on board was another, both of which served to make Lance puzzled, but then the fact that Brad Stevens or Winston Devereaux, the non de plume he appeared to prefer to be known as, was nowhere to be sighted possibly served to puzzle him even more.

"What cargo were they looking for anyway?" Jose nodded as he watched as the Spanish authorities decided to abandon their hopeless quest.

"The proceeds of one major jewel robbery in the U.K.!" Lance adopted a serious tone. "It was anticipated that the Sea Witch was possibly chosen as being an ideal get away craft as it had a legitimate reason for coming out to these Islands!"

"A jewel robbery? But surely there must have been more than one interested source in those contents!"

"My Superior appears to think that such articles were destined for one place. After all one can purchase quite a considerable amount of armaments with a collateral that goes well past the double figure in millions! No it would appear that the vessel must have been intercepted on route. See if you can find out if and where the craft docked on the way here, will you Jose?"

The other man looked rather puzzled at Lance's request. If the ship had been destined to make Tenerife and it had arrived, it took some time to convince him that the ship's master would have any ulterior motive to dock at any port on the way here unless a storm had blown up at the time and the skipper has been forced to seek refuge. Still Jose was nothing if not resourceful. He was already well known amongst the boating fraternity and certain questions placed strategically were bound to produce some fruit.

"According to old Tom they made port at Vigo. Apparently their master had previously told them to make a leisurely trip down here. He paid well for their services and also if old Tom is to be believed handed them an expenses paid card to stop off at Vigo on route!"

"So did they unload the cargo there do you know?"

Jose shook his head. " Sorry but I can't answer that one! To the best of old Tom's knowledge they were carrying no cargo. The whole idea of the voyage was to bring the craft to the Devereaux hire outfit over here. They were of course delayed by that storm and had to seek shelter off Maderia for a session, which was the reason that lay behind their late arrival."

"So I presume their employer did not sail with them at any stage on this trip?"

"No he actually claimed that he was far too tied up with other matters but would catch up with them in Tenerife!"

"And yet the man was not here to receive his craft!" Lance pursed his lips, so the switch if one had been made looked likely to have taken place in Vigo especially if the two members of crew were otherwise occupied at the time. But there again it was extremely unlikely that such a cargo would have been left in that city for the authorities there would have been far too vigilant for that, therefore the only other alternative was that it had been switched to another vessel whilst the crew were out of sight. He frowned for this was a matter he would now have to report back and Lance knew from past experience that his masters would be non too pleased with his reasoning, especially as it was a theory only and he had no tangible proof that this had happened!

His suppositions were correct for after Lance had dutifully reported matters as he saw them, he quickly found that he was summoned back to Whitehall. For a moment his mind switched onto Rachel as he supposed that this could provide an opportunity for him to see her once again. Yet upon perusing about the girl as well as the man she had previously worked for, the thought did cross his mind as to whether she had been party to what had been going on. And even though he tried to forget this, for he could not believe that the girl could be so two faced, the idea still rankled at the back of his mind.

⋆ ⋆ ⋆ ⋆

Chapter Five

The monotonous drone appeared to continue incessantly within close parameters on the octave scale and thus had the effect on Lance that made him begin to study the pin stripes of the suit worn by the man from whom these sounds emanated. The man in fact who occupied the chair across the desk from him in an office that appeared to be more akin with the early twentieth century than with current day décor. One could almost imagine that should one of the books be removed from off the stack of shelves that occupied a single wall of the room it would result in a tsunami of dust particles that could possibly choke any occupant who happened to be sitting there possibly at the time in all innocence! Of course he was well aware of why he had been summoned here and what was more at that time he had firmly arrived at the decision that should the Ministry be seeking to dispense with his services then the future outlook must surely prove to be more conducive in its enticement than these on going reverberations!

Still maybe Lance had not reckoned on the fact that the Ministry was normally loathe to dispense with any of its members and therefore his thoughts were jerked back into reality and away from the pin stripe suit with its trouser creases knife pressed, when he suddenly realised that the faceless one across the table had now ceased his rhetoric and had moreover now stood, whilst at the same time the individual was holding out a paper to him.

"Your contact!" The voice was still remarkably expressionless and as the man appeared to be fascinated in glancing around the room almost as if he was searching for something Lance could not help but wonder if he was indeed looking for his bowler hat to complete his uniform before he took his leave, for surely such a person would not deem to sally forth improperly dressed! "Chad Edwards will be working very closely with you in the future in an attempt to trace the missing cachet. Your own mission however is primarily to find this Brad Stevens or Winston Devereaux as he now prefers to be called and arrange if possible for him to be removed from the scene. I only hope that I have made myself quite clear on that point because now I am afraid I must leave you due to the fact that I have a prior appointment in Whitehall!"

He was obviously expecting Lance to leave the office before he did and moreover the one in question felt only too eager to oblige for now his prime motivation of thought was to search out some coffee house so that he might seek to quell the dust he felt accumulating in his throat and naturally enough whilst he was there to spend some time considering his brief not to mention a great deal of thought!

Lance allowed the mug of coffee time to percolate his senses before he decided that his first objective must surely be to seek out this man Chad Edwards before he could do anything else. In truth the person was not completely unknown to him and he also had a good idea as to where he was likely to find his counterpart. But upon arrival at the place where he had expected to find him it was to spy this individual in the act of preparing to leave his surrounds. Still the man was prepared to listen to Lance's rhetoric, although in truth Lance felt convinced that it posed no surprises to this individual.

"From what you have told me then it would appear that my first destination must be Vigo itself if as you surmise the cargo was removed at that place and possibly transferred to another vessel. Still at the moment I do have to keep an appointment in the Midlands so maybe it would be in both of our interests if you accompanied me and we would then have the opportunity to talk some more on this issue!"

Lance nodded for it was apparently anticipated that this was what would happen for obviously the man had previously been well briefed on the situation. "So you are saying the person whom you seek never arrived in Tenerife even though he was expected?" Chad Edwards pursed his lips at the notion even as they were driving out of the city.

"That is correct and much I suggest to the chagrin of his two hirelings who had brought the boat from England and were expecting to meet him there in all probability to receive their dues!"

"Then if a switch of vessels was made at Vigo then it could realistically follow that this Brad Stevens had no intention of making that port in Tenerife as he had led others to believe for no doubt the man knew full well where the cargo was currently heading. And of course if the seamen were invited to take an unexpected break at that place en route then it would afford a switch to take place without fear of being noticed!"

"But where exactly the acquired vessel is now supposed to be heading is something that I will need to establish for myself if I am ever to trace this person!"

"But of course, that is probably where our paths will come together. Perhaps we will talk some more over lunch for I am afraid that my current engagement is something I can ill afford to miss!" They were presently pulling into a car park in the Birmingham area. "I do not think it will take me very long however so perhaps we can meet back here in say sixty minutes time?"

Lance nodded. At the time he had no firm notion of any other options in mind. Perhaps indeed biding his time wandering around the city centre for a spell might at least bring something to mind. Thus left alone with his thoughts he began to question where exactly he was now supposed to find this elusive Mr Deveraux and Lance became more and more convinced that the present destination of this person could only be currently in the Midlands. Again he remained puzzled in his thoughts as to how this Stevens, supposedly blown apart in that explosion had not only managed to survive but had also succeeded in adopting this new identity. Even so he did not have to wait too long before the first part to this puzzle was solved by way of the mobile that took it upon itself to shrill its tones from within his pocket.

Listening to the message that was imparted it was soon abundantly clear that it was coming from the security boffins and moreover what they had to inform him was really quite simple. Winston Devereaux had currently entered the country at an airport in the Midland Region with a legitimate passport that was made out in his name and had been checked thoroughly by the security screening process at the airport. Furthermore his own orders were now reinforced in that he was expected to find this man. Yet if in all truth this individual had entered the country legally as someone bearing the name of Winston Devereaux, then who was the poor devil who had lost his life in that explosion and furthermore if security had known so much about this man then why on earth had he not been detained at the airport upon his arrival? Lance drummed his fingers as he chewed the matter over. One thought possibly gave an answer to his question, perhaps indeed the whole exercise had been set to test his own efficiency!

"You appear morose my friend?" Chad Edwards chided him on the matter over lunch after his own meeting had obviously passed to his satisfaction.

"Then tell me one thing if you can. How is it possible for someone who is apparently blown up in an explosion to suddenly return to the country with a new identity and moreover gain admittance through Security?"

"Maybe I could suggest that the man was not blown up at all! If you are speaking of the man Devereaux, as I believe you are, then I would suggest it would hardly be surprising if money was unable to provide him with the means to gain admittance. Indeed quite possibly money could have also provided someone to step into his shoes on that flight and assume such an identity on a false passport. It would not be the first time that ruse had been executed although I doubt that the poor sap who was involved realised at the time that he was a walking time bomb!"

"A bomb which now I presume you are now suggesting he took through the security check on his way to board the craft without anybody noticing?"

"Not necessarily. It would not be the first time that someone belonging to the airport security had been conned. Still don't ask me how it was managed with all the current checks in progress. Maybe there was even a mole somewhere within the airport concourse itself, in which case this person posing as Brad Stevens must surely have been of limited intelligence not to have been aware of a switch in brief cases or whatever! But there again I suppose one could say that anyone who was recruited into that role in the first place must have been either daft or extremely short of funds!"

"I still cannot come to terms with the point of blowing up an aircraft if Stevens intended to make a re-appearance using an assumed name!"

"That is something one can only hazard a guess about, which I believe you have already done for yourself. For reasons known only to himself, Brad Stevens obviously needed to disappear permanently from the scene. He also needed to make an effort to please his new masters and from what has happened he appears to have succeeded in achieving both with this one action! Still that ball is now in your court mate for I myself am heading back to the digs now in order to throw a few things in a case and prepare myself for Europe after I have succeeded in booking myself on the first available flight to somewhere closer to Vigo. Are you coming back with me?"

Lance shook his head. He didn't know whether he was doing right at the time but the Midlands appeared to be a suitable place to commence his search. "Perhaps that would be pointless much as I enjoy your company, especially after one takes into consideration that our man did actually land here in the Midlands only a short time ago and with a bit of luck he could still be in the vicinity!"

Chad nodded his head in some form of agreement before finally taking his leave. It was as he watched the car depart that Lance remembered that this was also the area where Rachel's family lived and this thought immediately brought something else to mind and moreover the thought did not sit too comfortably upon his shoulders especially when he remembered the name of the second person whom his Superiors had haphazardly recited as being one of Steven's contacts. Was it possible that Rachel was now aware that Brad was back in this area for it did appear most convenient for that man to choose to fly into an airport that was so close at hand! Moreover the Midlands had been the place where he had habited his original office. Almost in desperation he tried to wipe such seeds of suspicion away, but the seeds appeared to have taken a firm hold and he was therefore left with a lingering doubt in his mind, which seemed to gather a momentum of its own volition!

Moreover such suspicions were to be further cemented when as he sat still enjoying his coffee being in no great hurry to follow Chad's example, he happened to spy a familiar figure emerging from one of the nearby buildings. In truth, after managing to find a job as a temporary secretary for a nearby firm Rachel had taken the opportunity to bob out to the shops for one or two items during her lunch hour but Lance was not aware of this. His first inclination had been to make himself known to the girl for surely or so his thoughts told him, Rachel could never be guilty of any conspiracy; yet his training halted such intentions for now it would be far better for him to play this game with caution. He needed to follow at a distance and yet remain completely unnoticed for the time being. That of course was the reason why Lance was to find himself in the middle of a supermarket desperately searching now for something to put into his basket whilst Rachel herself was by this time at the check out paying for her goods. Thus she left the place without noticing the man who was following her and Lance was left to try to rethink his own position especially once he had left the checkout with a load of goods he really did not want!

----------Perhaps it was fortunate that after tea that same evening Doug had retired to watch his favourite television programme whilst Mandy and her sister were still finding something to occupy themselves with in the kitchen, because this was the factor that allowed young Jake to be in the position to spot the person who almost appeared to be hesitating outside of the house. The child moreover expressed little surprise when curiosity getting the better of him he went outside himself and saw that it was Lance standing there. Indeed his childish eyes lit up as he associated the memory of Lance with having a great time when they had been on holiday.

"You're the man we met when we were on holiday!" The child greeted the other in a profound manner having now come to the firm decision that this was indeed the man and not some figment of his imagination. In truth Lance having caught sight of Rachel disappearing into her place of employ had followed her when she had left that evening, after first booking himself an hotel reservation to complete a task he now found to be quite intriguing.

"I decided that I was missing you all!" Putting on his most beseeching expression Lance decided that perhaps the best thing to do was to pander to the child's emotions. "But tell me something will you, is Rachel here?" That was a dumb question, he knew full well she was here for hadn't he followed her to this place when she had left her work.

"Why do you always want to play with Rachel? Oh, if you must know she is in the kitchen with my Mum at the moment. But she doesn't live here of course, she is just visiting!"

"Then how good are you at keeping a secret?" Lance looked around anxious less anyone else could overhear the conversation. Perhaps he had almost given the game away by coming here as it was, but then what else could he have said to the child under the circumstances? Still the boy responded by nodding his head as if in the midst of some conspiracy, and adopted a more sombre mode. Well he supposed that was what grown ups did when they were asked to keep a secret. Yet for this man to actually ask if he could keep a secret must surely mean that he was treating him like a grown up because actually only grown ups kept secrets from one another.

"Well it goes something like this. You see Rachel doesn't know that I am here and I would really like to surprise her, so please don't tell anyone that I have been here will you? I promise I will catch up with Rachel later for what I want to say to her is rather personal!"

The boy nodded again by this time trying his best to ponder profoundly on the situation. He still wondered why this man, if he wanted to surprise Rachel had not bothered to see her here for even if it was something personal he wanted to talk to her about Jake was quite sure his Mum would have let them use the parlour for their tete a tete. But then he supposed that all grown ups were well known for doing the strangest things!

"I suppose so. Why have you bought Rachel a ring or something?" The boy prided himself on the fact that at least he believed he knew something about the ways of the adult world especially when they wanted to surprise someone and if he wanted to speak to Rachel on her own this surely would provide a reasonable explanation. Moreover it was much to the lad's surprise that the current expression such a question elicited on the man's face indicated that perhaps he wasn't in full agreement with this sentiment. But then Jake supposed he wouldn't be, not in the first instance anyway for adults usually didn't like people guessing all their secrets!

"Something like that I guess!" Lance was not for revealing anything else about his current quest. "But now I am afraid I must take my leave. Can I rely on you to keep our little secret though?"

Jake nodded still deep in thought. Of course he supposed it could be regarded as being something of a privilege for a man to trust one so many years his junior. And thus he watched as Lance without further ado made to leave, not that was until the lad became conscious that his mother was now calling him.

"Was that someone at the door that I heard Jake?"

"Oh it was only one of my friends mum!" The child crossed his fingers behind his back as he spoke. It was not natural for him to speak anything but the truth but then he supposed he could regard Lance as being one of his friends.

Outside of the house in the front street Lance took a deep breath. At least he supposed he had discovered where Rachel's family lived and where she herself was currently visiting, not to mention the fact that in all probability the girl herself would shortly be leaving this place to wend her way back again to her own habitat. Indeed to discover where this was all he had to do now was to wait for he still needed to find out whether Rachel had indeed made any contact with this Brad Stevens since his return and yet in his heart he now hoped that this could be proven not to be the case.

Perhaps his hopes on that score were justified when he finally was able to follow the girl back to her own flat in the area. At the time prior to her arrival the place had appeared to be in total darkness, yet in spite of his overwhelming desire to make himself known to her he was now compelled to wait outside until the place was plunged into darkness for the night and he realised that she had certainly had no visitors on that particular evening!

Jake Ogden glanced at the painting he had just completed on the easel in the pre-school playroom and then after deliberately dipping his brush in the dirty paint water he applied the same to erase all recognisable features in that work. In truth Jake was bored for now he was ready to go to the big school, he had done all the things that this playgroup could offer him and he had now to watch younger children going through the same motions as he himself had completed at an earlier age. The sad thing about it was though that the big school had still not decided to offer him a place declaring that his birthday wasn't in the right month or something like that and therefore he had been left, much against his will, to spend a further term here in this place.

Still he supposed there was one good thing to look forward to, his Aunt Rachel was going to pick him up from the group tonight because Mummy and Daddy were going somewhere. And Jake did not mind that in the slightest for Aunt Rachel was always good fun and they normally had a great time together. Slowly he removed his apron and put his sodden painting, or what remained of it to dry. It would soon be story time now and that meant that home time could not be far off coming!

"Is that your painting Jake?" The teacher had moved across to where he had just placed his masterpiece and was looking at it with a rather puzzled expression. "But I can't see anything on it Jake, what is it supposed to be?"

"A foggy day! You can't see very much when it is foggy!" At least the lad was pleased at having the wit to be able to defuse the situation for the teacher merely shrugged and moved on. All he had to do now was to wait for home time coming!

As promised Rachel was stood at the gate waiting for him when he emerged from the door and gladly he ran to place his hand in hers. It was a warm loving hand that took his, one that he was familiar with, but wait a minute------- His thoughts went back to the night the man had come round to the house. He had said that he wanted to surprise Rachel with a ring, but now Rachel had no ring on her finger and that was the place where most adults wore them.

"What's the matter pet?" Rachel sensed that the boy had suddenly tensed.

"You are not wearing the ring Rachel?" Jake was puzzled.

"Ring ----What ring are you talking about Jake?" Now it was Rachel's turn to question.

"The one the man was going to surprise you with!"

"What man?"

"Oh you know the one whom we met whilst we were on holiday, the one you seemed to like!"

"Do you mean Lance?" Rachel's face flushed. Of course she still had no idea what the child was talking about. As far as she was concerned she had left Lance behind in Tenerife and of course she had heard nothing from him since. Not, or so she told herself, that she was expecting to hear anything from him, so where Jake had got this ridiculous notion from must have been inspired by some fairy tale!

"Yes he came round to my house the other night asking about you but he made me promise not to tell anyone because he wanted to surprise you. Did he not give you a ring after all then?"

"I haven't seen anything of Lance not since we came home!" Now it was Rachel's turn to appear puzzled.

"But he was waiting outside of my house for you because you were talking to my Mummy at the time and he wanted to surprise you!"

"With a ring?"

"Well I asked him that and he said something like it!"

"I bet he did only his something like it must have been to follow me home!"

"Why did he want to do that Rachel?"

"I'm afraid I don't know the answer to that one Jake, I guess I'll have to try to find that out!"

Rachel's thoughts however were not quite as placid as what her tone made them out to be at that time. How dare the man, she could have practically have screamed out aloud? What gave him the right---? Yet something inside of her told her even then that Lance must have been following her for a purpose, and the only possible purpose why he should want to follow her and remain unknown could only be something to do with Brad Stevens. And then the ludicrous thought hit her. She had really believed that Lance Turner had thought something about her for herself, how wrong could one be, for if that had been the case then surely he wouldn't have needed to resort to having to follow her around in secret?

By the time Mandy and Doug came to collect their son Rachel had time to spend fuming over Jake's revelation that Lance Turner was apparently not only here in this country but he also appeared to be watching her movements for reasons only hazarded by herself. For to her mind this hardly reflected the behaviour of a so-called real estate employ even though she admitted her thoughts in the past had strangely enough decried this as being his sole occupation. Perhaps because of her morose state of mind Jake began to realise that his Aunt was not exhibiting half the fun he remembered her by, in fact even his mother noticed that the girl had obviously something on her mind when they came to collect him after sharing the meal out that they had promised themselves.

"Oh she's just upset because that man hasn't given her the ring that he promised!" The voice of wisdom rang out in explanation when he caught his mother's glance in her sister's direction.

"What man?" Now Mandy was intrigued besides being more than a little mesmerised by her son's outburst. Jake sighed, what was it with adults that they always required everything explaining to them in minute detail before they even attempted to understand?

"Lance Turner, the man we met on holiday, don't you remember? He said that he had a ring to give to Rachel, only he hasn't done it and so she is upset!"

"That is a load of stuff and nonsense. The only ring Jake can be on about is a telephone call but so far I have received none, so maybe Jake was mistaken!" By this time Rachel had decided to come to her own defence.

"Oh no I was not!" The boy tried to defend himself. "That was why he followed Rachel to our house and then waited for her outside because he said it was a secret! Oops, if it was a secret then I shouldn't have told you should I?"

"That really depends on what it is all about!" Mandy adopted a solemn mode. "But you said that Lance followed Rachel to our house?"

"Yes he told me that he saw her in the supermarket and then when she finished her work he followed her to our house because he thought she was living there. But when he found out that she wasn't he said he would wait outside for her so I thought that he must have given her a ring!"

"Why did you think that Jake?"

"Well isn't that what adults usually do when they are keeping things a secret and I know that he liked Rachel very much when we were on holiday?"

"Perhaps that is one reason Jake, but only one I am afraid!"

"Oh!" The boy appeared deflated. Quite rightly so, for was it not the case that yet another of the things he was looking forward to had come to nothing?

Rachel watched them go deep in thought. From what had been said it still appeared that Lance Turner, for reasons of his own, was intent upon following her, and now, as she was involved, she wanted to know the reason that lay behind such actions.

Her opportunity came possibly sooner than she had anticipated for as she was seeing the family to the door she was convinced she saw that shadow hanging around and avoiding the street lamps that could have illuminated his features. Not feeling particularly brave and yet now determined to find out what was going on, she waited for the family to completely disappear before she left the place herself.

Aware to possibly expect some sort of visitation, she heard the sound of his steps behind her and getting herself in a good position under a street lamp that now illuminated the path she suddenly turned.

"Perhaps you would like to explain just why you are following me Lance Turner?" Her voice was on even keel even if her heart was pounding at the time although she put this down to sheer annoyance on her part.

"I gather the child's secret was secretly eating away at him then?" He came into the light rather ruefully without attempting to deny he was there.

"My nephew appeared to be rather confused. But you have not yet said how a real estate agent from Tenerife not only happens to be here but is also persisting in following me. If there is something you wished to know from me then surely you shouldn't have to resort to any such kind of subterfuge!"

Her words had obviously found their mark for he smiled rather ruefully in her direction. "You are right of course. Can we talk?"

"Maybe I consider it is high time you did some talking. For starters why was I led to believe that I had left you in Tenerife?"

"Not here in the street, please Rachel!"

For a moment she was in two minds whether to refuse him but then she sighed almost reluctantly as she allowed him to accompany her back to her own front door. Once inside with the door closed however she turned on him again. "And now explanations if you please Lance Turner!"

"Then what would you say if I started by telling you that your one time beau Brad Stevens is not as you presumed dead?" He watched her reaction carefully. For her part however all that Rachel could now see was the image of that shadow she had imagined she had seen earlier and shouted after without receiving any response. Still her response when it came was to be expected.

"That is just plain silly. Of course Brad is dead, he was killed in the air disaster, the one where no bodies were ever found. But as fragments of the plane were later discovered over a wide area it was ruled impossible at the time that anyone could have survived that explosion! Anyway I have just been to the solicitors for the reading of his will. They would hardly have been doing that if he was still alive would they?"

"That depends upon their reasons for you see Brad was never on that plane!"

"Of course he was. The airport records at Gatwick showed that he passed through their customs with his own passport!"

"A passport that had been doctored in order that another person could take his place and innocently take on board a brief case with explosives in it when such cases were switched after the security check!"

"You are trying to say that Brad was the one who caused the air crash? No that I cannot believe!"

"Shall we say that his masters organised it for their own reasons and Brad went along with the scheme for again, reasons of his own!"

"Now you really are talking in riddles. Quite frankly I don't believe a word of your trumped up story. Don't forget you have still to explain your own presence here to me and please don't try to fob me off with tales of real estate or even that you are working for some ministry, for I am afraid that won't wash anymore!"

"Those explanations can wait for a while yet. You see Brad also had a second identity that of Winston Devereaux, and that is the name and identification he used to get back into this country from his exploits in Morocco!"

For a moment Rachel was silent, in fact Lance's latest gambit had left her with her mouth wide open! She knew of course of Brad's secondary interest in Devereaux Industries, a company that provided a fleet of sailing boats to operate around the Canary Island's during the season, craft that were suitable for hiring out to the visitors who fancied a spot of sailing. After all she had needed to deal with that side of his business in her secretarial role. And she also knew that he liked to keep the two businesses separate and had adopted the name of Winston Deveraux in his dealings with this side of the firm. But what Lance was now suggesting was totally preposterous.

"But what was he possibly doing in Morocco? We had no dealings with that country, always presuming of course that it was Brad."

"You can rest assured that it was. He was visiting his contacts in the Sahara Desert at the time of the crash!"

"His contacts? He had no contacts in that place, why should he have? I mean how can you sail hire yachts in the Sahara?"

"Again we will come to that point later. The main question I now need to put to you is, have you seen Brad since his return to this country?"

"No I haven't!" She vehemently denied the thoughts of that shadowy character she had spotted pushing the memory to the back of her thoughts. "Nor am I likely to for I am not in the habit of seeing ghosts!"

"I was rather under the impression that Brad wanted to contact you. Apparently you have something in your possession that the man now requires!"

"And what is that supposed to be?" Now thoughts of the envelope with that thin slip of paper inside of it came to mind. Could this be what it was all about?

"That is what I intend to find out, all of which brings me back to my reason for trying to follow you around in secret so that if this man did contact you I would be on the spot at the time!"

"Let me get this straight, you were following me about just in case a man whom I know to be dead decides to contact me because I have something in my possession that he wants?" She watched incredulously as he nodded his head quite sombrely in response. "Of course this must lead me back to my initial question. Who exactly are you Lance Turner? Who gives you the authority to pry into other people's lives in this manner?"

"You ask far too many questions Rachel and some of the answers it is better that you do not know at this moment!"

"Then if you don't tell me I am very much afraid you must not expect any co-operation from me!"

"Oh I don't know about that, some things you see never change!" She had never intended to find herself in his arms for she felt too damned mad with this bloke but then Lance was not one to take no for an answer. Not only that but she suddenly found she was responding to those lips in much the same way as she had done in Tenerife. Cursing herself she forced him away to arms length.

"Explanations first!" She was surprised at the strength of her own voice. Still her words appeared to have the desired affect on the other, for he wandered over to a chair as if collecting his thoughts together.

"I can tell you little about my job Rachel apart from the fact that it involves the security of this country. Hence when I told you that I worked for the Ministry it was not totally a lie and moreover some pen pushing is often involved in the job!"

"You mean you are a spy?" The words possibly came out before she really thought about them.

"Spy is rather an emotive word Rachel for one side of my work also involves the recovery of certain estates, hence the second job description I gave to you, and the estate I am now attempting to trace is real enough except that it is not dwellings we are talking about but the disposal of certain jewels from an audacious robbery you must have recently read about. The profits from such goods would provide quite a substantial funding for some of our less desirable acquaintances especially certain individuals who are currently residing in Morocco. To transport such goods however one requires the means, considering all airports and ports are under scrutiny for such an eventuality. But then Brad Stevens or Winston Devereaux as he now appears to want to call himself is quite adept at moving his hire boats from these shores as far as the Canary Islands! Indeed I believe I am right in saying that one such vessel, one called the Sea Witch has just completed such a mission!"

"But if what you say is true and Brad has transported such a vessel how can he possibly be here in this place trying to contact me as you suggest?"

"Simple, Brad had others to steer the vessel to its final destination for he had no intention of undertaking the task himself, only I have heard that when the craft arrived at its ultimate destination in order to join the other boats in the fleet the cargo had been previously removed. After that Winston Devereaux is reputed to have taken a flight to an airport here in the Midlands. What for I ask myself if not to relieve you of something that you might be holding for him however unwittingly you have acted in this manner. But now I think that I have told you enough at least to justify my own position. There is one thing however that I must do and that is to swear you to secrecy over what I have already said!"

"And what makes you think now that I will agree? After all when we met just a short time ago I was under the impression that you had your suspicions concerning my own actions!"

"Because I actually think you are quite innocent in all of this Rachel and secondly I think I know you well enough to be able to trust you!"

The paper lying in the envelope still in her bag came yet again to mind. Should she mention it to him? It was possibly of no significance and yet the item held little meaning to her as things stood.

"There is one thing Lance. You mentioned that Brad might possibly want something off me earlier on? When I went to the solicitors earlier on I was handed this. Not exactly a legacy even though the envelope with my name on it had been left with the papers appertaining to his estate!" She finally made the decision and fished in her bag to produce the same. "I'm afraid that I can make neither head nor tail of the contents, although Doug did say it resembled a fishing chart of some kind. Maybe you can make some sense out of it." She slowly unfolded the paper still a little unsure as to whether she was doing right and Lance took it from her with a frown.

"Perhaps these numbers are of some significance after all Rachel although exactly what I admit escapes me at this moment. Perhaps this is even the item that your friend has currently come in search of!"

"Then if you are right what do you think we should do about it?" Again she was testing him.

"Perhaps we ought to sit on it for a while whilst we get our thoughts together. In the meantime of course maybe we have some catching up to do with the business we left unfinished in Tenerife!"

Rachel lay awake long after the sleeping form besides her had finally settled for now a whole preponderance of questions assailed her thoughts. First and probably the foremost of these was the question as to whether she had been right to listen to the beating of her heart, which in turn had motivated her body into emotion. For in truth it could be levelled that Lance had expounded an almost impossible story for her mind to be able to comprehend. Yet glancing at his figure now as he slept the sleep of the innocent she was sure that she had been right to yield to her emotions whatever the rights or wrongs of the case for she was truly in love with this guy.

She stretched out her hand and tenderly moved it along his hairline as he slept and he stirred long enough to grab hold of the hand that had rested upon him and lovingly hold it firmly to his person. Perhaps indeed it was the warm glow of this man's presence that finally served to lull her to her slumbers for she roused quite suddenly some hours later and realising that the light in the bedroom was now on she turned to notice that Lance had already heaved his form from off that mattress and was currently sitting solemnly studying that paper once again as if trying to unravel the mystery that lay behind it.

"Sorry, I didn't mean to rouse you!" He spoke ruefully as he realised that she was now awake, blaming himself for having disturbed her.

"I'm fine ------Have you made any sense out of that paper yet?" She was surprised at the tonality of her voice for it had now adopted an air of softness around it. Slipping her legs over the side of the bed she made an effort to join him. "I told you that Doug did say it looked as if it had something to do with a shipping chart although why on earth Brad would want to leave me something like that I cannot possibly hazard a guess!"

"Perhaps your brother in law did have a point!" The other nodded solemnly in agreement. "But having said that

I think I consider this to be rather special and in my opinion Brad left it for you to keep with the intention of collecting it at some future date!"

"But the paper simply contains rows of isolated numbers?" By this time she had joined him and was looking down at the paper for herself yet again.

"Maybe they appear to be spaced in that manner on first glance. Nevertheless once you have worked out the sequence of these numbers then the whole thing becomes far easier to understand."

"And you are saying that you have already worked out such a sequence?"

"Well I have attempted to make a start. Look suppose you take the first two numbers on the first line and place them against the last two numbers on the second line. This actually provides us with the co-ordinates of a certain port in Spain that is of interest to us at the moment. I say that because this happens to be one of the ports of call that the Sea Witch made during her voyage down to the Canaries. Not only that but it was also the port where the crew of that vessel were destined to take a well earned break!"

"Surely you don't think that Brad was there at that place when the vessel docked? You're not suggesting that it was him who removed the cargo from off that vessel single handed are you?"

"He could always have had the cargo transferred to another vessel whilst it was at that place. After all jewellery as such does not usually present such a heavy cargo to shift. If I am right this means that we need to study the chart further and attempt to decipher a further port of call that this second craft would be making towards. Do you mind if I use your telephone Rachel? I'm afraid my mobile is in the state of requiring a recharge!"

"Of course. All the same remember that some people are funny at being woke up at this time in the morning!"

"I doubt if that will apply to Chad. No doubt he will be glad to receive news of our find especially if he is in a position of wracking his brains out for nothing at the moment!"

"And who then is Chad?"

"Oh a colleague of mine employed on the continent at the moment!"

"But even supposing you are right this still doesn't explain why Brad decided to leave this paper with me. As it was it could have easily have found itself into the rubbish recycling bin!"

"Maybe he took a chance of you holding onto things Rachel, especially once you had got hold of some incomprehensible puzzle. Don't forget he gained a good insight into your habits when you worked for him. Maybe he even considered that this was one way he could keep a record of the sequence safe knowing at the time that he could always collect it from you at a later date!"

. She waited as he made his anticipated phone call whilst the questions once again crowded into her mind. But it was when he returned from the telephone still looking more than a little puzzled that she decided that perhaps it was time to voice some of those questions. "You mentioned Morocco before Lance. If Brad is still alive, which I still find hard to believe, why would he wish to transport this cargo to this place?"

"Simple, because that his where his masters currently are!"

"And they wanted jewels?"

"Expensive jewellery converts into cash quite easily and cash is necessary for them to be able to purchase weapons for future skirmishes!"

"But surely the Moroccan authorities are the ones to deal with this matter?"

"I believe there is currently a cell somewhere in the Sahara Desert upon whom the Moroccan Authorities have little control, for the organisation they belong to is quite powerful in the Middle East!"

"So you are intimating that Brad has something to do with this so called cell?"

"I believe he has been coerced into it yes. Whether this is for monetary gain or because he shares their ideals is something different. But the fact of the matter is that he must be stopped before he can succeed in providing them with fuel for future exploits!"

Rachel fell silent. The whole idea seemed to be far too ludicrous for her to take in at that time. She knew Brad for some of his less than ideal tendencies but to consider the man to be a traitor to his country was something that was far too difficult a pill to swallow.

★ ★ ★ ★

Chapter Six

In truth Rachel did not know how to now respond to Lance's assertions. In fact she didn't really want to believe a word of it for people in her walk of life simply didn't behave in such a manner. Therefore she searched her mind for something to say in the hopes of changing the subject. That was when she remembered the expression on his face when he had returned from that telephone and now it seemed to be the right time to question him about it.

"There was no reply!" The words of explanation were issued in a flat sounding voice almost indeed as if he expected her to understand the significance of this statement. "I really cannot for the life of me understand why though!"

"Well I can, the person you rang is probably still fast asleep at this hour!" She tried to make light of the situation sensing that for some reason he was worried.

"Chad asleep? Never! Neither as a mater of fact would he willingly be separated from his mobile. It's a lifeline to him. No it's my opinion that something has happened to him out there!" She wondered if it was almost a look of suspicion he cast in her direction. Well even he must realise that she could hardly be in two places at once so how on earth was she supposed to know what had happened to his mate?

"What do you mean? Lance I really have no idea what you are talking about. This person you were trying to phone, the one you called Chad; who exactly is he and how does he fit in with your plans and why does his apparent absence now seem to trouble you?"

"If you would like to place what I am about to say in inverted commas Chad and I so happen to be currently working for the same boss and we are also both employed on the same case but in different locations!" Again his words held a hostile ring within them!

"Well if what you have previously said is true and Brad Stevens is currently in this country under whatever particular name appears to turn him on then he can hardly be blamed for the disappearance of your friend at the same time!"

"Shall we say that there are others who are involved in this matter even if, I submit, it is Stevens who acts as their paymaster!" Surely he didn't suspect that she was one of these people he now spoke of?

"And you said that your friend was last seen where?"

"As a matter of fact I didn't say where but for what it is worth the answer to that question happens to be Vigo, which is also the same port that lies on the first set of co-ordinates we managed to decipher from that paper of yours. Anyway because the man refuses or is unable to answer my call the crux of the matter is that I'm afraid I am going to have to go out there myself Rachel!"

"If people are in the habit of disappearing from a place without any explicit explanation as to their whereabouts then perhaps you can think again!" She shifted closer to him as she spoke anxious now to feel the warmth of his arms reassuringly around her and to make belief her earlier suspicions were unfounded. But by this time Lance was obviously determined on exactly what he was going to do.

"Sorry, but much as I would like to stay here with you I am afraid that I do have to go to try to ascertain what has happened to him Rachel! That is all part of the job and I am afraid it is something I need to find out for myself. I don't think that you fully appreciate just how much is at stake in all of this!"

"Then maybe I should come with you just in case you take it into your head to do a disappearing act on me the same as this friend of yours has, especially now as soon as I have found you again!"

"Sorry, but if that was a request the answer is a most definite no. Anyway you have your work here as well as your family to consider and besides in your spare time you could always start plotting a storyline connecting spies and intrigue!" Perhaps his tone had softened a little but he was still eyeing her rather critically.

"The job I can assure you is merely a means to an end. It simply provides a living that stops me from relying on hand outs from my relatives!"

"But there is more than your job involved in this place Rachel. Don't forget you are still holding onto that paper so whilst I am away you could do me a favour by trying to decipher further co-ordinates on it that will provide us with a clearer picture as to where this shipment is heading! That I can assure you is most important to us!"

She pouted trying her best to show her disagreement but now he appeared to understand her motivation in trying to persuade him to change his mind on the issue.

"Sorry, but the answer is still a definite no!" He moved across to where he had placed his net book and logged in.

"Now what are you doing?"

"Trying my best to arrange an available flight. Now that one looks promising, the one from the airport in the Midlands!"

"What the one that is going today, you mean you are leaving straight away?"

He nodded. "I consider that there is little point in me wasting any more time. The sooner I can get over there and find out for myself what has happened the better. Oh please stop looking so morose. I promise you now that I will be back just as soon as I can. I've no intention of deserting you not when I have found you again. Besides by the time I get back perhaps the solution to the puzzle I have left for you will be on hand! Just one more phone call that I have to make however!"

So that was to be it. She had seen Lance Turner again for one night only and now he was ready to go away again. For a moment she clung to him and he in turn held her tightly in his grasp. He finally broke away from her with a sigh. "And now that is enough of that, at least for the time being!" He reached out for a towel ready to take a shower. "But don't worry for I am sure that we will be able to carry on where we left off in the not too distant future!" She never knew whether he made that phone call like he said that he had to make or not but at the time she had far too many other things on her mind to worry over it.

She supposed that she felt and behaved something like a zombie after his eventual departure. Perhaps if she had not been in such an emotive state she might have questioned the telephone call she received begging her to meet the caller after work that night as she could possibly learn something to her advantage. Normally Rachel would have been wary of such an undertaking but in fact she was so wrapped up in her own emotive state that she failed to notice the figure waiting for her outside of her workplace when she left, nor intent as she was to make the rendezvous that had been indicated, did she sense the other's presence until she felt a hand clapped over her lips to stop her from crying out whilst at the same time her arms were pinioned behind her.

"I believe you collected a paper that rightfully belongs to me!" The voice issuing forth in guttural tones she did not immediately recognise, not that she could have responded even if she had wanted to at the time, not with that hand still clapped across her lips. Still perhaps her assailant finally realised this for now having established his presence he began to slightly ease his hold.

"Who the hell are you and what are you talking about?" In spite of her faltering emotions Rachel almost spat the words out, for in truth she had not immediately recognise him, nor did she associate him with the phone call she had received earlier that day.

"I thought the answer to both of those questions would be pretty obvious!" Her retort had now apparently angered her assailant. "I thought I made it quite clear that I wanted to see you. If you require an explanation as to my reason for this Jarvis told me that he had passed the letter on to you as was requested."

The name of the solicitor who had required her presence as well as the name of the individual who had previously left the letter for her sprang to mind and she cringed. She supposed that Lance had intimated that he was in the area at this time. She admitted that she hadn't really believed him when he had told her. Lance's attitude towards her before he had left came to mind, is that what he had thought, that she was still in contact with this person?

"I understood that you were dead!" Somehow she had managed to wriggle free and had spun round to confront this man. This appeared to be the only thing that came to mind to say to her assailant and in truth perhaps Brad Stevens was taken by surprise at her action for at least he made to remove his hands from off her person.

"Such thoughts have often been found proved wrong! Besides dead men do not often make phone calls as far as I am aware!" The tone he adopted was still rather unpleasant. In fact everything about this man seemed to be unpleasant and Rachel began to wonder what she had ever seen in him! "The reason for this clandestine meeting concerns the paper Rachel. At the risk of repeating myself I believe you have this and consequently I now want it back!"

"But your estate was settled after your supposed death!" She tried to think of something to say to the man even if the whole occasion was completely ludicrous. She had to admit she had been intrigued by the phone call even though she realised now that she should have completely ignored it, slammed the receiver down at the time and most certainly not have been determined to keep this assignation.

"That I am afraid was a necessary part of my disappearance, but then the envelope was given to you at the time or so I was later informed. A matter that I expected for after all those had been my instructions!"

She thought back to what Lance had intimated about the paper being some sort of coding system for certain co-ordinates as well as the task he had set her to try to unravel the puzzle whilst he was away. "Oh that thing! Well to tell the truth I couldn't understand one word of it and therefore I assigned it to the waste bin!"

For a moment she thought he was about to strike her for this utterance. This stranger was not the Brad she had known and she wondered whether the taking on of a new identity had served to alter his character as well. "But then you were supposedly blown up in that explosion. How on earth did you manage to escape and were you the only one who was so lucky?" She remembered now what Lance had said about the likelihood of Brad paying someone to undertake the journey in his name on a forged passport. She realised now that she needed to play for time whilst she hoped and even willed someone to come along who would recognised her and interrupt this little scene. Unfortunately however nobody did!

"Maybe you ask far too many pertinent questions than what are good for you Rachel. Tell me though has your garbage been collected recently?"

"My garbage?" For a moment his question floored her until she remembered what she had previously said. "Yes I expect so. Yes I believe it was collected today. I'm sorry if I did wrong but then at the time I didn't expect you to come back for it especially as it was left to me. Therefore I considered it was mine to do what I wanted with!"

"But you see now I am back and as you must be aware I am not dead after all although for convenience sake and also to avoid a lot of silly time wasting questions from people who ought to know better how to spend their time, I have found myself adopting a different identity. Actually I am now calling myself by my trade name. No doubt you will remember that!"

"In that case Winston unless you can convince me with a more sincere story than the one you are currently fabricating, I think you must understand that I have now no wish to dwell upon such details!"

"I think you will now do exactly as you are told Rachel. Let me see there is a nephew of yours of whom I believe you are very fond. I don't suppose you would want to see anything happening to the boy!" The mention of Jake in such a manner served to make Rachel's blood run cold and the other was certainly not slow in realising that he had hit upon a raw nerve ending. "Perhaps you will now realise my dear that I am quite determined in my resolve and therefore perhaps you would do well to heed my words and strive to assist in any demand I should make of you!"

"What is it that you want?" Her voice came out sounding little more than a mere whimper.

"Now that I consider is a little better. But you will still do well to remember the outcome if you should fail in your endeavour to assist me! First of all shall we start by enquiring what has happened to your new boy friend? Surely even you must command enough attention to be able to keep a man beyond the confines of a single night!"

She cringed as the words bit into her and she felt a tell tale flush rising in her cheeks. "He just happened to have a business appointment and he had to travel to the Continent!" Well she supposed this could be considered to be the truth for somehow she needed to get herself out of this predicament without placing Jake at risk from this man.

"I consider the Continent to be rather a large expanse Rachel. Perhaps you could be a little more specific!"

"I'm afraid that I can't help you on that one!" She prayed that her lie would go undetected.

"Can't or won't Rachel?"

"He tried to make a phone call, only there was no response. That was when he said that he believed he would have to take matters in his own hands!" No, she determined steadfastly, she would not tell him the destination of the flight Lance had taken.

"I am afraid that I must interrupt you at this point Rachel for I actually think you could be slightly more specific on your detail. Where exactly did he intend to go to?"

"He didn't say although I anticipate it could have been to Toulouse!" Now she deliberately lied. If only she could get away from this being. The more she thought of it she realised how ludicrous the situation had become for wasn't this the same person that at one time she had been toying with the possibility of marrying? She wondered now how she could have been so naïve in the past. Not only in the past either, but leaving work today at that precise time knowing full well that the man was in the vicinity after the phone call she had received.

The expression now in his eyes however told her that quite frankly he did not believe the story and her fears for Jake became aroused yet again. Yet the retort she had anticipated did not come for instead he grabbed hold of her arm in a tight hold.

"What are you doing, where are we going?" She realised that he was now attempting to propel her along the pavement.

"Oh I thought we would go somewhere where it is quiet, somewhere where I can leave you in order to allow you time to recharge your thoughts and decide to speak the truth. The sooner that you realise that when I ask a question then I expect an accurate response, the better it will be!"

She made no attempt to struggle as he made his way with her in tow down the quiet street for to have done so at the time would have been totally pointless. This was an area of the city with which she was not familiar with its rows of back-to-back properties that were waiting their turn to be condemned but which often provided shelter to some of the dregs of society and this sobering thought did nothing to boost her morale. Yet Brad on the other hand appeared to be quite familiar with the area.

He finally stopped outside of one of the houses that appeared to be on first glance totally deserted. This was when he produced a key to the property from out of his pocket.

"Don't look so shocked Rachel. I can assure you that this accommodation is only on a temporary basis! I could only obtain a short term lease on the property but sufficiently long enough I believe to suit my purpose!" He laughed almost coarsely when he beheld her expression as she entered the room from off the street with its bare floorboards that looked as if they were well past their sell by date. The room itself was completely devoid of any furnishings however threadbare one would have imagined they would be. "Not entirely the Ritz I must agree with you there, but I have no doubt it will suffice in its efficiency by giving you enough time to jog your memory. Still unfortunately I cannot stay around to watch for this light of reason to begin to express itself in your eyes after you have had ample time to think about your own predicament. Therefore I will have to leave you to your thoughts. Oh yes, one other thing, there are no longer any comfort facilities in this place and the services are now no longer available. One cannot be too careful about attracting squatters nowadays. Therefore I do hope that you have decided to come to your senses upon my return for I would hate to have to leave you in this place indefinitely!" He left taking the key and Rachel was left to listen as she heard it turn in the lock. She heard the sound of his feet growing fainter on the pavement outside as he left and perhaps she began to realise for the first time the predicament she had found herself in!

For in truth she was left to look around the empty place in desperation hoping now that the vermin around the place were only of the two-legged variety. Seven paces one way and eight the other; Rachel paced those floor boards for the umpteenth time convinced in her own mind that they were in imminent danger of splitting beneath her weight for the flooring was ancient and bore the marks of ingrain patina almost as a mark of their authenticity. Realising that by this time the hours of daylight had begun to fade and there had been no further sign of the person who had been instrumental in her abduction she began to panic. It was not so much that she desired to see this scumbag but more of her isolation that now troubled her for in one matter the man had been right. This area already waiting for the bulldozers to move in was totally deserted and therefore there was no one about to hear any calls for help. She viewed the windows wondering whether she could smash one of them with a shoe and affect her escape that way, but the sashes to those frames had been securely nailed down and boarded and she lacked the strength to make any sort of an exit. Finally desolate and both tired and thirsty with her efforts she sank to the floor that held no comfort in it for her and buried her face in her hands as she desperately tried to think of a way out of her current situation.

Crouched in this position she did not immediately see the beam from a torch flickering backwards and forwards along that street. Indeed it was only after she heard the smash of the glass as a brick was hurled through the window by someone who obviously could muster a great deal more strength than what she had that she realised she was no longer on her own. For a moment she cringed down in a corner of that room wondering what was about to come and then there was the guttural tones that she recognised.

"Intending to stop here all night girl? Your sister has had me chasing all over the place to find you and when I finally track you down you start playing shy on me!"

Doug, what on earth was he doing in this place? She knew he had a hard job as a steel erector, but that could hardly account for him smashing windows in derelict property even if he was familiar with the area. Anyway how had Mandy, or anyone else for that matter, known that she had disappeared for she hadn't been due to go round to their abode that evening?

"Well come on then, you can get out through this window just be careful of the glass that's all. I don't fancy having to take you to A and E with bleeding and cuts as well as getting you out of here!"

She still hesitated much to her brother in law's consternation. "It's a good job that this street is deserted and nobody has come to investigate the commotion otherwise they would have me up for abducting you! Now come on shift yourself or are you waiting until I open the front door for you?"

"But how and why have you come in the first place?" She reckoned the question must have sounded most ungracious as she finally struggled to her feet and took the arm he now proffered to assist her through the gap in the broken window.

"I told you Mandy told me to come and find you after she had that phone call. I admit that at first I didn't know where to begin but fortunately I do know some guys down at the club that are familiar with these quarters. Aye and one of them said he thought he had seen a bloke coming this way with a female in tow and that she didn't look very happy about the situation!"

"Mandy had a telephone call?" By this time her feet were finally clear of those jagged edges and her body had reached the atmosphere of the street. She stopped yet again to pose her question much to Doug's disgust.

"What's the matter with you, don't you want to be rescued or something? If you don't be making a move we'll be having the fellow who took you in the first place coming back and I don't expect he will want to see his prize exhibit escaping from the place where he left her. Yes if you must know when I got home from my work Mandy had received a phone call and she was mighty cut up about it too!"

"A phone call from whom?" Surely Brad had never phoned her sister although now her eyes had been opened concerning that individual she had to admit he was capable of anything.

"Why that bloke you met in Tenerife. He intimated that you might be in some sort of danger and of course my Mandy got really upset when you didn't arrive home from work. She was checking up on you I guess. Anyway that was when she sent me out on the prowl. Not that I have nothing better to do mind you!"

"So where are we going now?" After carrying out a cursory glance to make sure she was all right Doug was now urging her up towards the end of the street.

"Fortunately I've got the car parked up at the top and as far as where I am now taking you, why that's back to your sister of course. At least once she sees you it should stop her from bleating about it down my ear hole; and she will be able to pester you instead!"

There were a thousand questions Rachel would at that moment have liked to have asked yet in her heart she realised that Doug was right in one matter, it was time to make good her escape whilst she still had the opportunity and for his part Doug gave her little opportunity to ask further questions for all he seemed to be keen on doing was completing the task that had been set for him.

Still perhaps her sister was to prove to be more forth coming after the initial furore of welcoming her back. "Yes!" The confession was finally wrung from out of her lips. "Lance did phone me. It wasn't from anywhere in England, I can tell you that because the operator kept butting into the conversation. But he claimed to have heard a rumour that there was a distinct possibility that you would be abducted and that you needed some form of protection until he himself could get back to the U.K. Well I reckoned that Doug knew the area well enough being employed on the likes of such property that lay close to the place where you were working!"

"But I still don't understand why Lance should have phoned you Mandy?"

"There is quite a long story attached to that one. Maybe I will explain it to you sometime!"

"What about starting now?" Rachel now was intent upon pursuing the answer. Perhaps the fact that the girl now appeared so adamant gave Doug his opportunity to make good his own escape with a wry expression on his face.

"Well now that I've returned the lamb to the fold perhaps I can be excused whilst you two girls do a little catching up on detail!" The one in question had poked his head around the door and showed no wish to be embroiled any further in the affair. "Anyway I promised to see Sid down at the club tonight. It's the planning committee meeting for that darts match I told you about!"

He watched as Mandy nodded her head, for it was only after he had departed that she had reason to wish that she had not! In the meantime however she had certain questions from Rachel to answer.

A cold wind heralded the shades of autumn in the wake of the early morning mist that day, forecasting that the season was almost upon them and Rachel shivered as she pulled the fleece closer to her form. The temperature drop since they had left Tenerife and indeed the difference in the temperature here to the Canary Islands seemed to be particularly relevant to her on that day.

But of course that was not the only thing that had changed. For from being finally settled back in her flat and fully occupied in her new job, she had, after the events of one certain evening, been suddenly uprooted and hastily brought to this place, which seemed to be miles away from any noted pockets of civilisation, in the hopes that no one would be able to trace her whereabouts. Still this move had happened when upon going along with Mandy to collect Jake from Beavers, partly because her sister was reluctant to let her out of her sight. Rachel switched her mind onto the happenings of that night. First of all she had witnessed the shot before she had seen her brother in law's figure slump to the ground whilst his life's blood had slowly seeped away from him! Doug had never made his club that night for someone had been waiting for him!

Now Mandy herself wore an air of solemnity and silence around her, something that Rachel had never witnessed before. Subsequent events had passed by in almost a mist of reasoning for her. She had been aware of the ambulance arriving, of Doug being taken to the local hospital and the doctors mournfully shaking their heads as Doug had been pronounced dead upon arrival. Yet it so happened that there were even more surprises in store for her. For Mandy had never sobbed on Doug's death or even afterwards almost as if she had bottled it all up inside of her. Rachel had expected the police to play a more prominent role in this murder enquiry but to her mind everything seemed to have been hushed up. And Mandy's own pensive mood had only been broken by Jake's persistent questioning as to where his father was, something that made Rachel feel that her own heart had been wrenched apart and made her wonder yet again how on earth her sister managed to hold it all together.

"I'm afraid that Daddy had another appointment with Jesus in heaven!" How on earth could she manage to issue these words and make them sound so matter of fact to the youngster?

"So will he come here then to this place when he has finished? Will he know where we are Mummy?" The boy looked around him now obviously obsessed with the idea that perhaps they should have left a note behind for his Dad saying where they would be. He was still not convinced as to why he had been taken away from his pre-school so abruptly. He knew he had previously intimated that he was ready for a move, but that was to the big school that was situated locally, not this place that was seemingly situated miles from anywhere.

"It all very much depends on whether the angels can manage without him!" Mandy's voice sounded flat even though there was still no evidence of tears springing to her eyes as Rachel had anticipated. She could do little else but marvel at her sister's apparent hard exterior.

It was quite obvious that the child didn't understand the scenario but then that was something he had in common with his Aunt for in truth Mandy had still never fully explained to her how she had become involved with Lance Turner or why indeed Lance had chosen to contact her in the first place. Yet with the death of Doug the time had obviously not been opportune to question Mandy any further on this nor even query why it had been necessary for them all to be uprooted and brought to this remote spot! In fact the whole situation had been quite inexplicable, what with the police never demanding more questions concerning this obvious murder and again in her mind the whole matter appeared to have been hushed up and that was something that she really couldn't come to terms with. She could understand Mandy being worried for Jake's sake but to insist that she herself accompanied them to this area of isolation did nothing to alleviate the thought process that ran through her own mind, especially after she spied Mandy speaking to yet another stranger.

"Who was that?" At length the words finally sought there was from out her lips. Mandy had previously insisted that nobody must know where they were now abiding and yet she herself appeared to be on relatively friendly terms with this individual almost indeed as if they had known each other in some past existence.

"Oh just someone who has our interests at heart!" Again her sister refused to be forthcoming, merely frowning at Rachel's curiosity in asking the question. She waited for a few moments before she decided to continue. "Michael just happens to be an old colleague of mine!"

"In the teaching profession?" Rachel frowned again wondering why an old colleague of her sister just happened to be in the area especially since it was several years since Mandy had married and left the profession and apparently lost contact with any of her colleagues from that branch of her life.

"Not exactly in the teaching profession, but perhaps it would be as well if you concentrated upon that thought as a sort of explanation!"

"I don't really think I can do that Mandy for you see I really would appreciate being allowed to know what exactly is going on!" Well at least she had spoken her mind and surely she ought to be able to do that with her sister. The timing and the thought gave her the courage now to carry on. "There is also something else I would like to know. Maybe you consider this to be too personal but how is it that you managed to keep the trauma of Doug's death so closely under wraps, and why did I get the impression that the police at the time seemed to be quite keen to hush the matter up? I'm aware that you will probably tell me that it is none of my business, but after all I was involved, yet all that I was told was that I had to come away to this isolated spot and bury myself away, yet at the same time some old colleague of yours apparently knows where we are and takes it upon himself to show his face! After all I am your sister Mandy, surely you know better than to try to pull the wool over my eyes!"

Mandy sighed as if she realised that an explanation was on the point of being wrested out of her. " I have been taught to hide my emotions well enough. Whatever I feel about the matter must remain totally private. Now however it appears that Lance wants you to join him in Paris Rachel. Michael, that is the person whom you saw, is simply the go between who is in the process of making such arrangements!"

"And who the hell is this Michael and does all this go under the job description of teaching. What else did you do besides teach Mandy? After all it appears you know Lance well enough for him to contact you even though you gave the distinct impression that you had not met him before when we were in Tenerife. Surely you are not insinuating that you were his teacher as well?"

"Lance ---? Certainly not, don't even think about that as an idea!"

"Then why did you pretend not to know him when we were in Tenerife even when I introduced you? Surely that wasn't extra curricula activities?"

"In the past, prior to my marriage I did at one time work with Lance!"

"In the teaching profession?"

"No Rachel. The teaching part was, one might say, a front. Oh I grant you that I qualified all right but when the time came I took up another job!"

"Which was?"

"Better for you to know nothing of that side of my life Rachel. Naturally after I met Doug and married I retired from those sorts of ventures. Before then however Michael was also one of our colleague and therefore Lance has now asked him to help in assisting you in getting to Paris!"

"Then I presume Lance never was in real estate?"

"Lance ----? Perish the thought, although on the other hand he has been known to assume a number of different guises!"

"Such as a sudden interest in boats, especially the one we spotted in Tenerife?"

"I did hear that there were some illegal immigrants around at the time. I understood that was all part of his job!"

"Yet you never said anything about it when we questioned you?"

"It was hardly my brief. But no more questions please. Perhaps I have already exceeded my brief in telling you the amount that I have! There was one other thing however; Lance mentioned a paper that you had. He said to be sure that you took it to Paris with you and whatever else you did not to let it slip out of your grasp."

"Just one more thing if you please. Did you know at the time that Lance was in Fuerteventura when that plane disappeared?"

"I believe he was attempting to perfect his surfing skills yes for he has a disabled relative whom he tries to raise funds for. What I didn't know until later was that the two of you had met. I wasn't even aware that the finger of suspicion was at the time pointing in Brad Stevens direction or you can rest assured I would have made some excuse to intervene in a certain relationship that appeared to be developing between the two of you. When Lance arrived in Tenerife and I realised that you had already met him it put me in a rather awkward position and the easiest way out of it was to claim complete innocence!"

"If I do go to Paris with this Michael you have mentioned it appears that it would leave yourself and Jake in a rather vulnerable position therefore perhaps you ought to consider coming along too!"

"Much as the temptation to get the bit between my teeth again appeals to me in a way I must consider Jake's well being first. As it is his schooling is already beginning to suffer and he has enough trauma in his young life with losing his Dad without subjecting him to anymore!"

"You mean if I depart with this man you call Michael, this will help to relieve some of the pressure from off you?"

"Yes Rachel I am afraid that is the truth!"

"Then you don't appear to have left me with any alternative!"

"Perhaps you have caught my meaning yes! Not to mention the fact that despite my exterior I do feel I need time to come to terms with what has recently happened on my own. Perhaps I should call on Michael and introduce you to your travelling companion, and don't forget that paper or the decoding work you have apparently been doing for Lance!"

So her sister knew about that to. Rachel looked at the other in a new light and wondered why she had never realised before that Mandy had a hidden life that she had been determined to keep secret from all the family

To Rachel's mind the one they called Michael appeared sullen and in no way appreciative at having to escort his new charge to Paris even if in appearance the man was dark and attractive looking. Not however that Mandy was shy and hesitant in making up for this lack of communication for she was obviously glad to see this young man again. Indeed she was so expressive about her feelings on the matter that Rachel couldn't help but wonder if she was missing out on something that had once existed between the two of them!

Still he appeared considerate enough towards her on the journey even if he did spend the whole of the flight engrossed in some document that he just happened to find in his brief case and as promised Lance was waiting at the airport upon their arrival. Yet after greeting Rachel with a perfunctory kiss Lance was to turn to the other in a more sombre mood that again made Rachel feel something of a spare part.

"Sorry about Chad, Mike, but I am afraid I arrived too late to prevent it happening!"

The young man nodded sombrely and Rachel sensing that something must have happened that affected her escort pinned her ears to try to ascertain more determinedly that this was possibly the only way she was likely to discover the truth for herself. "So I suppose you will now require me to step into his shoes?"

"Well you know the score but I will go through the details with you later. For now I suggest we all retire to the hotel I have booked!"

Still feeling a little left out of the proceedings Rachel hung back behind the others. Not that this motion was missed by Lance. "I presume that you brought the paper with you Rachel? Once it is deciphered it could prove extremely important to us!" She nodded in response although at the same time she wondered why he had not queried whether she had made any further sense out of the code. "I heard that there was a spot of trouble back home. How is your sister coping?"

"I would say very well under the circumstances!" It was not Rachel who responded to this but the one they called Michael. "But then one can expect it from Mandy!"

"Well I suppose you ought to know better than most!" Rachel paused upon these words her mouth now slightly open as thoughts percolated her mind. Had her surmises any substance then after all? Obviously Lance again noticed her expression.

"Michael knew Mandy quite well some time back!" The explanation was offered quite calmly as he was by this time ushering them out of the car and towards the hotel. "On the other hand I believe condolences are in order. I was sorry to hear about Doug. It was a great pity that a thing like that had to happen!"

"He saved my life before he was shot in the process. Otherwise I doubt whether I would have been here today with your precious paper!"

"Something I guess is now grieving you?" He stopped for a moment catching her arm and forcing her to face him.

"There seems to have been far too much bloodshed for one miserly piece of paper that consists merely of columns of numbers!"

"Perhaps even now you still don't realise just how important those numbers are and why Stevens wanted them back at all costs!"

"So what is the story about Chad?" The young man obviously felt he had been kept waiting long enough.

"Let me show Rachel to her room so that she can freshen up and then I will go through the criteria with you!" So she was going to be dismissed in the wake of this upstart? The thought didn't please her very much especially after what had happened back home. Again Lance obviously read her mind. "There are certain things Rachel that it might be better if you do not know anything about. I say that because I happen to be concerned for your own safety out here. You see we are not exactly dealing with a load of schoolboys who are intent upon playing pranks. Michael has come here to take over from Chad who has completely disappeared and upon whose fate we must fear the worst. Once we have had a few words and I can put him fully in the picture then we will get back to the problem of the mysterious numbers if that is all right with you?"

She nodded feeling she could do little else but once left on her own she toyed over the events of the recent past. She was still not sure what this was all about and to Rachel's mind that was completely wrong!

* * * *

Chapter Seven

Although the well-rehearsed adage indicates that Paris is the place for lovers, Rachel was to find precious little sign of this during her first few days at this place because it became increasingly obvious that the main objective was the deciphering of that code and this activity was to come before all others. In actual fact the exact methodology applied in her means to attempt and ultimately to solve this riddle seemed to be far easier than in actually interesting Lance in her presence, for the man obviously had a mission and her contribution was after all only one small step in enabling him to achieve this. As a matter of fact Michael began to show a new light for he seemed to be the one who appeared more concerned in her well being as well as the fact of how much she was missing out on in this place than did Lance. Consequently she finally presented the man who had given her this challenge with his required solutions in an almost haphazard manner.

"Splendid!" He still seemed to be completely unaware of how his charge had monopolised her time in this city of romance. "From this then we can assume that the boat made a detour after leaving Vigo, stopping at Maderia and La Palma before finally tying up in Tenerife!"

"It would appear so if my calculations are correct. Although there is one other place that is mentioned!"

"Which is?" He peered over her shoulder and Rachel reflected that this was the first time since making this trip that he had come into such close proximity.

"Fuerteventura!" She saw the flicker of disbelief pass across his face until he bent closer in order to ascertain the point she was making.

"But that doesn't really make sense. Why would the vessel wish to deviate so far from its original charter?"

"I believe you asked me to decipher the coding for you. Perhaps if you now have doubts on the matter maybe you would like to attempt to decipher them for yourself!" In truth Rachel was beginning to feel not a little annoyed. After all there were the coordinates to five different places within the coding.

"I have little reason to doubt your calculations Rachel. The important thing is that I can now instruct Michael to check up on these places. Even so I must register not a little surprise that Fuerteventura is also included in your calculations. As the Island is so close to the African mainland I would have deemed it to have been off limits even for that set up!"

"Well maybe I was wrong on that one for I don't pretend to be infallible!" Perhaps there was now a note of reproof in her voice for to be totally honest she was fed up with the blasted figures that Lance had deemed to be so important and the last thing she felt she needed now was a critique of her work!

"Perhaps after all you are not however!" For a moment she couldn't quite make up her mind whether the man was being condescending or not. “Anyway it will be Michael’s job to check them out for us!” She supposed the fact that he had used the word ‘us’ gave her some hope that she was not after all being excluded.

“Your friend, the one whom you called Chad, have you had any word from him yet?” It was something she wanted to know yes, but it also helped her to change the subject.

“No, I am afraid not, but there again you yourself have had an example of how vicious these characters can be. That is why I don’t want you going out in this city on your own!”

“But I thought that our so called enemy was residing miles away. After all what has Paris got to do with this case?”

“I don’t know why you choose to be so deliberately argumentative Rachel. But for your information I don’t presume that we will be here for very long at all. Not once Michael has got going that is and I know that he is keen to get to Vigo on account of his friend’s disappearance. Maybe we should call him in!”

Rachel shrugged her shoulders. It appeared pointless asking her opinion when Lance had obviously made up his mind. Still Michael was not long in heeding their call. “Vigo, Maderia and La Palma in that order as far as we can decipher the matter!”

The young man shook his head and Rachel reflected that perhaps this was the first sign of any emotion portrayed by this fellow. “I presume you have still no news of Chad then?” Maybe the man was not interested in the other places outside of Vigo, the port where his friend had disappeared.

“Sorry but the answer I am afraid is still no!”

"Then perhaps I was wasting my time in not heading there in the first place. Why did we have to meet in Paris anyway if Chad disappeared in this other place?"

"Because for one thing it is cosmopolitan and therefore possibly the safest place we could meet without our presence being noted and perhaps more importantly because I asked you to accompany Miss Aldred here. There is moreover one other thing you have probably not taken into consideration. If you had flown to Vigo direct from the U.K. then there is a good chance you might have aroused suspicion, a matter that might possibly be now avoided by flying into the place from Paris. Even so you are probably right in one thing, perhaps it is now time you got yourself to Vigo after all, so that you will be ready to take up the cudgel!"

Michael cast him a look that spoke more than a thousand words before he finally acquiesced. "In that case I will be on the next available flight always providing you have finished with my services here!"

"Good man!" Lance watched him depart from where they had met. "I'm afraid that Michael has taken it rather badly over Chad. The two of them joined the service together and they have always remained friends. But now Rachel it is your turn for we also will be looking to take a flight in the direction of Tenerife!"

"Tenerife, but what for? You said before that you had drawn a blank there!"

"I did but on the other hand you have not had the opportunity to try something that I have in mind for yourself yet!"

"Me, but what can I do?"

"The answer to that is quite simple. Perhaps after due consideration I have decided that it time you yourself paid a visit to the Devereaux Hire Company in Gigantes!"

"Are you crazed or something, whatever for?"

"The way I see things the answer to that is quite simple. You were until recently employed by Winston Devereaux and by acting as his secretary you were also well aware of the company that he ran in that place. Therefore it would be quite realistic for you to call at the offices there to enquire after your master. I don't expect they will have any knowledge of the fact that you have now left his employ and it is possible that they may have some idea of that man's present whereabouts! Oh don't looked so shocked I will be coming with you but the information I require will possibly be more easily elicited by the man's secretary rather than by an outsider!"

Rachel shivered. "After all that has happened lately I most certainly do not want to meet up with Winston Devereaux or whatever he cares to call himself ever again!"

"I don't in all honesty think that is likely. The best you will receive is information as to the man's current habitat. And after all Tenerife was one of the co-ordinates you managed to unravel from that paper so one could suppose it is the best place for us to start!"

Rachel still looked hesitant. The thought of meeting up with that person again whether Lance was there or not filled her with dread as she remembered the evil she had espied upon his face at their last meeting. Lance obviously judged her reluctance. "Just think of your sister if you need further inspiration. It is through the actions of that man she has been left a widow. Surely if there is something you could do to help to bring the fiend to justice then you must try if only for her sake for Stevens has killed and no doubt unless he is stopped he will do so again!"

Rachel swallowed hard. There was little doubt that Lance had hit a raw nerve by reminding her of Doug who had been murdered simply for helping her to escape that day. "You will be with me?" Finally she relented and Lance allowed himself to smile.

"But of course I will! Haven't I already told you so?"

The flight down to the largest of the Canary Islands she supposed was nondescript. Still Lance had caught her expression on the way to the airport that day.

"O.K. I am aware you haven't been given any opportunity to visit Paris properly but I promise you that once this is over then I will bring you back so that you can make up for lost time. Who knows you might even find inspiration for a novel there. Knowing the place no doubt it will be full of romance and so forth, but a promise is a promise after all!" And after that exposition he had lapsed into contemplative thought. In fact she was beginning to wonder if he regretted saying such a thing for a doubt still existed in her mind as to whether Lance was really cut out for romance!

Dusk was just about to fall when they arrived on the Island and realising how quickly the night followed on Lance took her to check in at a hotel he had booked on the Internet, claiming there was little they could do until the following day as the offices would now be all closed. Checking in as Mr and Mrs Turner, for they only needed the one passport to accomplish this, gave her some food for thought to start with, but apparently nothing could have been further from Lance's mind at the time, for no sooner had he deposited her in her room then he retired to the other side of the suite of rooms.

"Get some sleep I suggest so that you will be ready for tomorrow. I am presuming that you don't want anything to eat?"

They had eaten at the airport so Rachel shook her head. "A coffee would be very nice though!"

He rang the bell to order without saying anything to her and motioned the waiter to take it to Rachel when the man arrived with it. So that was that. Obviously she had been right in her premise, Lance was not into romance specially when he considered himself to be working. Funny but she had always thought that spies were the other way inclined. Still that idea must have come from watching too many James Bond films!

-------------She was actually surprised that she slept and even eyed the empty coffee cup suspiciously when she roused to notice it was already daylight. At the time Lance was in the bathroom having a shave so she propped herself up on her pillows as she waited.

"Oh so you're awake at last!" He eyed the fact that she was still in bed almost disapprovingly. "Guess you had better get a move on if we are going to make Gigantes this morning!"

Charming! Was her first thought as she slid her legs out of bed and tried her best to walk seductively towards the door to the bathroom. Not that the man appeared to notice her passing for he seemed to find far more interest in his mobile with all its gadgets.

Still breakfast passed pleasantly enough and she was surprised when the fruits of his morning's frantic phone calls arrived in the form of the same car she remembered him having before.

"Well you didn't expect to have to walk all the way to Gigantes did you?" He grinned at the expression on her face upon seeing the transport parked on the hotel forecourt. "All right I got a friend of mine to bring it round earlier on whilst you were tormenting me and trying to get me back into bed. But all that can wait until later, this morning we have a job to do remember?"

"By quoting us in the plural can I take it that you will be coming with me after all?"

"Into the den of thieves? I'm afraid the answer to that is no although I will be close at hand. If I did come in the place with you it could arouse suspicion and that is the last thing that we need right now. You yourself have quite a legitimate excuse and I doubt whether their teeth will be strong enough to eat you. No I expect they will be uncommonly polite to Winston Devereaux's secretary from the Head Office. Besides whilst you are there I have something else that I need to do. That is to find out if Ned Dorkins and his mate are still lurking around this place and if they are see what I can possibly glean from them!"

He left her a short distance from the front door to the building that housed the Devereaux offices and Rachel steeled herself for the ordeal she felt was lurking ahead. The boatyard lying close by appeared to be bustling with craft of all sizes being continuously hauled in and out of the water for various reasons. Rachel swallowed hard as she made to pass these workmen in order to reach the building. Again and again the thought tormented her as to what she would resort to doing if Brad himself was currently at this place. To turn tail and run from him would certainly not be good enough. In fact the only thing she decided she could do in such a situation would be to try to brazen it out, all of which left her cursing Lance Turner for ever putting her in this position!

On the other hand Brad, or whatever name he now liked to be known by, had been responsible for her brother in law's death all because Doug had assisted her in her own escape and her mind focussed once again on her own sister's reaction to the news and her apparent lack of emotion to the whole incident.

The open door to the building suddenly loomed up in front of her as she finally summoned up the courage to step over the threshold. Well, she supposed it could be said that whilst she had been at school she had always fancied acting so now was the time for her to allow those creative vibes off the leash.

"Miss Aldred!" She introduced herself to the surprised girl present on the desk in the front office. "I am Mr Devereaux's personal secretary from the U.K. I was given to understand that my employer was currently here on the Island!"

The mention of Brad's name and her own association with him appeared to stir the girl into action In actual fact she later reflected that Lance was to be proved right, for once she stated who she was and that she was looking for Mr Devereaux on a matter of some urgent business the staff occupying the place could not have been more helpful.

"I do hope that you haven't had a wasted journey Miss Aldred but I am afraid Senor Devereaux is not here on this Island at the moment. As a matter of fact I do believe he is currently on Fuerteventura. There has been talk about opening up an office there at Calleta de Fuste and he has gone there with that intention in mind!"

"Will he be away for long?" Rachel suddenly found she was beginning to enjoy playing the part. It was a little bit like being in some school production but she felt that the least she could do was now to try to elicit such information for Lance.

"Several days I believe. But if your matter is urgent and you feel unable to text him I suppose you could always take an Island flight out there to join him. I believe he is staying at the Fuerteventura Princess in Calleta during his visit and the place is not too far distant from the airport."

"Yes I do know the place, I have been before!" She really had to get out of here. She was beginning to enjoy the scenario far too much. "Thank you anyway for you have been most helpful. I knew of course that Winston was considering opening a branch on that Island and the place you mentioned is becoming quite famous for its water sports, but obviously he is much farther into the process than what I initially thought he was. Therefore perhaps I will take your advice and travel on there for my business is of some importance!"

Lance was waiting for her in the car when she left the building. Well not exactly in the car for he was talking to another figure she thought she recognised as she re-appeared but upon seeing her made his way back to the cat immediately "You needn't tell me I understand our quarry is presently on Fuerteventura!"

"Then if you know that just why have you made me risk life and limb by going in there?"

"But you didn't risk anything did you, and by the pleased expression on your face I would suggest that you put on a jolly good show? If you must know my information came from Ned Dorkins. He and his mate are still enjoying the sunshine around here and appear to be in no hurry to return home. He claimed that Stevens still owes him some money and had promised to pay him off on his return from that Island!"

"Well one must admit that the man gets around. One minute he is here, the next he is threatening me and my family back in the U.K and now he is currently on Fuerteventura!"

"The hallmark of his craft I am afraid. Still I don't suppose it will hold too many bad memories for you if we go back there?"

"To Fueteventura?"

"Where else would you suggest? After all it was one of the places marked on the puzzle of the co-ordinates. Maybe we will even find what we are searching for there!"

"You said you had seen Ned Dorkins, but that wasn't the man you were speaking to outside whilst you were waiting for me?" Alarm bells had suddenly started to ring inside of her head. She was now sure that this person was someone she had seen Lance with before around the time she had spotted the boat outside of the hotel where she had been staying earlier on that year.

"Do you miss nothing woman? Perhaps the tendency of yours is genetic. You appear to have the same qualities as your sister. If you remember the last time I was here we were investigating the arrival of illegal immigrants, not merely for their sakes but because of the ideology they might be trying to import!"

"Oh!" She sought rapidly to change the subject. Whatever that was all about was hardly on her agenda at the moment "So the jewel robbery, that is what all this current investigation is about then?"

"More importantly it is where a prize worth all that wealth is ultimately heading. I already have my own ideas about that and Fuerteventura is not its final resting place!"

"Where then?"

"Rachel you ask more questions than what is good for you. Some things it is far better that you do not know for if you do not know then nobody can ever force such information from you!"

"So you now consider that I am not trustworthy enough for such fine details?"

Lance stared at her for a moment. "You are beginning to sound exactly like your sister did you know?"

"Speaking of my sister perhaps now you will be good enough to enlighten me on what she got up to in the past and how this man Michael fitted into her life?" Right if he wanted to avoid giving her direct answers on the quest in hand then she was quite capable of posing even more pertinent ones.

"Why do you suggest there was ever anything between the two of them?"

"Because travelling with him to Paris was like an endurance test. His thoughts were most definitely somewhere else and I think I know where!"

"Mandy and he were good friends long before she met Doug. As a matter of fact Michael was missing when Mandy first met Doug. Unfortunately he had been captured on the job he was employed to do at the time and eventually presumed dead. When he finally escaped Mandy and Doug had already married, so that was the end of anything developing between Michael and her. Mandy left the Service and until very recently the two of them had not met up again, so perhaps their meeting was a bit of a shock to both of them which in turn would go some way to explaining the man's moodiness. But all of this is serving to deviate us from our next move and that is to catch one of those Island hoppers out to Fuerteventura for ourselves!"

"And if Brad is there?"

"Then he will have me to deal with this time around so stop worrying!"

"It has been a short stay!" The Hotel Manager frowned as Lance went to pay the bill.

"I am afraid that we have had some rather disturbing news from home!" Now she listened to him lie so feasibly that she half began to believe the story herself. "But do not worry Senor, I am quite willing to pay for the missed accommodation that we booked for surely the loss is our own as we now have no time to explore this beautiful Island of yours!"

"But then perhaps you will come back again Senor!" The manager beamed, Rachel was not sure whether this was because of the money Lance handed over to him or whether it was because he had passed nice remarks about his Island home.

"Rest assured we most certainly hope to!" Lance flashed him a beaming smile, an action that left Rachel not knowing whether to laugh or to cry.

It was only a short flight on the Island hopper to the place situated closest to the African continent and because the place was indeed so close it had seen the first wave of illegal immigration from off that Continent. Yet even before they left on that flight Lance received a phone call that presented its contents in a worrying frown across his features.

"It's Michael!" He noted her questioning look, which although unspoken left little to the imagination as to what she was thinking. "I'm afraid he has some rather disturbing news. Chad is dead!" The words obviously cut him to issue them but it was against his strict training to show any open emotion.

"What happened?" She was concerned and she wanted to convey her feelings to Lance.

"Hit and rum as far as Michael can make out. But I think we can surmise differently to that in the light of other things that have happened, don't you?"

"What about Michael then? You said that Chad was a particular friend of his!"

"He is proceeding to the second point isolated on the circumnavigation paper as previously indicated. Yes Chad was a good friend but Michael is far too professionally motivated to ignore his own orders!"

"Then I take it that Chad discovered something at Vigo and was silenced because of it?"

"He reported back that the loot had been transferred to a second vessel whilst Dorkins and his companion were enjoying their unexpected break, so that they were none the wiser that their precious cargo had been shifted from off their vessel upon their return!"

"So I take it that this second boat was itself then heading towards Fuerteventura?"

"Not necessarily. There were other ports of call listed if you remember, this of course is now what Michael intends to investigate!"

"The fact that Michael reports back to you each time I suppose makes you his Superior?"

"You ask far too many questions woman. But to be truthful I don't think one can consider anyone as being superior in our line of work. It just so happens that this time around I am in charge of this case. Next time it could possibly be Michael or someone else. It all depends what strategy our masters decide at the appropriate time!"

She remembered the airport and the long walk to where the coaches were parked because of the extension work going on there. This time however Lance hailed a taxi to take them the short distance to Calleta.

"Well you didn't expect me to have had my car transported over as well did you?" He took note of her face with a grin. "I suppose there is a bus passing by the airport but perhaps this is infinitely more convenient!"

Still once in the taxi a wave of apprehension took hold of her. What if Brad was already present at this hotel? His staff in Tenerife had intimated as much! Once again however Lance seemed to be able to read her mind.

"The hotel if you remember is well laid out over a large expanse. Large enough I would suggest for one to be able to avoid anyone one doesn't wish to come into contact with!"

"But I thought that was the general idea?"

"My task, not exactly yours Rachel!" Then if she had nothing now to do with it then why exactly had he brought her here? She watched as he again registered in under the name of Mr and Mrs Turner.

"That is becoming a habit!" They followed the boy and their luggage down the mass of corridors leading from one block to the next.

"So you wanted to register in your own name so you could be easily recognised, is that it?"

"No, I don't think so!"

"Then perhaps you ought to give that tongue of yours a rest for a while!"

Unsure whether she was now being chastised Rachel lapsed into a silence as she took in the onus of the building and whereabouts in the set up they were to be stationed.

Still the room that they were allotted with its sea view did much to allay such thoughts and thus moving out onto the balcony she took in deep breaths of the beautiful air and pondered back onto the time when she had first spotted Lance right there on the beach in front of her. All that now seemed to be a lifetime ago.

"Which bed do you want then?" The twin beds had been pushed close together so that one could make one queen-size bed if required. The fact that they would be sleeping together suddenly hit home. Not that she objected sleeping with Lance, it was just that lately he had seemed either unwilling or unable to show his emotions and somehow he expected her to understand this situation.

"Either will do for me!" She wandered into the bathroom that was worthy of taking note being made up of two distinct areas with the bathing area well separated from the grooming mirrors and watched as he followed her.

"I thought we would eat in tonight. The Restaurant here is quite good and it will also give me the opportunity to organise a car for our stay on the Island. Tomorrow however will be somewhat different. I have heard it rumoured that the new branch of Devereaux Hire is due to open in the region of the Atlantique Shopping Mall, which is situated not too far away. This time however I think I will be going there on my own Rachel!"

"Why was my performance not satisfactory or something the last time around?"

"Perfectly satisfactory. But on this occasion I feel it could be infinitely more dangerous and therefore I am not willing to let you go!"

"In that case what would you be expecting me to do then?"

"I suppose you could always take the opportunity of weighing up surfing talent on the beach here. If I remember correctly you are quite good at doing that!"

She clenched her fists now ready to land out at the insufferable man, but realising her intent he started to laugh. "O.K. I know that I am being provocative, but I meant what I said about the situation possibly proving dangerous and I am not willing to subject you to that. Once I have cased out the place perhaps the car will have arrived and we can then go to the port in Puerto Rosario, the capital, just at the other side of the airport and see what we can observe there. But now as I am already beginning to feel the pangs of hunger beginning to gnaw at me I suggest you get yourself ready for dinner!"

She found herself obeying him as if in a dream and caught his eye of approval for her efforts as they descended down to the Restaurant. Although buffet service it was a rather special night as the cast of the show from the hotel amphitheatre were advertising the evening entertainment and had even decorated up the entrance to the place so that in Rachel's eyes it almost appeared as if she was entering wonderland even if Lance did steer her well away from the hotel's photographers whose main interest lay in capturing the couple on film and then displaying it for all to see in the foyer the next morning in the hopes that they would purchase the same.

Lance himself seemed to relax through that meal and she was hardly surprised when leaving the dining room he slipped a protective arm around her. "You look especially desirable tonight!" He whispered the words in her ear and all their recent disagreements seemed to fade into the background.

"Well thank you kind Sir. Had you anything in mind then?" She was being totally provocative now and for once he appeared happy to be encouraged.

"Were you bothered about seeing the show or shall we settle for an early night then?"

"Perhaps the latter!" She watched as he went over to the bar to return with a bottle and two glasses.

"Merely a night cap if we feel we need it!" He explained as he took her arm and Rachel was content.

Well so much for a queen size bed when a single would have served their purpose adequately! Rachel giggled to herself as she untwined his sleeping form from around her the next morning. At least though she felt that they were back together again and the thought elated her. Her movements obviously disturbed him for he opened one eye and gazed at her actions and noticing that he was now awake she planted a kiss on the end of his nose.

"Guess I broke my resolution!" He moistened his lips as he spoke.

"Which was?"

"Never to mix business with pleasure and never to become emotionally involved with a colleague whether she had been coerced into that position or not! But all that was before you, you little minx came along to shatter all my good resolutions. I don't really think the Department would approve!"

"Do you care?"

"For them? In a word no, but I do care about you and the fact that you are involved now up to your neck in this little drama!"

"Then I am coming with you to the shopping centre this morning?"

"No you are not, I thought I made myself perfectly clear over that notion. Besides if Stevens did happen to be there and went for you I would probably blow my own cover mighty quick!" He managed to extricate his legs and swing them out of bed. "So for once you are going to do as you are told this morning but after lunch that will be a different matter!" He was now heading towards the shower. "Well come on then get yourself out of bed. The sun is already up in the sky and I am dying for a coffee!"

She dressed in blind obedience to his command and a few minutes later they were both heading to retrieve their breakfast from the Restaurant now devoid of its nighttime finery. To be truthful Rachel did feel a sense of unease as they passed through the doorway just in case Brad happened to be there but fortunately her fears were quite unfounded. Lance himself spoke little over their meal, instead he kept watching her and did not seem to be content until he finally parked her in one of the deckchairs overlooking the massive swimming pool.

"I promise that I won't be away for long, it's only a short stroll along the beach. But at least we will have something to go on I suppose!"

She nodded, not that she really felt in agreement with him but this time around she had to let him do things in his own way. Maybe she ought to make the most of this situation by a little creative writing. She glanced at the pad she had brought with her but the page remained unfilled with any words during his absence. Still fortunately that was not for long before she saw his form returning and she steeled herself to stop her running to greet him as he came across the gardens.

"The office as such still appears to be in its embryonic form. Just one person in attendance who appeared to know very little and no sign of Stevens there at all which under the circumstances of our present close proximity might be just as well at the moment!"

"So I could have come with you after all?"

"I said no Rachel and I meant it. Anyway time now for our elevens and then I will see to this hire car I have booked ready for this afternoon's jaunt!"

For those initiated into the merits of other capital cities, even those of other Canary Islands like Santa Cruz and Las Palmas, the capitol city of Fuerteventura probably would prove to be something of a disappointment, for there were no lush new buildings lining the quay. Indeed both the port and the town appeared to have remained in its own undeveloped state. Yet to Rachel with its alcoves and old-fashioned cobbled streets it proved to hold something distinctly fascinating about the place that had once swore upon the trade of its goat populace.

The port itself was not large. Earlier on in the year there had been a call for a ferryboat to transport people across to the African continent and back. Yet the route had not lasted for long for barely a month after it had been opened the run across the narrow channel to meet the Sahara Desert had been abandoned. The official reason that had been given was that the boat had provided a tendency to career into the structure of the jetty and ultimately it had caused quite a lot of damage that was not easily repaired in the one-man company!

"I presume that is the vessel over there. At least it appears to be the only one that is presently not ready to go anywhere!" Facing the port he indicated one such vessel that was moored apart from the rest. It appeared to be deserted apart from one or two figures round about on the quayside. Rachel did not say anything. To her mind the man whom she was with appeared to have an unusually keen eye for she doubted whether she would ever have singled out this craft as being anything special.

"So are you ready to do your stuff again?" Lance now regarded her quizzically.

"My stuff?" For a moment she did not follow his argument.

"As Winston Devereaux's secretary it would be quite acceptable for you to make enquiries as to whether he is on board. Spin the yarn about some urgent business matter you need to see him about. I don't think for a moment he will be there so if I am right your next job will be to cause a distraction whilst I get on board myself. You should find that quite easy, after all you seem to be remarkably good at being able to distract folk. Oh, just sport yourself around and do a lot of chattering, that ought to keep them fully occupied. Don't look at me like that, remember if the worst comes to the worst I have you covered!" He reached into his pocket and perhaps for the first time Rachel realised that the man most definitely meant business as she heard a weapon click ready to fire.

"So you intend leaving me on shore whilst you board the boat on your own? If you are searching for something surely two pairs of hands would be better than one?"

"I intend to board on my own because that happens to be my job. Secondly you can be of far more use to me on shore causing your usual commotion so that I will not be observed. Don't worry it won't take me long I promise you. All that I need to do at the moment is to ascertain whether the jewels are on board. After all we can hardly continue with our plan if they are not, now can we?"

"Our plan?"

"Oh do stop either repeating or questioning everything I say, you are far worse than your sister ever was. Just go and get on with your task!" For good measure he slapped her across the rear almost playfully and Rachel decided that perhaps it was just as well that they were involved with a case for that alone tamed her actions from turning upon him.

As Lance had previously anticipated she reached a blank with her enquires about Brad. Obviously the man was expected but had not yet arrived on the scene. With this news she looked winsomely in Lance's direction, maybe under the circumstances it was not advisable for him to board the ship in case that person arrived. In turn however he motioned her to get on with the second part of the project as they had planned.

It took him almost ten minutes before he finally reappeared from off that craft and after that length of time Rachel was convinced that those present on the quayside must really have begun to believe that she was some eccentric female, whom they were polite to only because of the fact that she claimed to be Winston Devereaux's secretary. No doubt they all sighed with relief when she finally took her leave of them claiming that they were the ones who were holding her back from her work. How this translated into the local dialect she had no intention of waiting to seen but instead hastened to rejoin Lance by the famous statues of the goats near the main square.

"They are on board all right!" He glanced in her direction as if questioning the fact that she had taken her time in getting here.

"They are on board and yet you made no effort to move them?" What he had said just didn't appear to make sense to her.

"That will come later after you have done some shopping my dear. I did however manage to take some photographs of the goods for your perusal!"

"I don't understand what you are talking about now!"

"Quite simple. We can hardly remove the jewels without putting something in their place otherwise that would arouse a great deal of suspicion. Therefore I want you to see if you can replace these items with some paste costume jewellery which we will the place on the boat in their stead. There must be enough trinket shops in the vicinity for us to be able to acquire some likeness of the real things and I do believe a woman has probably a finer eye for such detail than a man. Then if we can manage to get them back on board before either His eminence arrives or the boat sails, I am sure his masters, wherever they might be will appreciate our efforts!"

Rachel gulped as he handed her the camera with the shots still enclosed. The plan was simply audacious, but then she decided that was only what she could expect from Lance. "In that case I guess I had better get busy. How long have we got?"

He glanced at his watch. "Shall we say around an hour? The shops have already opened again after their siesta and in one hours time it will be growing dusk which will give us a further advantage!"

She nodded as she took the bit between her teeth, reminiscing as to where they had passed such trinket shops on the way down to the port. If Lance was rusting her on this then she definitely was not going to let him down!

★ ★ ★ ★

Chapter Eight

At least she presumed that he was satisfied with her purchases although he wasted no time after giving them a cursory glance, in indicating that now was the time that they must get back to the boat to effect the exchange. In addition she was quite surprised when she watched as he deftly implanted some small device into one of the stones on the false tiara she had purchased.

"Simply a small tracking device!" He was obviously assuming her unspoken question. "With a little luck it should enable my superiors to be able to define the final destination of the cache. That is something that they consider to be extremely important!" He did not go into further detail but simply decided that he had said enough.

"So how do you envisage getting back onto that boat?" An unexplainable fear now crossed her thoughts. What if Brad had arrived during their absence? She knew him now for what he was and that included being unaffected by the taking of life and what was more to the point she felt fiercely protective towards the man at her side.

"The same way as I managed to get off it I suppose. But stop worrying. By now it is long past the normal working hours for any gallant minders so there will be no necessity for you to portray your femme fatale act again. More is the pity for I actually missed the floorshow the last time around!"

"In that case maybe I ought to come on board with you. I could always hold your torch or something and even keep a look out for any strangers that could be approaching!"

"The answer to that Rachel is a resounding no. I don't even think health and safety would support you in that notion. But the torch idea is not a bad suggestion. Stay in the shadows and if you do see anyone approaching then you can always give me a flash from it. Only be careful you are not observed acting so by anyone who is venturing close otherwise you yourself could be spotted. Once you see me leaving the vessel however the most useful thing you can do at that time is to bring the car around so we don't have to carry the loot too far!"

"But will you be able to manage it on your own?"

"We are not talking about a massive trunk Rachel. Even jewels of that magnitude can occupy very little space!" He tossed her the keys to the hire car. " I presume that you have remembered where we parked it?"

"Of course!" For a minute she objected to being spoken to like a dimwit. "And if we are talking of risk then it is you who needs to be careful!"

"O.K. then let's move and get it over with!" He nodded with that by now familiar grin on his face and she wondered if he always reacted in this manner when he was on a job. They parted without any more ado except perhaps for the slight tweak on the cheek that he now gave her and the veiled reassurance that the matter would not take long.

Still with her eyes glued in the direction of the boat she had never been more relieved than she was when she saw him reappear. Perhaps however it was unfortunate that at the time of this reappearance one executive car could be spotted approaching the scene and even without thinking Rachel flashed her torch just hoping that Lance would notice it and take evasive action. But now her own orders had been to fetch the car from the parking lot and her feet sped across the promenade to where the vehicle had been placed.

"O.K. I wasn't spotted!" She felt a surge of relief as he finally climbed into the vehicle carrying his precious cargo.

"The car I saw approaching?"

"Thanks for your timely flash. I am not sure but I suppose it could have been the man himself!"

"You mean that Brad is here after all!"

"I was under the impression that it was him, yes. Fortunately I left before he had a chance to spot me rifling his precious cargo!"

"But he will notice the exchange surely?"

"Shouldn't think so old girl. In fact I will go so far as to say that it is not the cargo, however valuable that might be, that he is currently interested in, but rather the pay out from his masters when they receive the goods!"

"Then you don't think that he will want to check them?"

"Only cursorily I am hoping if that, just to assure himself that they are still there. I don't suppose the man has any eye for jewels at any rate. His own value rests with the amount of money they are likely to fetch him!"

"So where to now. What are you going to do with the genuine articles?"

"Beyond claiming the reward for their safe return do you mean? First of all we make back to the hotel and then I will have some text messaging to do. One thing is certain I doubt if we will get these back to the U.K on any plane!"

"How then?"

"I have some ideas. For instance have you ever contemplated taking a leisurely cruise back to the U.K?"

"But you would still not be able to get them through customs without the pertinent questions one would wish to avoid!"

"I do believe the girl is learning. But who said anything about a regular service? That is why I need now to do a little text messaging. After all we have the perfect pair of fishermen ready for action and more to the point currently based in Tenerife. Crossing their palms with silver would I suggest produce a change of heart on their behalf and persuade them to move from enjoying the balmy climate out here and returning to the pleasant rain of England. Plus as fishermen I doubt whether they will be inclined to declare their wares at any official post on the way there! This is also something that I need to let Michael know about as well otherwise he might start wondering where we have got to on our travels."

She lapsed into silence on the way back to Calleta. Upon arrival however it was Rachel who found that she was the one entrusted to carry the precious packet indoors. "But where do you now suggest we place it?" She glanced at the safety deposit box in their suite in dismay. The packet wrapped in its oilskin could possibly be considered to be manageable but there was literally no way that the object would fit into that small container even if it was empty at the time. Such a facility was meant only to house travel documents, passports and possibly a small amount of Euros. Lance followed her glance but did not remain perplexed for long.

"Guess it will have to go into one of the suitcases for the time being. Wrap it in some travel clothes or something. In fact better still wrap it up in the dirty washing. That is one place where nobody would ever deem to look!" He had retrieved his mobile and was now in the act of starting to text someone. Rachel frowned. If this was the fishermen he was attempting to contact then she doubted that they would have the facility to receive the message. He smiled again as he noted her expression possibly reading her thoughts. "There are others I can text on the Island, those whom I can trust to pass on the message. You yourself have questioned my other employ when I was staying there!"

Still the message was obviously received for he finally turned in her direction. "Well at least that is settled, although I suppose it will take them at least a couple of days to get here with the Sea Witch, so in the meantime we might just as well enjoy a welcome break here!"

Whether he considered a break feasible or not he was soon on voice mail to another person. This time he turned away so she did not fully understand all that he had to say but she gleaned enough to realise the person he was now contacting was Michael in an attempt to bring him up to date with events.

Strangely enough she was left with the impression that Michael was rather frustrated with the results of their own efforts feeling that his own mission had been rather pointless. "Well if you fancy a lift back to the U.K. then I suggest you get your bones over here before our transport arrives. Sorry if your own quest proved to be a wild goose chase, but nevertheless it is something that I believed had at the time to be checked out. Anyway now we have got hold of the goods to continue with your efforts appears to be rather pointless. The names of the points of contact will most probably be enough to satisfy our employers!"

There was a grunt that issued back down the fibre optic cable yet although he knew his colleague was none too pleased with the way that things had worked out, Michael was also aware that Lance being his Superior had spoken and to his mind this was an order. "Be with you later tomorrow then!"

"Good! I wouldn't want you to miss the boat!" Lance replaced the receiver and turned to Rachel with a smile. "Now that is all completed I guess it is time for us to sort out a meal for ourselves!"

After spotting the car at the port Rachel felt uneasy at eating in the Restaurant that night for now she was more than half convinced that Brad would be there. She was however relieved to realise she had been quite wrong in her assumptions for there was currently no sign of his presence.

On the other hand Lance appeared determined to play the perfect escort to her that night and after following the meal with dancing it was already quite late when they finally retired. Still if she had expected them both to sleep in just one of those queen size beds again she was sadly mistaken for after a brief nod Lance turned on his side and fell fast asleep!

The morning broke with the first rays of sunlight penetrating through the flimsy net curtains at the window and Rachel, keen to witness this advent of a new day made her way outside onto the balcony to be able to experience this first hand. Yet stood on the balcony the girl suddenly froze, for parked alongside of the other vehicles belonging to folk staying at the place there was a new different vehicle, in the form of a large shiny black saloon. Choking back her emotions she roused the still sleeping Lance.

"That car, the one I spotted before is here Lance. Maybe after all he has caught up with us!"

"Oh yea of little faith. Of course he will be staying here. After all it is possibly the nearest hotel within easy access to both the port and the airport. But don't worry for I doubt whether he will see and recognise us in a place of this magnitude! After all he will be far more concerned with his own problems to even anticipate that we are here!"

Rachel however did not feel quite as convinced in her own mind as what Lance sounded. Moreover the latter showed no intention of attempting to hide himself away that day, for after breakfast he quite blandly announced that he saw the day as an opportunity for him to catch up with a couple of wind surfing lessons whilst he was here.

"You are actually thinking of going out there?" The girl felt mesmerised at the man's audacity.

"Of course. There is little else we can do whilst we are awaiting the arrival of absent friends. You yourself have a choice of course. You can either, come and watch me in my exploits from La Castillo, or you can sun yourself around the pool, or if you are energetic you could always take in the local shops. Not that there is a great deal there to keep you occupied for any length of time although I don't know ------ women always seem to find plenty to occupy themselves with when there are shops at hand!"

"Well thank you for giving me such a wealth of alternatives to choose from. But on reflection I think I will come and watch you. Why with a little bit of luck I might even see you finish up in the water!"

"And no doubt that sort of event would serve to cheer your dispiriting heart?"

"The last time around you mentioned perfecting your skills in order to raise funds for some disabled children whom your friend has an interest in. Is that still your reason for wanting to go?" She decided that perhaps it was best to attempt to change the subject onto something obviously closer to his own heart. Not that he had mentioned anything about this of late!

"That is still very much on the cards!" He adopted a more serious tone. "You see the friend I spoke about before, the one who is disabled, happens to be my brother Pete. He was injured after a serious rock fall when he was out climbing in the U. K. and consequently lost the use of his legs. In fact he is lucky to be alive and because of this and the treatment he received he has been determined to put something back into society. The idea behind the surf board, a sport that I personally have always enjoyed, is that when I feel myself proficient enough I want to raise sponsorship money for the world championship that takes place right here on this Island. Not that I expect to win anything but to be considered proficient enough to take part will assist me in raising enough funds to help the children Pete cares for in some way. I guess that is the least I can do to help him under the circumstances!"

They fell into a silence after his rhetoric whilst Rachel began to examine her own conscience. It seemed to be so refreshing to hear this man speaking of trying to do something for others. Eventually he grinned in her direction. "Well if you are still determined to watch whilst I become a cropper I guess it's time we made tracks!" He took her arm and the warmth percolating from his veins infiltrated into her being. Quite suddenly she had realised that there was another side to Lance Turner, one that she had never known about!

The breeze that chose to blow in a tormenting fashion over her wad of notes that morning appeared to be almost in defiance of her desire to at least try to unlock the words from her memory board and write them down on the paper she had brought, for this element chose to toy with the edges of her pad playfully and thus ripple it in order to make the sort of noise that would easily distract her and deny any thought of such creativity. All of which she felt appeared to be a great shame for she had allotted this time whilst Lance was embroiled with his surf boarding to do something constructive. But it was not only the breeze that served to disturb her for now in her mind's eye a child had seemingly nudged his way into the spotlight, a child whom she initially believed to have some sort of handicap but then upon closer inspection discovered that it was the likeness of young Jake whom she now had in mind!

Her initial reactions were followed by something that resembled rebuke for now in all honesty she realised that recently she had not given her nephew a single thought and naturally she now worried as to how the boy was getting on!

"Don't try and tell me you were asleep in the sun? You know that is bad for you!" She jumped up from her position almost guiltily as a voice suddenly accused her of this terrible demeanour before she realised that Lance had returned from his morning's sojourn and what was more, in spite of all her promises to the contrary she had not witnessed his prowess that day.

"No, I was not asleep, merely contemplating that 's all!" She denied the fact that the perpetual motion of the tide and the flapping of that paper had lulled her into an unwanted slumber.

"But looking at your paper I can see that you have not written a single word and I have been away for almost an hour at that!" He screwed up his nose disdainfully at her efforts as he caught a glimpse of her empty sheet.

"Well one needs time in order to allow the ideas to gel!" She spoke now in her own defence, determined as she was to wipe the smug expression from off his face. "Anyway how did your lesson go?"

"Are you trying to tell me that you couldn't even find the time to watch me for yourself? Especially today when I proved to be the star pupil!" Laughingly he pulled her up to her feet. Maybe indeed if they had not at the time been so wrapped up in one another one of them at least might possibly have observed the fact that the gate that led from the gardens of the hotel onto the promenade had opened and a shadowy creature had made an exit. As it was however it was the mobile in Lance's pocket that served to bring the pair of them back to reality.

"It's Michael! Apparently he has just arrived at the airport and has therefore decided to make his way here by the local bus. Well I guess it isn't a very long trip for him to make from that place so perhaps we ought to think about getting ourselves along to the local bus stop so that we can meet him. I suppose one can consider that it is quite a walk from here up to the main road where the nearest stop is situated!"

She nodded as she remembered the place from her last visit. In fact that caused her to smile for she also remembered rushing up the last part of the hill because she thought she had missed her transport, only to find that the in coming vehicle had only stopped to let off passengers before it had finally moved on to the terminus at the next stop by the Atlantique Shopping Centre before it made its return journey and picked up the waiting passengers on the way back.

Maybe it was an act of stupidity on her part but the only reasonable excuse she could offer was those earlier thought of Jake and thus as she was passing the shops on the way up to the main road, Rachel suddenly remembered something she had spotted there.

"Give me a minute!" She almost begged. "I don't actually think that the bus is quite due yet and I have just remembered something that I must get for Jake!"

He tutted but after waving his arms in the air as if this action was all one could expect from a woman he finally nodded. "One minute and then I'm coming after you. Sometimes I don't really think you fully understand the importance of our own position!"

"Well I'm sure a minute will make little difference in out quest. After all we are out to meet a bus that isn't even due yet!" Her voice held a plea within it that others found hard to resist.

"Oh all right then have things your own way. I'll wait here for you!"

Perhaps however Lance would not have been quite so tolerant to her request if he had been able to see what was to materialise next however: For as he waited patiently for her to return back onto the main road it was time for another to make an appearance.

Gazing in that shop window where she had spotted something of interest to one small boy, and debating with herself whether it would be feasible to buy it for the lad, Rachel was quite unaware of the shadow that cast itself across her path. Not that was until she heard the voice that she could only describe as coming from hell accosting her.

"I have heard from several sources in these Islands that my secretary is attempting to trace me on some urgent business matter. Perhaps my dear you would be now good enough to enlighten me on this matter?"

Rachel felt her mouth go excessively dry as she wondered whether Lance had spotted the intruder. The man she had feared to meet was currently present here on this Island after all. A man whom she knew from the past was capable of anything to enhance his own being and that included murder if it was necessary. To her mind it seemed to be impossible that Lance from his current position would have noticed anything was amiss and her mind fought to seek out inspiration to make some sort of reply to her ex-employer.

"It is a query concerning your new venture in opening up an office on this Island!" Perhaps it was the first or rather the only thought that came to mind for her tongue seemed to be incapable of issuing anything else. "Apparently there appears to be some legal obligation and the official papers have not yet been received for your signature!"

"You never did make a very good liar Rachel but unfortunately for you I am afraid that I am not a character in one of your books, much as I enjoyed our one time relationship. I actually believe that you have quite a great deal of explaining to do, not least why you are on this Island and more importantly why you are in the company of a certain individual whom I do not count as being amongst my friends!"

"We are currently on our way to meet an old associate of Lance's and what is more Lance is currently waiting for me on the road there as we happen to be in rather a hurry. I have now imparted what I had to say to you so as I am already late perhaps we should leave the matter there!" Her own tonality served to surprise her and she felt quite pleased with the result although in all truth it seemingly failed to impress Brad Stevens.

"I do not think so my dear. Once before I believed I had impressed upon you the necessity of keeping your nose out of my business when I gave you the chance to cool down. Unfortunately you appeared to have a man present at that place, a person whom you thought that you could rely upon. Perhaps you failed to learn even then that I do not tolerate anyone who attempts to interfere in my affairs!" She realised, much to her horror that as he referred back to Doug the fiend had now produced a gun, which he held threateningly in her direction. " You can believe this however I will not fail to use it Rachel if you do not do exactly what I am about to say for it is high time you confided in me on certain matters!"

"What do you want?" Desperately she tried to look over her shoulder to determine whether Lance was looking for her, but of that person there appeared to be no sign.

"First of all we will walk back to the hotel together. There you will find I have parked my car and therefore we will go together to visit the port and then you can tell me exactly what you were doing snooping around a certain vessel yesterday afternoon. You need have no hesitation that I will use this weapon if necessary, so if for old times sake you wish to prolong your life you will do exactly what I say!"

"I don't think so!" Another voice rang out to join in and Rachel thanked her lucky stars that Lance must have noticed. Yet her thanks did not express itself for long for a shot rang out as Brad turned the already primed weapon onto her saviour and she herself was in time to witness his crumpled form sink to the ground!

-------------Now without thinking of herself Rachel tried her best to move towards this still figure on the ground but in attempting to do this she had reckoned without her assailant.

"Move!" He had grabbed hold of her arm and was now waving the gun in her direction and threatening to use it. But Rachel no longer cared for her own predicament; so determined was she to get to Lance's side. "I said move!" This time she felt the blow across her face yet even as her eyes streamed with tears down her stinging face she refused to yield whereupon cursing like hell the devil incarnate then begin to forcibly drag her back out of the shopping street and back towards the hotel car park. Why had someone from those shops not noticed her predicament, she moaned as she felt her arm practically wrenched from out of its socket as she was pulled roughly along the pavement. In desperation she willed her feet to find some rock or stone where she could wedge them and stop this charade. Yet the position she now found herself to be in seemed to be hopeless. There were no such stones to anchor her feet behind. No one came forward to witness her cries and the car park loomed ever closer as her assailant seemingly enjoyed metering out his will upon her.

She thought she heard the police sirens even as her head was forced through the open door of the vehicle after it had received a further punch that almost rendered her senseless and thus quite incapable of stopping this car once it was in motion. But then there was an apparent silence and she thought she had been mistaken as she sank down abjectly into the interior of the vehicle. Her eyes now closed with the stinging they had received from his fist she was not aware at first of yet another sound approaching, that was until she realised that a fight was currently in progress. But still stupefied from those blows she had received it wasn't until she became aware of her assailant's body hitting the ground outside of the car and a pair of arms reaching into the vehicle to pull her out that she realised her rescue was afoot.

At first her bemused mind told her that this must be Lance, a factor that was quite ridiculous as she had witnessed him taking the shot earlier and then turning her bleary gaze upon her rescuer she saw that it was Michael, the silent disapproving one who had escorted her to Paris, an act she had deemed at the time to be very much against the fellow's will.

"Come on let's get out of here before he comes round!" He was emptying the man's gun of its remaining cartridges and now he implied an urgency to get her away from the scene.

"But Lance, he has been shot!" She had to get back to him. She was grateful to the man for rescuing her but now it was Lance and the crumpled form that she had left that was the thought that occupied her mind.

"He is being attended to. We have got to move!"

She had heard that word move before and shivering she now determined that she had no intention of doing so not if such an action on her part meant leaving Lance behind. Yet with this pair of strong arms fastened around her she now found herself being carried against her will. She had no recollection of anyone telling him where they were staying, but Michael seemed to know, he also appeared to be aware of where this place was situated. How, she had no idea, for if he was familiar with the layout to this resort then why on earth had they gone to the bus stop to meet him?

"A fine reception I received when I arrived at the bus stop I must say!" Perhaps something of her thoughts had conveyed themselves to him. But by this time he had carried her into the foyer and perhaps, she decided, he was possibly making words of consolation.

"I need to get back to Lance!" Her voice moaned again almost inconsolably. She didn't want this person commandeering her life, for as far as she was concerned she simply yearned to get back to the figure she had left still slumped on the ground

"I've already told you that the man is all right. He is currently being attended to. It's a flesh wound or so I am led to believe!" She didn't believe him of course for by this time she was convinced that someone was trying to keep the worst of the news from her. "Whereabouts is your room?"

Rachel stopped wailing for long enough to appear aghast. What on earth did this fellow think he was doing? She wanted to go to no room anyway and what was more she had no intention of telling him where it was.

"No matter!" They had cleared the reception area and Rachel was almost relieved to see that the person on duty paid little attention to them for the whole charade was proving to be an embarrassment to her. Eventually however he put her down but still keeping a firm hold on her he then grabbed hold of her bag quite deliberately. What she did not realise at first was that the evidence was present there for him to glean what he wanted to know by glancing at her dining card inside the bag that also had her room number neatly typed across the front of it. Still she supposed he still hadn't got the key to that room! Her reasoning however was to prove to be unfounded for propelling her down the corridor as if he was familiar with the place he suddenly produced a selection of keys from out of his pocket. Perhaps if she had not been so surprised she would have yelled out in her objection, but before she regained her composure she was to suddenly find herself deposited upon that bed.

"Now see if you can calm down!" At least she supposed he made no effort to touch her. "I doubt if Lance will want to see you in such a frazzle upon his return!" He parked himself almost uncomfortably in one of the chairs that also graced the room signifying perhaps that this was decidedly not his scene. "At least if you continue yelling like some amateurish schoolgirl one must approve of that fact that few if anybody will hear you in here. Here's a handkerchief anyway for good measure and when you decide to shut up then I could suggest you attempt to repair the damage to your make up before Lance arrives!"

"How can you be so sure that he is all right, and that he will come? You forget I saw him lying there on the ground!"

"I think I know Lance well enough to know that a flesh wound will not stop him from doing exactly that. He will be here just as soon as the wound is attended to and in answer to your next question it is being attended to for it was I who sent for medical assistance to tend to it for him as unfortunately even I could not hope to see to two things myself at the same time. The main question I would like to ask you though is how on earth did that satanic fiend spot you in the first place? Anyway as you have not blubbered for the last few minutes shall I get you a drink?"

The effrontery of this chap. Not only does he arrive on the scene uninvited but then presumes to take over even to inviting himself into her bedroom. "No thank you I am not thirsty!"

"Who said anything about thirst. I believe tea is good for you after sustaining a shock!" She didn't believe what she was hearing when he picked up the phone for room service. Whatever the waiter must have thought upon seeing another man in the room whilst she was still laid prone on the bed she almost dreaded to think. Still apparently Michael saw little that he deemed unusual about the situation and therefore she was left to sip the tea still feeling disconsolate!

Upon one thing however Michael appeared to have been right for she had scarcely time to finish the drink before they heard a key turning in the lock as Lance let himself in. The first thing she probably noticed was the sling he was wearing, but this did not stop her from throwing herself off that bed towards the newcomer.

"Your arm, are you all right?" Perhaps this was a silly inference, the man could hardly have walked into the place if he had not been.

"The bloody thing is tender so watch it!" Perhaps he thought she was about to land upon his sling. Then perhaps sensing her concern he hastened to add. "Of course I'm all right, would I be standing here if I wasn't? It is a flesh wound only. I took the bullet in the shoulder and it passed right through but damaged little apart from pride. Good job that bus arrived when it did anyway Michael. Hope she didn't prove to be too much trouble for you for I am afraid our friend here appears to often make up her mind to play the obnoxious!"

"But I saw you laid on the ground?" It sounded stupid maybe but it was the only thing that now came to mind.

"You appeared to be lying there motionless and now you say it was only a flesh wound?"

"A tactical manoeuvre I can assure you!"

"You mean you laid down and left me to the whims of that man?" She suddenly felt a wave of anger percolating through the initial relief at seeing him that had at first beset her and feeling somewhat dejected flung herself back on the bed.

"Well after all I knew full well that Michael would be on that bus!"

"You mean you hoped he would be! Why didn't you just shoot the fiend and have done with it? After all he was the one who shot Doug and what is more you are carrying a gun for I have seen it!"

"What and spoil all our future plans? That my girl was not an option! You see we don't exactly work like that for the matter happens to be a police affair and therefore it is up to them to bring the accused to trial! So I suppose judging from this little outburst you had trouble in persuading the lady Michael?

"Considering I rescued her from our mutual friend that matter could be deemed to be debatable!"

"And our so called friend?"

"I left him out cold!" He fingered a bruised hand. "Although I must admit he was a hard target!"

" I still don't understand why didn't you shoot him before he could do any more damage. After all I suppose you had a gun as well!" This time Rachel quite undeterred with what had gone before was determined to make her voice heard even if she was forced to shout over their voices!

It was Lance who regarded her through tightly drawn eyes. " I thought I had just made that perfectly clear. To have done that and exceeded our brief would have ultimately defeated our whole objective. You see we still require your publishing friend to stay alive in order for us to carry out our mission!" Rachel swallowed hard not a little surprised that Lance appeared to make far more fuss of Michael than he did of her! Tactical manoeuvre, my foot!

"So your mission, as you would call it, is all that matters to you?"

"I suppose it is what we are paid for yes. Anyway I never doubted that you were in any kind of danger in the first place. Still perhaps it is time we considered lunch!"

Rachel looked at her watch. In truth she was surprised that the clock had raced around so quickly. "Then we are all going to the Restaurant?"

"Not such a good idea under the present circumstances. I suggest we ask for room service at the moment!" He took hold of the internal phone with his good hand. "Although perhaps it would appear more seemly if you didn't appear to be lounging on the bed with two men in the room when the waiter arrives!"

Positively fuming she thrust her way from the bed and over to the French windows. "Then perhaps it would appear even better if I disappeared out onto the balcony and left you two boys to it?"

"Not advisable my dear!" Now he had placed himself between her and the window outlet and she was left to wonder just what the waiter would deem to think when he espied a woman alone in this suite with two men anyway!

Rachel toyed with the strings of lettuce left on her plate as she finally sat at the small occasional table in the room and came to the conclusion that she had never liked lettuce and even if she was starving she could never face the mistakes of a salad that others appeared to go in raptures about. One thing however still served to amuse her and that was the expression on the waiter's face when he had brought in this luncheon and eyed her together with two men, the same two who were presently talking together in low subdued tones on the balcony outside, the one she had earlier been forbidden to go upon.

Well if they wanted to talk secrets out of her earshot they were welcome to it. She refused to strain her ears to catch any snippets from this conversation that was going on although at the same time she could not avoid catching certain phrases that appeared to float to her sensory organs on a breath of a gentle breeze. She could not help but overhear the name of the Sea Witch being included in that conversation as well as the names of Ned Dorkins and his sailing companion. Maybe Lance was now trying to fill his colleague in with some of the finer detail. Michael responded by saying something about Brad Stevens although what that actually consisted of she had no idea except for the fact that it appeared to amuse the two conspirators. Well she was sure she wasn't interested in their boyish talk and spiked a tomato with her fork. She supposed she would have to eat something!

"Then you are sure that the exchange will not be noticed?" That was Michael playing his role of caution quite proficiently and regarding his companion with a terse expression.

"Rachel showed that she had good choice when it came to selecting items to put in place of the items on the vessel!" Oh so she was appreciated for something after all! Alleluia!

"And the originals what did you do with them then?"

"They are quite secure until it is time for us to relocate them!" Well that was a laugh anyway. She would never have stated that she considered a suitcase of dirty washing to be a secure place. Michael however did not question further for he obviously wanted to change the subject to something closer to his own heart. She attacked her salad yet again as she heard them move and realised that the pair of them were now heading back into the room.

"Guess you've not made such a good job of that!" Lance paused as he eyed her plate. "Has no one ever told you that the green stuff is good for you?"

"I believe that rabbits go a bundle on it but unfortunately I am not one of their breed!"

"Have it your way then but don't start complaining you are hungry this afternoon!"

Did that comment mean that they had already something planned? Rachel gazed up into the face of the person currently regarding her. It was then more than ever that she realised whatever kind of fix they were in she loved this man more than anything else!

* * * *

Chapter Nine

It was Lance who finally took the call that informed them that the Sea Witch had finally made the Puerto de Rosario and for her part Rachel did not know at the time whether she was glad or sorry! She supposed she could claim in a sense that she was glad for after been cooped up here in this place with these two men, one of whom merely regarded her with a critical eye whilst the other appeared to ignore her completely which in turn left her in a state of some demoralisation, that something was about to happen. But on the other hand she was sorry that in her timidity the thought of having to sail back to England across the wiles of the Atlantic with merely two of a crew she found both frightening and unrealistic. In fact she was forced to admit that in truth perhaps this was a far worse scenario than being kept here as a virtual prisoner merely because Lance in his infinite wisdom had reached the decision that because of their forthcoming mission it could prove dangerous for them to be spotted around the place.

In the intervening period too she had on several occasions noticed Lance flinch, as his wound appeared to be troubling him, and yet when she had offered to tend to it all she had received in return had been a sharp rebuff. Indeed in retrospect, she reflected, Lance's whole attitude appeared to have changed towards her. Whether this was a result of his long conversations with Michael that had conveniently ceased whenever she came within earshot she did not know, but for his part Michael himself had preferred to remain much the silent partner in the unlikely threesome. Indeed she was given to wonder what the man from the hotel had thought of all this when he had been given the task of bringing sustenance to them instead of them visiting the Restaurant. But that was something she was not going to be enlightened upon. That coupled with the fact that Lance frowned disapprovingly if she even thought to venture out onto the balcony in an attempt to catch that scarce commodity in the form of a little sunshine that was seldom to be found back home in England!

But now it appeared that all this was about to change. "We will be leaving tomorrow. According to the call I have just received the Sea Witch is presently making port!" Lance spoke the words without showing the slightest sign of tonality to give shape to them and in response the silent one merely nodded. If only that man would say something, but after his initial outburst when he had first brought her here his lips were now sealed as far as she was concerned. It seemed all too easy to imagine that this man resented her presence and had somehow persuaded Lance to act in a similar manner and she was forced to question whether in truth she served as the number one nuisance factor that somehow interfered with their schemes! One she supposed could present an argument that if she had not been there then they would have been able to have had a bed each in that suite instead of one of them having to sleep in cramped conditions upon a chair, not to mention the ritual of them tossing a coin to decide which one of them could command such a privilege!

"You will need to pack!" It was an order but at least she supposed that it was something for it meant that Lance had now actually exercised his tonsils in her direction. "Be careful however that you manage to keep that lot concealed in your efforts!"

"You are suggesting then that I leave the parcel in the suitcase?" His words never ceased to amaze her.

"Well I certainly have no intention of walking around Rosario with such a parcel in my hands! Anyway I thought I had already commended you on your choice of concealment for the goods?"

Rachel shrugged. It was pointless arguing with the man she supposed. In the eventuality all their arrangements seemed to go according to plan, for despite looking warily over her shoulder as they left the confines of the hotel in order to travel to the seaport they appeared to be unobserved and once they were on board the Sea Witch cast off with little hesitation.

It was after they cleared the harbour that Rachel finally ventured from the small cabin she had been allocated to get some sea air and rid her nostrils from the stale smell of fish to become aware that she was not the only one on deck at the time but that Lance was regarding her through eyes that appeared almost clinical in their appreciation.

"Tell me, how did you get to know him then?" The man was pensive almost morose in his questioning and yet she knew this was after all a matter she had told him on a previous occasion.

"I have already told you. I worked for Brad as his secretary!" She knew exactly to whom he was referring but after she had imparted the knowledge already she was left to wonder exactly what had motivated this current outburst.

"But how did you come to be employed by him in the first place?"

For a moment Rachel fell silent. How could she tell Lance of that other affair, the one she had initially be running away from? Surely he would conclude that running away from employers was the story of her life. How could she tell him that Brad's office had been conveniently situated close to where her sister lived?

"I suppose it was because he advertised and I happened to be out of work at the time!" This seemed to be the least complicated way of answering his question.

"And his office was situated close to where your sister lived. Was that a coincidence?"

Rachel swallowed hard. What on earth was the man getting at? "Well yes, I suppose that is true. As a matter of fact I wanted to move back into the area!"

"Why?"

"Well Mandy is my sister and as they are the only family I have now got I suppose it made common sense! Not that I knew his offices were situated there when I first answered his advert however!"

"Ah yes you applied to be his girl Friday on the Internet!" His voice scoffed now at the notion, still it reminded her that he already knew the circumstances before he had asked. "But what puzzles me is why you didn't apply for a position in London where you were already working, there must have been opportunities for a secretary there, unless of course there were mitigating circumstances as to why you gave up your previous position!"

Rachel glanced at his expression determined now that she must have got hold of the wrong end of the stick, Lance could not really mean what he was saying, and surely it must be a joke. But there was nothing in those eyes she met that gave her any confidence in that. Indeed after viewing the protagonist Rachel was quite abrupt in her return.

"At the risk of repeating myself the firm I worked for was one of the victims of the recession!" She idly wondered whether she needed a sledgehammer to drive this point across, yet at the same time she was still unwilling to reveal anything of that previous liaison for as far as she was concerned it was none of his damned business! Lance however still did not appear to be satisfied.

"You said earlier that you welcomed the chance of getting closer to your sister and yet you had been apart from her for some time. Why the change of heart?"

"Because she was family of course even if I hadn't seen her for some considerable time. Therefore as far as I was concerned taking the job in the Midland area seemed to be ideal at the time. Tell me, do you find that very unusual?"

"And was that your only reason?" He chose to ignore the question she had posed.

Rachel coloured up to the roots of her hair. Why on earth did this man possess the ability to prise matters out of her that she would have much preferred not to have to speak about. But he was waiting expectantly for a response from her. "If you must know, not that it has anything at all to do with you, but at one time there was someone else. A relationship moreover that had just finished. That is all that I am prepared to say on that issue except that it seemed to be apt at the time to move back closer to my family when the opportunity came my way!" She steeled herself almost expecting an onslaught with Lance now demanding to know about the other person in her life but she still felt she had said enough to satisfy even this one and she was determined that he would get nothing else about this affair from her lips for she was still not prepared to admit even to herself what a complete fool she had been at the time.

Surprisingly enough however Lance did not appear to want to pursue that line of enquiry further. Perhaps he had already gleaned from her expression that she was adamant when she had said that it was all she was prepared to say on the matter for at this time he appeared to turn his point of questioning onto something totally unexpected.

"So you are saying that was your only reason for leaving London and moving to the Midlands? You are trying to say that Doug had no part in this decision?"

"Doug! What are you talking about? Doug was my brother in law, the father of my nephew, married to my sister! Doug had nothing to do with my decision! Surely you are not intimating-------?"

"-------I am intimating nothing, merely imparting the facts that I am aware of. I suppose you will deny that you knew he was an associate of Brad Stevens even before you came to the area?"

"Don't talk such absolute rubbish: Doug was the one who saved my life, remember? He was also the one who Brad Stevens shot simply because he had helped me to escape. What gives you the damned right to speak of him in this manner?"

"I am already aware that your brother in law rescued you from that derelict property and was consequently shot for doing so, but the reason for that was because the guy, even with all his faults, happened to love his family and you just happened to be his wife's sister. Even so that didn't make him less a confidante of Brad Stevens!"

The boat chose that precise moment to give a sudden lurch as they finally hit the waters of the open Atlantic having cleared the shelf of the archipelago and Rachel found she had to cling onto a rail which in turn helped to dispel some of the rejoinder she had been about to make.

"I think I have heard just about enough Lance Turner. I don't know whether it has all come from those private conversations you have been having with Michael of late, but whatever has been said between you, in future I would be obliged if you would leave me and my family out of it!"

Thus having imparted such thoughts Rachel decided to move to the confines of her cabin leaving the other standing there in a perplexed manner. Furthermore once she was inside of her temporary oasis she firmly locked the door determined that she would have no more interruptions on her thought process. Even so, although she had not intended to leave the cabin to suffer any further linguistic abuse of whatever nature, Rachel was soon to discover that she could not have left the place for a good twenty four hours afterwards anyway for after that first lurch that had found her clinging to the rail up on deck, the weather conditions had turned decidedly foul with a stiff breeze blowing upon the sea and causing the waves to build in crescendo like fashion and consequently the boat to pitch and toss as it was buffeted to and fro. Thus Rachel had to be content to lie back on that bunk and brace herself against the motions of that craft and whilst she was thus occupied she had little time to give to the complex workings of the minds of others!

Content that was until there was a knock on the cabin door several hours later and she heard Ned Dorkins bellowing out but not in a sea shanty fashion. "Well come on open this door because I've brought a drink for you. Get it down before you dehydrate or something worse and try and catch a mouthful of fresh air as well if you don't mind. That will do you far more good than being cooped up in here for hours on end. Besides I need to get into that cabin to change my gear. It's bad enough having to give up the best cabin on the ship and having to spend my time kipping in with the boys without finding myself deprived of a change of clothes when I am already wet through!"

There appeared little else she could do now but crawl off the bunk to oblige the seaman and open the cabin door. Perhaps when she did so she half expected to see a posse of Lance and Michael waiting to pounce on her with more questions, but of them there was now no sign, merely one rather irate seaman who simply wanted the opportunity of retrieving his gear!

"If you're looking for your friends those landlubbers have taken to their bunks as well. Not a pair of sea legs between the lot of you!" The seaman was scornful as he pushed past her into the cabin she had vacated. She took the drink he had brought her and made her way along the companionway and up the steps perhaps realising for the first time exactly how parched she was.

Finishing the drink she cautiously made her way up onto the deck. Despite the perpetual motion of the boat she realised that the sky had now cleared to reveal tiny pin pricks of light in the heavens made by the stars from some far off galaxies. The deck itself as Ned had intimated was currently deserted and she took the opportunity to breathe in the fresh oxygenated air and rid her lungs of the stale substance she had been breathing down below. She was still there as if transfixed by the night sky when Ned returned to the deck and glanced appreciatively in her direction.

"Guess we are over the worst now Miss although when we come to cross the Bay that will probably be a little bit choppy, so time to make the most of it whilst you can I would say!"

Rachel agreed with him although her reasoning on this was probably slightly different to the man's expectations. She intended to make the most of it before the other two stirred, for once either of them appeared on the deck then she was determined she would seek out that cabin once again!

If Rachel had desired to separate herself from her two fellow travellers as much as possible on that voyage she was surprised in how easy this decision of hers was to keep. Moreover the problem of food or rather eating in the galley did not worry her unduly for she felt herself well capable of sneaking in that place at an off meal time and helping herself to whatever was available. Yet the whole of her endeavours appeared far too easy for her to accomplish even in her own eyes but it was still a good forty eight hours into the four day journey when she finally realised that far from her being the only one who wished to avoid her fellow travellers, these companions also appeared to be in similar mode as if they wished to avoid her. In fact she saw little sign of Lance until the frigate appeared just off the Channel Islands to relieve them of the cargo they were carrying and even then the words he spoke were to the Captain of this vessel whose interruption had obviously been well planned. What surprised her more was whilst sneaking a cautious peep at the proceedings through a nearby doorway she watched as Lance himself was lowered into the craft and moreover the cheery good bye he waved was not for her benefit but rather to Ned and his mate and Michael whom for some reason he left behind on the boat to make their way back to their assigned port in England. Now despite her determination to keep herself separate from the other two Rachel was furious which was probably the reason why as the frigate moved away from them she forgot all about her earlier resolution and went in search of Michael.

"Perhaps you will be good enough to tell me what the hell is going on?" She must have looked like a female possessed for Michael blinked at the sight of her. But then perhaps she had been wrong coming to the silent one expecting some sort of explanation. Therefore she was quite surprised when he actually spoke, even forgetting her venom for a moment.

"I thought that you understood. The cargo we intended to remove before we made port. The customs people do an excellent job but at this time we did not desire to be tied up in a wave of explanations, particularly as the robbery was initially high profile news. Lance has travelled with the cache to determine that it gets back to the right quarters. But surely you knew that this was to happen?"

"There appears to be quite a lot that I have not been made party to!" The words came out almost as a mutter under her breath and Michael eyed her rather clinically. "Then tell me, why did you not go with them as well?"

"Because Lance instructed me on a further charge, that was to see you safely back to your sister's!"

"And I presume he considered I was not capable of doing that for myself?" These words too were spoken almost before she realised she had uttered them. Perhaps indeed Michael had a different motivation for wanting to travel back to the Midlands for she presumed her sister would have returned there after she had left.

"Maybe there was a slight suggestion that you might have decided against it!"

"So he decides to go off without saying a word after I had been just as active in getting that cache back as what he was?"

"In truth you have not been seen for anyone to explain anything to you!"

"I could well say the same for you two!"

"We have been present in the galley at regular meal times. You yourself have not!"

"Only because I wasn't hungry. My stomach decided that it was not over fond of sailing!"

"It was fond enough of sneaking into the galley at other times and helping itself though!"

Rachel flinched as she made to change the subject quite rapidly. "So now I presume you have been left behind in order to escort me back again to my sister's?" In truth it did strike her at the time that she had now spoken to this man more in the last ten minutes than in all the time she had known him. The thought made her sniff.

"I have been asked to escort you, yes, and possibly ease your own arrival back into the country as well!" There was a serious tone now to this voice that lacked any semblance of humour within it.

"And no doubt keep a wary eye on me until after he has delivered his bounty safely! One must be forgiven if the word trust is omitted for seemingly that factor no longer exists between us, that is if it ever did in the first place!"

"I think that you have got matters totally wrong Rachel!" He spoke with a determined expression in his voice but Rachel felt she had heard enough for she no longer wished to bide her time out here on the deck vying with this one.

"Whether I have got it wrong or not I believe that I have heard enough therefore please excuse me for I have matters I wish to attend to back in the cabin!" She found the man totally insufferable. What Mandy had ever seen in him was well beyond her comprehension. Perhaps in truth her sister had felt she had suffered enough of him when she went and married Doug. But at the time your sister believed this man to be dead! A little voice inside of her head pleaded to be heard but Rachel wanted none of it. As far as she was concerned the advent of Michael had brought about a change in her own relationship with Lance and that she swore was something that she would never forgive this man for!

Even so Rachel was forced to stifle her surprise at the way they were received after the vessel they were on finally eased its way back into the berth at Poole Harbour. The surprise possibly emanated when the customs official ritualistically came on board before anyone was allowed to depart and nodded in acknowledgement in Michael's direction. Furthermore as they finally left the craft unheeded there was a car waiting for them that whisked them away from the dockside quite quickly, leaving Ned and old Tom behind to see to berthing the vessel on their own.

Still the official looking car was not destined to take them far; merely as a matter of fact to the other side of the dock gates where Michael's own car just so happened to be parked.

"Well get in then!" He held open the door a trifle impatiently as he waited for her.

"I suppose it would be in order for me to ask a silly question? How did your car just happen to be parked here?"

"Only the one question? Really perhaps you are slipping Rachel. But to answer your question can I say that I arranged for it to be brought here for us after Lance and I had talked matters through!"

"That seemed to be quite a distinguishing habit of both of you, talking things through I mean as well as talking about people without confiding such considerations to them personally!"

"Have it your way if that is what you wish, just get in the car!"

"And suppose I say that I won't, if I respond by saying that I object to being ordered around like a schoolchild?"

"Then perhaps you might start by not behaving like one. On the other hand I credit you with more intelligence than wanting to cause a scene here, therefore perhaps you should try and grow up a little instead and do as you are told. Now get in please!"

Her face flushed Rachel found herself reluctantly climbing into the Renault motor vehicle. She supposed upon reflection that it was after all an infinitely better way to get back to the Midlands than relying on public transport. Once she was there however she vowed that she would dispense with the very sight of this man. In fact if her sister was daft enough to want him then she was more than welcome to him!

Thus apart from polite but necessary interchanges the journey back to the Midlands passed in silence. It was a silence that was broken only when she saw the small boy running towards them and she felt that at least someone cared. Jumping out of the car she noted that her sister had remained several paces behind Jake and was now looking almost shyly in her escort's direction. Rachel determined she would be physically sick if these two greeted each other with platitudes and she cushioned the small boy in her arms as she made to remove the pair of them away from the scene!

The Training Camp was situated some considerable distance from any other live habitation in Morocco but nevertheless it had received the consignment it had been waiting for earlier on that day. Now however the once still desert air shook like someone trembling as it was hit by a voluble tirade of voices.

"The man is demanding payment for completing his part of the project!" A robed and bearded figure addressed his leader bowing almost in reverence as he etched out his words.

"Is he indeed?" The reverberation that issued forth was almost powerful enough to shift the desert sand. There were more words spoken in a foreign tongue, which if the reaction of those surrounding him was anything to go by, contained a lot of inflammatory phrases before the leader controlled himself enough to breathe further instructions to his minions.

"Tell the Englishman that if he requires payment for this trash then he must come here himself to receive it. I would dearly like to take a look at the one who seeks not only to betray his country but also to betray us with this cheap rubbish he thought we would not recognise. Let us find out exactly who he thinks he is. That is my decision. I leave you now to act upon my words!"

The minion who had spoken in the first place bowed his head now almost allowing it to touch upon the sandy surface below. "Then it shall be as you have commanded Master!"

----------"I'll catch up with you later, I really need to get back to my flat!" Rachel refused to tarry at this stage. It was not that she had anything against Mandy, just that man who had steamrolled himself into their lives. In truth young Jake had clung to her and it and it had upset her to put the boy down again so quickly, but she would make amends to the child later, for now with that fellow still being around the place she doubted whether her nephew would have seen her at her best. Besides there was some truth in her words, she did need to get back to her flat, for now she had to sort out her future, whatever that held in store for her! For starters she wondered whether she would still have a job to go back to or whether she would be back in the dole queue, which was not a pleasant scenario considering the vast number of unemployed in the country.

Much to her surprise however she was to find the flat very much as she had left it. In fact the only disturbance to the property appeared to have been the postman delivering the usual quota of junk mail whilst she had been away. Therefore after switching on the heating to air the place a little she made herself a cup of tea and settled back to allow the warm air to percolate out of its respective vents and gave herself time to think. In truth all that had happened now seemed to pass as if in a dream world and her mind became focussed on more immediate things such as her position on the job front.

Again however she was to receive a pleasant surprise. The manager of the firm where she had worked actually appeared pleased to see her. Apparently her absence had been related to the personal tragedy in her life that evolved around her own traumatic experience followed by the untimely death of the man who had come to save her. To her work colleagues the story was all the more poignant because as yet no one had been caught who was responsible for this crime, and Rachel unwilling to fill them in with any further detail allowed them the benefit of expressing their feelings on the matter.

"Then you really do feel that you can cope with coming back to work now?" Her boss spoke with a concerned voice.

"But of course, that is why I am here. I will start just as soon as you require me!"

"Then would tomorrow be a good day for you?" The man still expressed some doubt but his fears were motivated around whether Rachel felt fit enough now to be able to cope.

"Tomorrow will do just fine. I expect that I will have quite a lot of catching up to do!"

The man nodded his appreciation before she left. Well, she supposed it did give her at least today to sort herself out. And she supposed there was still the question of her sister that she had to come to terms with for there had never been any been any bad blood between then before and furthermore, any quarrels in the past had been sorted out within the twenty four hours! Consequently upon leaving the firm she found her feet treading their way back towards where her sister lived. She imagined that Mandy would have quite a story to tell, how for instance they had managed to get back from that other place where they had been prior to her leaving the country. There was however still one fly in the proverbial ointment and that was wondering if that other man would still be around the place when she arrived. Fortunately he was not and Mandy had obviously forgotten her own behaviour of the previous day for soon the two sisters were in each other's arms glad enough to be back together again.

"So tell me what happened?" It was Mandy who was the first to break and demand to know what had been going on.

"That was the question I was going to ask you?"

"But I was the one who asked first. The last thing that I know was when you left to catch that plane with Michael because Lance had commanded it!"

"And Michael said nothing to you?"

"Why should he? After all it is my sister's story!"

"But he was the one who brought me back!"

"A factor you appeared to strongly disapprove of I must say. But why should he now bring you back? After all it was he who took you away in the first place!"

Thus Rachel found that she was now in the process of concocting a story around factors that had actually happened without dwelling too much on the salient points. Why she did this well she considered perhaps that Lance would not approve of her relating the whole story for his own reasons, although why she had to consider that person at this time completely escaped her.

"At least you appear to have been able to live life!" Perhaps there was a tinge of melancholia in her sister's voice as she finished. "So where is Lance now?"

"Time for your side of the story I think!" There was no way she was going to start speculating about that one's movements even to her sister.

"I'm afraid it is in no way as exciting as your own. After you had left with Michael, Jake and I returned home on account of Jake's schooling------!"

"And what of Doug's death?" She needed to know how her sister really felt about things. Was the woman simply bottling it all up inside of her or had she really come to terms with what had happened.

"I still miss him like hell of course, but I am more worried for Jake than for myself!" Of course that was more like the Mandy she knew. Always concerned for others before herself. "I suppose a boy of Jake's age needs a father he can rely upon. Sometimes I catch him wistfully looking in other children's direction especially boys who might be having a game of footsie with their fathers!"

"Perhaps I shouldn't bring this up at this time but Lance did say that at one time you were actively involved with the service and he believed that there was something going between Michael and yourself?"

"That was a long time ago Rachel: A time possibly best forgotten. It happened long before I met Doug and I was n love with my husband make no mistake about that!"

"I never suggested any different!" Rachel realised she needed to change the subject. "By the way I called in my work this morning and I have got my old job back again!"

"Good for you. At least this means that you will be staying in the vicinity now?"

"But of course. I wouldn't have it any other way!"

Previously working for that manufacturing firm Rachel had very quickly found herself in charge of the office by a man who was far more interested in what he was manufacturing than any paper work associated with it and as he was in line for many export orders there had been no shortage of paper work accompanying this. Upon her return it was soon apparent that during her absence a great deal of this work had been neglected and she sighed realising just how long it would take in order to catch up!

Still it happened to be Amy, one of the other girls who worked under her direction who first drew her attention to the newspaper cutting that related to a local network T.V. station who were currently asking for scripts based on true life experiences.

"You like to write don't you Rachel? What's more I guess there is enough in your life to write about. So why don't you give it a whirl. One thing though, you will have to be quick for the closing date is at the end of this month!"

At first Rachel perused the cutting with little interest for to her mind it appeared that there was sufficient enough for her to do here without taking on anything else, but Amy was nothing if not persistent. Besides there was another reason and that centred on the fact that the girls in the office had decided that this was probably the only way they would ever learn anything of her story from those tightly drawn lips! And what was more to the point was that they were curious in a nice sort of way, for nothing ever happened to them in this place that ever warranted anyone putting pen to paper!

"Oh all right then I promise that I will think about it although to be fair I believe I have quite enough challenges in front of me with this lot you have left for me!" With that Rachel tried to dismiss the idea from her mind yet much to her annoyance this opportunity for her to be able to lend words to paper did not want to go away quite so easily. She knew even then that names and incidents would have to be disguised but even after all that was done it still left quite a lot for her to be able to work on!

She was in fact in the throes of rediscovering her literary talent when Mandy called to ask if she would baby sit for her and Rachel readily agreed without really considering it for such thoughts of distraction were not permitted in the midst of the process of creativity!

"But what are you doing?" Mandy eyed the files and laptop Rachel took around to the house that night with not a little suspicion. In truth she had expected questions concerning her forthcoming date but her sister's mind was obviously now divorced from reality and on some other planet.

"Oh I've had the gem of an idea for a plot actually. It was Amy from work who first suggested it for apparently the local paper is running some sort of competition for the local T.V. network!"

"Guess I read about it although I didn't really think it would be your scene!"

"Well I suppose I have to start somewhere and maybe this opportunity is as good as any other to get me going again!" For the first time Rachel noticed that her sister appeared to be all dressed up. "Where are you going to anyway?"

"I told you, I have a sort of date. You are here to baby sit Jake remember?"

"You have a date? Is it anybody I should know?" A seed of suspicion had suddenly implanted itself into her mind.

"As a matter of fact yes!"

"Him! ------I thought that he had left the area!"

"Officially he has, but he still gets some time off! Rachel I know you don't particularly like Michael although I still do not understand why. But it is after all my life we are talking about!"

"I don't like him because I think he is both arrogant and conceited and anyway he used what influence he had over Lance to destroy our own relationship!"

"Now you are being completely childish. Michael only appeared arrogant and conceited in your eyes because he felt that he was dealing with some wayward schoolgirl. As far as Lance is concerned, I am positive he had nothing to do with the man cooling off towards you if indeed he has. There's another thing too, have you ever considered that Lance might have been trying to protect you?"

Rachel fell silent, there was nothing she could say in answer to this except to get out her laptop, whilst at the same time she was convinced she was writing absolute rubbish! Still she had to admit the man appeared well groomed and debonair when he arrived to take her sister out, not that she was interested of course. She merely grunted in his direction and then found much to her consolation that another more youthful figure had etched closer to you.

"Grown up stuff again!" The boy gave vent to his feelings once the front door had closed behind them.

"Surely you don't mind your mother going out with a friend for once?" Rachel surprised even herself with her words. It was ridiculous really saying something like that to the child when in truth she was the one who minded very much.

Still Jake solemnly shook his head. "No, I don't mind Aunt Rachel for it gives me the opportunity to spend more time with you!" So that, she thought grimly was to put paid to any thought of her doing any writing that night, but then she supposed the child was worth it!

------------It was in fact the deadline date when Rachel finally went to hand in her manuscript at the newspaper offices only to be rewarded by a rather suspicious look that was based upon her late submission. Still the girl now felt that she didn't particularly care anymore. For starters she had not been able to find the time to proof read the script and had merely relied on her computer's wizardry with its spelling and grammar check, which from the past she realised she could not always be dependent upon. The fact of the matter was however that the script was now finished and in all honesty she felt relieved to be rid of it!

Perhaps one of the reasons for her delay centred on the fact that she now appeared to be spending far more time with Jake as her sister now seemed to regularly favour a night out with glamour boy! Thinking this she sternly reminded herself not to be so bitchy. In truth she herself might not care for this Michael but her sister obviously saw some quality in the man that she had missed and perhaps Mandy did deserve a little consideration after suffering the previous trauma.

Once she had left her offering behind she never expected to hear anything else about it for she most certainly believed that it was not good enough to warrant any further attention. Thus the news that the man from the newspaper wanted to meet her came as something of a shock and she went there with a sense of reluctance leaving the matter until after she had finished work one evening and without saying anything about it to her fellow workmates.

"Your story is good!" The rather corpulent frame of the man who had summoned her to this place protruded over the top of his desk as he spoke. "Are you sure that you have had no formal newspaper training?"

Rachel shook her head. "I admit however that I have written before in an effort to do my own thing but nothing so formal!"

"And you are saying that the story you have submitted is based on the truth?"

"Basically it is although I felt compelled to disguise some of the characters in it as well as the events as a matter of some expedience!"

"Well I can tell you now that we submitted your manuscript to the television network and they are now showing a great deal of interest in it. How does that make you feel?"

"Possibly relieved that it will finally get the girls from the office off my back!" Her counterpart looked at her in a puzzled manner probably because he had never expected a response such as this.

"And should the television people decide to make a play out of your script, how would you feel then?"

"I understood that was the general idea that lay behind submitting the piece!"

"They will of course naturally want to meet you!"

"Well as far as I know I am not due to go anywhere!" By this time Rachel was rapidly beginning to lose interest.

"In that case I will inform them of your decision and they will be in touch with you!"

She left after deciding that was that. It was two days later when she received a letter inviting her to go along to the studios. Because this involved taking even more time off her work Rachel hesitated at first, that was before Amy found out and practically propelled her into the manager's office. But Bob the manager appeared more than affable in agreeing to let her go. Indeed there was a distinct air of excitement that now bounded around that place of work and it was this more than anything else that finally persuaded her that she had to go through with it if it was only for her colleague's sakes.

Maybe however she might have reacted very differently if she had been forewarned about that meeting; for walking casually into the outer office to the studios the first figure she cast her eyes upon did not appear so enchanted by the sight of her as he held something out in front of him

"I am afraid Rachel that as this piece you have written centres around confidential information I am going to have to remove the same from any competition for the contents within your story are not for public consumption!" And as he spoke the words there was a coldness in Lance Turner's voice that could well have emanated from the inside of a fridge.

* * * *

Chapter Ten

Glancing at the person who now confronted her, once the first shock of seeing him there had subsided, Rachel could not help but feel that her hackles were beginning to rise. How dare this man deem to take command over her writing in such a manner and what gave him the right to come here in the first place? How dare he dare to face her in this manner when she had not caught sight of him since the time he had left them when he boarded that frigate? In truth there had been not one phone call from him, not even a letter in the interim period, yet now he appeared before her in confrontation almost as if he was bringing some sort of judgement to bear and after she had come here in good faith presumably to meet with the production team from the film set? It would have been oh so easy for her to throw herself in the ides of the rage that followed at his form in some sort of desperate attempt to snatch the damned script out of his grasp, for in truth what made the whole matter worse was that it had nothing at all to do with him. She still had no notion as to how he had found out about it in the first place but surely in all truth the manuscript belonged to her personally therefore what right did he believe he had to pass any judgement on the matter? In the positive fury Rachel found herself in she never thought to ask about his shoulder, in truth the matter never even occurred to her and she supposed that if it had she would have hoped that the damned thing still hurt him for he deserved no less! It was still whilst she was incarcerated in this moment of hesitation of how to respond that the door to the place opened to admit yet another person who entered the room.

"Is this the young lady whom you spoke of then?" The newcomer appeared to be slightly frustrated, an attitude perhaps motivated by the very thought of such an incident taking place in his studios.

"The same!" Lance's voice still held the semblance of grit within it and Rachel wished with all her heart that she had some commodity close by her so that she could have willingly flung it into his face.

"Then I am afraid Miss Aldred that as much as we have liked your story and we would therefore under normal circumstances recommend it to our team of scriptwriters so that they might turn the whole into a script that was feasible to be broadcast on the media, there unfortunately appears to be several incidents included within the same that we are not at liberty to broadcast. Having said that however all is not lost, for Mr Turner has himself kindly offered to go through the script with you to subsequently iron out any of these discrepancies; and as Mr Turner is a trusted member of our Security Forces I feel sure that you will welcome this opportunity of working closely alongside of him. More especially I might add when I say that once he is satisfied that any such relevant changes have been made to his satisfaction then we will be only too pleased to be able to proceed with the production without further delay!"

"Strangely enough I was on a previous occasion given to understand that Mr Turner was merely a pen pusher for the Ministry. In that capacity therefore I really do not see how the man can possibly be of help in the circumstances!" Rachel's voice had adopted a more icy tonality so that it froze her words allowing them to chip out from her lips almost like a frosty fall.

"I suppose one might consider that the description of him being pen pusher could be considered to be an operative explanation Miss Aldred for one would assume that the fact that he has been immersed in such a role then he is more than adequate in handling that instrument for our mutual benefit!"

"If it happened to be a red pen I have no doubt that you would be right. Yet previously I was under the impression that his pen pushing skills revolved around real estate!"

At least she now had the satisfaction of seeing Lance flinch as she watched his expression change, yet whilst she in turn scanned him from out of the corner of her eye this in no way served to deter her from stating her piece. In fact if anything it served to encourage her in re-emphasising her defence. "Perhaps I ought to point out that although my story is based on fact I also insist that I have also gone to great lengths to disguise anything that could be considered suspect within it!"

"Not exactly everything!" The one she faced now appeared to be acting the role of his most sardonic self, a further factor that caused her blood to positively boil. If the other man had not been present at the time she was sure that she would have kicked out if only to watch his supercilious attitude change. "The fact remains Miss Aldred that whatever terms you care to use in order to describe me and my employment I am still interested in certain aspects of your work particularly those that relate to the security of this country and more especially in those that could prove to be most damaging if they were allowed to become public knowledge!"

"Well it appears to me that the answer is obvious Miss Aldred for you now have a choice. You can either work with Mr Turner here until the man is finally satisfied with the contents of your story, in which case we will be only too anxious to use it in a production, or otherwise allow Mr Turner to remove what he considers to be an inflammatory script in which case you will consequently lose the contents of your work altogether!"

Rachel wanted to scream out abuse especially at the sardonic smile that now appeared to grow as it spread across Lance's face but then she rapidly realised that for her to do so would in all probability have served to please the man. Therefore the only thing she could do at the present time was to acquiesce, an action that obviously satisfied the production manager.

"I believe I am right in saying that you are now working for Whittaker's Miss Alder, in which case it will be my privilege to arrange to pick you up from your employ this evening and maybe we can then start to look into ways we could possibly refine your script for I do believe that Artie here is anxious to get started on the production of it. Therefore I suggest that the sooner we make our own contribution the better it will be for the film company's point of view!" Did this man really always refuse to take no for an answer? "In any case I will hang onto the script for the time being if you don't mind. You need not worry for I promise that I will look after it!" Those brown eyes had adopted a determined expression as he picked up the manuscript ready to take it with him. A part of her wanted to scream out that he had no right to even touch it, that it was her own possession yet she had the uncanny feeling that for her to object would somehow please him and the last thing Rachel currently desired to do was to seek to give this man any satisfaction on the matter!

Instead she posed another question that was puzzling her. "Perhaps before we proceed any further you would be good enough to tell me just how you came to be involved with my story in the first place Mr Turner?"

He eyed her steadily, a move that made her forget momentarily of her own chagrin at how this plot had developed. "Your story Miss Aldred? Actually I was under the impression that someone else was involved. But as to why I am currently present the reason is quite simple. You see I happened to receive the information in the first place from a colleague who is still currently in this neighbourhood!"

So it must have been Michael who had informed him. But why, she asked herself? Was it because of some mutual understanding that existed between members of the Security force, or was there some other reason for in truth she could never admit to being comfortable in Michael's company! Still she was not to be enlightened upon the matter for after a brief nod in her direction and a timely reminder that he would be waiting for her when she finished work, Lance took it upon himself to leave still holding onto the papers and defying any thought she might have had of snatching them out of his hands.

---------"How did you go on then?" A bevy of questions was awaiting her upon her return to her employ. Amy in particular was jumping up and down in her exuberance at what she considered must have been a momentous occasion.

"Oh O.K. I suppose, although it appears that they will require a few alterations to the script before they start production after all!"

"But surely that isn't fair! It is your story isn't it so why should they want to start altering the plot?"

Rachel sighed. It seemed to be difficult to explain the situation when Amy had just voiced her own opinion on the matter. "Because it just happens to be the way of the world especially in the publishing profession I'm afraid. Such alterations are not unknown for I have been subjected to them before. Still I suppose it could be worse. At least one of them has promised to give up his time to go through the plot with me and outside of working hours as well! In fact he proposes to meet me from work tonight!" Rachel swallowed hard as she attempted to put a brave smile on her face. At least to her mind this should shut any speculation that was currently rife in that office and furthermore she was not prepared to say anything more about the situation in order to fuel their imagination.

Even so her words appeared to be enough to stimulate an excuse for window gazing as the office hours drew to a close.

"Is that the man now, the one waiting by the gate? Rachel you never said, he's absolutely gorgeous!"

Gorgeous was not a word that Rachel would have used at the time in providing any description of Lance for there were plenty of alternatives she could have found at that moment. The fact was however that her hands were now tied and she therefore had to go along with the idea of Lance monitoring her plot. What he expected to find that was completely out of joint was a different matter although she supposed that she did have the satisfaction that she could in no way be excused of jeopardising the security of the country whatever he had initially thought! Therefore when she eventually left the place once the office had closed for the evening and after dawdling for as long as she dare in the hopes that the others would leave before her, she was to find that there were still at least a dozen pairs of eyes following her progress almost as if they were in envy.

"Who are they then, your fan club?" Lance, missing little and noting the onlookers looked vaguely amused. Still she supposed it made a pleasant change from the blackened mood she had witnessed in his appearance earlier on in the day.

"They apparently think you are a gorgeous hunk of masculinity but that is obviously because they don't know you!" There was a cutting edge to her voice and she hoped he got the inference.

"So you are still deeming to act like a bear with a sore head?"

"Well supposing I am, don't you think I have a damned right to be?"

"Why? Is it because you cannot bear the thought of your plot being altered in anyway?"

"No, my main question to you is why you have decided to stick your nose in just in order to dissect a perfectly innocent story? After all even you must admit that I was extremely careful to disguise anything that anyone could regard as relevant in jeopardising the security of the country within my writing!"

"Well I suppose one could say that it gave me the perfect excuse to see you again; at least in the hope of seeing the girl who I had to leave behind on that boat. But now I find myself confronted with one raging strumpet who has already told me in the past all about the publishing process of changing things around and so forth but now deems she wants to have no part of it!"

"Oh since when have you been a publisher to learn such finer points of the process and in any case how did you get to know about this story in the first place?"

"Because it so happens to be my job. You see after I was contacted concerning this unusually good account of matters relevant only to the Ministry, naturally the powers that be were curious as to where the author had managed to acquire her research. That was when I realised that there could only be one person who was both in the position as well as being capable of producing such a documentation!" If he meant his final phrase as flattery his words failed to cut any ice with Rachel. Instead she turned her mind onto the task in hand.

"Such flattery does you no service Lance especially since you have already mentioned Michael as being the initial guilty party. Anyway changing the subject where had you in mind that we should commence this matter of copyediting for want of a better word? I say copyediting for it sounds far more polite than the word vetting!"

"How about your place?"

"Sorry but I am afraid that I happen to be baby sitting my nephew tonight!" Now she was being deliberately obstructive although in truth she had sort of promised.

"Like that is it? Still I don't suppose the lad will mind us holding a discussion over papers especially if there happens to be something good on television!"

"What did you mean exactly when you said it's like that?"

"As a matter of fact you mentioned that Michael still happened to be in the area and I suppose that he and Mandy did have something going at one time!"

"That if I might say so is completely despicable. I shouldn't need to have to remind you that my sister has just lost her husband, and whether you lot ever valued him as a human being or otherwise, Mandy and Doug happened to care a great deal about one another!" She knew full well that Mandy had seen Michael on more than one occasion recently but even though she did not have much time for the man himself, who to her mind was still a sullen commodity, she had concluded that if Mandy enjoyed his company then her sister deserved to relax occasionally.

"Then perhaps I can be permitted to rephrase my thoughts. I was meaning that the presence of an old friend at such a time might indeed have provided some measure of consolation for her!"

Thus Rachel was left to seethe at his sentiments, and yet it now appeared that there was little else she could do but to go along with his intentions. If the others were surprised to see Lance when he returned home with her then they were for saying nothing apart from exchanging glances before the elder two departed, leaving Jake apparently embroiled with his children's television. At least that was how it first appeared although in truth the child was not quite as immersed in his programme as what the adults had first estimated for Jake was after all wily enough to know that adults seldom had the habit of stating anything that was of interest if they believed that they were being overheard. Therefore because the lad exhibited a certain curiosity as to what was currently transpiring, he had adopted the air of an impartial observer who appeared to find the television programme more to his liking yet at the same time he did not hesitate in allowing his ears to flap in a different direction.

Still eventually the time came when the youngster felt it only right to expound upon his own thoughts and lend a voice to the situation and in order to accomplish this a single factor came to mind and the boy was quick to seize upon it. "As a matter of fact I happen to quite like Michael because he can be a lot of fun. You used to be fun at one time Lance before you went away and now since you have come back you have turned quite crotchety!" The child had obviously some difficulty in getting his tongue around the word crotchety but there was little doubt that his two listeners knew exactly what the child meant even if they could not decide what had provoked this outburst.

"Perhaps it is time you were thinking of bed Jake. Don't forget you have school in the morning, especially now you are in the big school!" It was Rachel who initially adopted the strong tones, for the conversation, even if it was issued from a child, was not particularly to her liking.

"Why is it that everyone wants to send me to bed when there is something interesting going on?" The child now adopted a deliberate pouting expression.

"First of all because I think that if you have had enough of television for tonight it is time that you made tracks in that direction and secondly I can hardly see that what Lance and I are doing can be of any interest to you toying around with these sheaves of papers we are using in order to adapt my story. The whole exercise must be a complete bore to you!"

"I don't think that it is boring Rachel because I liked your story therefore why does Lance now want to alter it?"

"Now who gave you the idea that I was going to do that?" This time it was Lance's turn to move forward and in doing so to scoop the boy up in his arms. "And if as you say I appear to be crotchety, then I apologise!"

"Then are you going to make it up with Rachel then? If you want to know what I think then I believe that you have upset her!"

"Now is that a fact?" Lance's arms tightened around the child. "To tell you the truth I was under the impression that your Rachel had quite different ideas. Not that it is anything for you to concern yourself about for grown ups very often have differences of opinion. But now sunshine I believe Rachel said it was bedtime for you, and for god measure I think that we will be capable of sorting our own problems out!" He made towards the door with the child still in his arms.

"Well I'll tell you something for nothing. I am not going to go to sleep if you two keep on arguing!"

"Then in that case I solemnly promise that we will have no more arguments!" Lance nodded in the child's direction as he started to escort his reluctant onlooker towards the stairs.

"I'll be up in a minute to tuck you up. Don't forget to clean your teeth now!" Rachel attempted to offer some words of consolation. At least she considered these to be better than criticism under the circumstances.

"Will you come after you have kissed and made up then?" Rachel heard Lance's throaty chuckle as the two disappeared and at the time she felt very glad that the elder of the two who disappeared could not see her face. Still once he had returned back to the room Lance picked up the script again as if this was the only thing he had on his mind and certainly had no intention of obliging Jake by showing any affection. Moreover she found that he was a hard taskmaster until she yielded to the alterations he wanted her to make and after that he left with a mere simple nod as he bid her good night. No doubt Jake would have been most disappointed this was all that had materialised and thus Rachel was left to ponder upon the true motivations that lay behind his action!

Once the alterations were in place Rachel found the production team were more than anxious to commence upon their part in the procedure, yet to Rachel, in spite of the aura exhibited by her work colleagues at what they termed as her success, something to her mind appeared to have been lost forever and she found that her initial interest in writing no longer enthused her. For his part, his job now apparently completed, Lance had yet again made one of his disappearing acts from off the scene. In truth Rachel did not know what she had done to deserve this change in his attitude especially if one stopped to consider how well they had worked together obtaining that illicit cargo. Yet even as she pondered on the matter one name stood out above all others and that was Michael's. It surely must have been this person who had acted to separate them. After all of his own admission Michael had been the person who had informed the Ministry about her story. Why was it then that once he appeared on the scene Lance had reverted back into behaving as if she was some mere casual acquaintance? She pondered even more upon the matter, forgetting for a time her own feelings concerning the sullen one but then at the time she had no way of being party to the questions that were currently being asked about Chad's untimely death!

In time the production now completed, the premiere of the low cost film created by this embryonic company was held at a local venue whilst all those concerned waited with baited breath for the reaction of the public to this creation that they had toiled over for so long. Their fears however were completely unfounded and remarks were indeed passed that the output was worthy at least to be entered in its class for the forthcoming Cannes Film Festival.

"After all!" Deemed one critic who appeared to be well versed in such procedures, "Nothing ventured nothing gained. You could be refused an entry, for a great deal depends upon the amount of material that is submitted in any given year, but on the other hand I for one feel that this epic deserves some sort of promotion!" There could be little doubt that upon these words her contemporaries were over the moon yet Rachel shared little of their enthusiasm for by this time she had allowed herself to become convinced that Lance would himself have been present for that premiere and in that she had been quite wrong. Thus developing a state of melancholia because she had neither seen nor heard from him, it was surprisingly enough Michael who was the one to finally seek her out.

"Surely you must have realised by this time Rachel that there are other things at stake beyond a film, which in all fairness Lance previously took the time to go over with you!"

"To my mind there are always other things at stake!" She answered him almost petulantly and had Mandy shaking her head disapprovingly at her current attitude. "There is one thing of which I am certain however and that is he always chooses to leave without offering any explanation!"

"Have you ever looked at it from Lance's point of view? Maybe the man doesn't want to worry you unduly rather than wanting to keep things from you just for the sake of doing so!"

"So by that I presume you know where he is?" Like a dog wrestling a bone Rachel refused to let go. If Michael knew and wasn't for telling her then he was no better than the sullen desperado that had been her first impression of him. In fact she didn't know what her sister saw in him, how could the Mandy she knew bear to spend time with this Job's comforter?

"Suppose I do?"

"Then why are you keeping it to yourself?"

"I know you were an asset to Lance out in Fuerteventura. In fact the man could not sing enough of your praises. But there is still an awful lot to our job that you don't fully comprehend Rachel otherwise you would not be asking such pertinent questions on matters of State. Still as there is little need for an element of secrecy to surround what he is doing at the moment, on this occasion only I will tell you that he has been asked to investigate Chad's death!"

"But I thought this man Chad was your friend, why isn't it you who has gone to investigate?"

For his part Michael had the manners to now cringe. "Don't you think I wouldn't have given my high teeth to have had the chance? In this case however Chad was working alongside of Lance when the matter occurred and therefore it is Lance who has been ordered to carry out this investigation and in the Service that is something we have to learn to accept, to do as we are instructed!"

Rachel fell silent as a sudden wave of remorse stole across her. For a moment her success in the realms of the theatre appeared to be as nothing when compared with the tasks that these two were compelled to undertake. "Then I suppose I ought to apologise for my behaviour?"

"Well that is a start, especially as I have heard on the grape vine that you are to expect a visitor shortly!"

"I am to have a visitor?" Immediately her mind fixed upon whom this could be. Her initial reaction that this after all could be Lance soon passed however. Not only that, but with Michael being the one to break the news to her a certain element of foreboding attached itself to her response.

"So I have heard. Therefore if you are willing to take my advice then try to be careful not to be too eager to wear your heart on your sleeve in his presence and please try and keep your tongue in check during this meeting and try not to lose your temper please!"

"Correct me if I am wrong but I get the distinct impression that you knew all about this well before the event?"

He shrugged but did not attempt to deny what she had suggested. It was just at that time that Mandy came back upon the scene and sensing that something was wrong appeared eager to join in the fray. "I suppose I am right in presuming that this is Curt we are talking about?" The voice of her sister adopted a decided chill as she spoke the name.

"Of course, the same!"

"And you are trying to say that you have invited him here to see my sister?"

"One doesn't invite Curt, Mandy. After all you should know that. Once the man makes up his mind upon an issue then he is determined to carry it out!"

"But nevertheless it was you who informed him?"

"I had no option in the matter!"

"There is always an option Michael and quite frankly I consider my sister has had enough to contend with other than entertaining your Superior in the force!" At least Rachel supposed that Michael had the guts to look sheepish but this certainly did not dispel the coldness Mandy now exhibited to the other. In the meantime Rachel was left to wait and wonder.

---------Not that she had long to wait however for their visitor arrived the very next day and was present when Rachel came home from her work. At the time the stranger was apparently commiserating with Mandy upon the loss of her husband but this did nothing to alter the fact that Mandy was still non too pleased at having to entertain this individual here on the premises. Indeed the girl had been tempted to cringe when she first spotted the pin striped trousers emerging from the interior of that car and to make matters worse the visitor had attempted to immediately commiserate with her over her loss.

"I don't need you to come here with your false tears for what is past if you don't mind Curt. Maybe the whole of the situation would have been avoided if I myself had not at one time been involved with you and your little games with people's lives!"

"But if you had never been involved in the Service then the chances are that you would never have met Michael. Don't tell me that the boy has not been of some consolation to you in recent weeks! I was actually led to believe that you were currently in the process of renewing your former friendship. After all one could say that you have something in common for Michael himself is currently recovering from the trauma of the death of his friend!"

"So I suppose that was his justification in dragging you here in order to investigate my sister?"

"I would have thought that you of all people knew that the safety of the state is our prime motivating force. That is a matter that you of all people should know that even if it was once levelled at you that you lapsed when you married!"

"Perhaps you have forgotten Curt but by that time I had already left the Service. Therefore I was under the impression that I was free to marry whom I pleased!"

"On the other hand however Lance Turner still happens to have an active role within the Service, or had that fact slipped your mind?"

"If you want my opinion then I really would apportion no blame to Rachel if she told you to go to hell for quite frankly I fail to see that it is any of your business what she chooses to do with her life and moreover as far as Lance is concerned, let's face it, that one hadn't even the manners to tell her he was leaving before he completely disappeared on her. Just how do you think that made her feel?" She broke off as she realised that Rachel had arrived and had probably overheard a large part of the conversation. Still introductions had to be made she supposed!

"Curt this is my sister Rachel whom you wished to speak to. Rachel please allow me to introduce someone who considers himself worthy to be judge and jury to all those who cross his track just because he is employed as Lance and Michael's Superior Officer!"

"Perhaps that is a little unfair Mandy!" Rachel glanced at the well-pressed pin striped suit and the highly polished shoes and decided that it probably was most fair. "Anyway as I have already been forewarned of your visit how can I help you?"

"It is the question of one or two matters I need to clear in my own mind Miss Aldred. Could I begin by asking you exactly what your relationship with the person you knew as Brad Stevens was?"

"While I cannot see that the matter has any possible significance to you, he was at one time my employer!"

"May I enquire in what field you were employed Miss Aldred?"

Rachel found she needed to steel her voice in order to perfect the correct tonality in her answer. What the devil had it got to do with this man whom Michael appeared to feign around over? To give good measure to these thoughts Mandy sniffed her displeasure in a laudable manner. "As a matter of fact I was employed as the man's secretary although in addition Brad did assist me in the publication of several of my novels as he appeared to have the right contacts in that profession. Still I am afraid that I fail to see why this appears relevant to you at this moment in time?" At least that ought to shut him up, she gloated to herself. Unfortunately however it did not, in fact it appeared to excite the man's curiosity even more.

"So was it this that first persuaded you to go to Fuerteventura?"

"No, as a matter of fact I went there initially on holiday. Most people are entitled to take a holiday just in case it has escaped your notice!"

The man questioning her eyed her in an almost clinical manner as if he was attempting to pry through the machinations of her brain cells before he made his next remark. "So I suppose that Brad Stevens had arranged to join you out there?"

"I would like to correct you on that assumption. He never arranged anything of the sort!"

"But I understood that you were at the airport presumably waiting for him on that particular day when the disaster happened?"

"I had received a message that he intended to come yes and therefore I went to the airport that day in order to meet him. There was nothing unusual in that for after all he was my employer!"

"What reason did he give you for coming out in the first place?"

Rachel turned away; this man was surely going too far in prying into her affairs. The whole business was a private matter and therefore could have no bearing on his department whatsoever.

"You appear to be finding some difficulty in answering the question Miss Aldred?"

Rachel sighed. "If you must know it was a private matter. Brad was coming out for a response to a question he had put to me!" What more was she compelled to tell these people? Already they were well on the way to baring and tarnishing her soul.

"I see!" She wondered if her questioner actually did see or whether he had finally realised that he had gone far enough. "I believe that is the place where you first met Lance Turner?"

"Yes, as a matter of fact it was!"

"Then don't you think it is rather strange Miss Aldred that you were expecting one man but instead found another in that same airport? A man who also happened to be a member of Her Majesty's Security Service as well? What was it that motivated you in these circumstances?"

"What circumstances are we talking about now? For your information however I was led to believe that Lance was a sort of pen pusher for some Ministry who was also in charge of real estate!"

A slight glimpse of a smile touched the other man's lips. In retrospect she supposed she could have marked this as some sort of success for the man in question seldom allowed his facial features the luxury of a smile "I suppose one could consider that we are all pen pushers in one way or another! Still I believe that you met Lance Turner again when you were on Tenerife?"

"She was there on holiday. She came with Doug and myself along with our son Jake and what was more she initially needed some persuading to come!" For her part Mandy had heard enough and could see no earthly reason why her sister was being put through this ordeal.

"Now is that correct? But then of course your husband Mrs Ogden was an old associate of Brad Stevens!"

"You really are taking matters too far Curt. I most certainly will have something to say to Michael about this. Where is he now by the way?" Mandy had suddenly realised that Michael had disappeared from off the scene, and in her eyes most conveniently at the time.

"He is currently preparing to work under my direction Mrs Ogden. It so happens that I have a task currently in mind for him!" Further conversation was however halted by a ring from the direction of the telephone. After picking up the receiver however Mandy made to pass it to Curt, her expression now being one of blackened fury. A few moments later their Inquisitor replaced the receiver and turned to face them. "If you haven't already guessed by his voice that was Lance, Mandy. He wishes to make it quite clear that after duly investigating the circumstances he is now convinced that Chad's untimely demise was a sheer accident. Apparently the man stepped out right in front of the car, this was according to an eye witness and the driver of the vehicle has now been apprehended!"

"You are saying that Lance was on the phone and yet he felt no inclination to speak to Rachel?"

"He seemed to be far more concerned in setting Michael's mind at rest. Perhaps Rachel you have not realised exactly what strictures you would be placing on yourself if you were to marry a serving member of the Service!"

"In the world I live in it is considered manners to wait until one is approached on such a matter and even if I was what makes you think I would ever consider tying myself to someone who appears to prefer a life of mystery?"

"Then maybe I was mistaken after all Miss Aldred. If that is correct then I must offer my sincere apologies!"

"I find that remark to be rather tongue in cheek coming from you. After all when have you ever apologised for anything before?" Mandy stood her ground. "But after considering all this to be a sheer waste of our time I must inform you that Rachel and I have now something to do that excludes all men, so perhaps you will show yourself out Curt and oh yes, make sure you take that snivelling lap dog of yours with you when you go will you? I fear that there is nothing left for him here now!"

Curt faced two determined women and took several moments before he came to the conclusion that probably the best thing he could do was to beat a hasty retreat. Rachel watched him leave still partially mesmerised with what had transpired.

"Sorry Mandy it appears that I am now guilty of ruining a forthcoming romance between Michael and yourself!"

"That is nonsense sister. I admit it was good to have Michael around for a while but the past can never be rekindled; you see I happened to love my husband even with his many faults that I recognised. One seldom has the chance to choose who one falls in love with and that is something that I believe you have already found out for yourself. Now after his latest trick in bringing Curt here in order to harass you, I don't particularly want to see Michael again. Maybe you were right after all when you described him as being surly on your first meeting, maybe that is something I should have realised for myself sooner. But Lance is a completely different case, you are in love with him aren't you?"

The question obviously floored her for a moment and when she responded it was in dismal tones. "Perhaps I thought I was at one time but apparently he had different ideas!"

"And how can you be so certain that these ideas were of his own choosing. After all you are well aware of the job he does and how he has to be beholden to other's orders. No Rachel, I consider that I know you well enough to believe that you still love him in spite of anything he has done or said!"

Rachel nodded rather soberly; not that she was under any impression that such an admission would make any difference to the final outcome.

"Perhaps I thought I was at one time but he apparently had different ideas!"

"And how can you be so sure that they were of his own choosing? I think that I know you well enough to know that you still love him in spite of everything he appears to have said and done in which case go for him girl and forget all about Curt Broad and the rest of his kind!"

"Perhaps that is easier said than done. How can I be sure that Lance feels the same about me?"

"I feel pretty positive that he does, but if you do want to know for sure then I think I have a plan!"

★ ★ ★ ★

Chapter Eleven

"You say that you have a plan?" Rachel eyed the speaker with something that could be said to resemble a tinge of suspicion. After all she knew Mandy from the past and the last thing she now required was the other person interfering in her life especially where matters of the heart were concerned.

"Yes, now forget Lance for a moment if you can bear the trauma!" Mandy knew what was presently percolating in her sister's mind only too well. After all she had watched her grow up and the younger sister had been able to keep few secrets away from her older sibling. "As you know the kids will be breaking up for Christmas very shortly and I have been pondering upon whether this year we should make an effort to get away for the festive period!" She waited a moment for the meaning of her words to sink in.

"But whatever for? You have always declared that you preferred to spend your Christmas' at home!"

"Well for starters things happen to have changed a little this year Rachel and maybe I myself feel it is time for me to flee the nest given the opportunity. Don't forget I have lost Doug this year and Christmas spent at home without having him here would be in the least traumatic. There is also something else. I have been offered a contract to go back teaching in the New Year so maybe it will enable me to get my ideas together!"

"You never mentioned applying for it?" She didn't want to sound accusing. It was just so unusual for Mandy to do anything like this without saying something about it.

"Didn't I? Sorry, it must have been an oversight on my part. But now that Jake is firmly installed in mainstream school it just seemed an ideal opportunity for me to affect a change in my own lifestyle!"

"Having said that I am now under no illusion that you also have somewhere in mind for this planned little jaunt?"

"As a matter of fact we have heard so much about that Island of yours that it is somewhere you have made me want to visit. Therefore as far as the destination is concerned you could say that you are the guilty party for having such a vivid descriptive power within you. And there is also another point in favour of that destination. I believed you mentioned the safe bathing there, that plus the added sunshine at this time of the year should do Jake a power of good!"

"Just a minute, before you went into this dichotomy of a Christmas break you mentioned Lance. Exactly how does he figure in your plans?"

"Lance? Oh I thought that I would drop him a Christmas card and inform him where we intend spending our Christmas this year!"

"And you imagine that he will be interested? Come off it Mandy, that man couldn't be less interested not now that he has completed his so called assignment!"

"Now don't be too sure. I myself believe he'll be slightly furious when he thinks of you out there without him!"

"So now you are even suggesting he might take it into his head to follow. Sorry Mandy, even if your idea sounds romantically enticing in practise it is something that will never materialise. Besides I thought that I had already made it quite clear that what existed if anything between Lance and myself is over and done with and quite frankly I couldn't care less now if I never see him again!"

"Then I suppose that only time will tell on that one. On the other hand you did say that you wanted to know how he felt about you!"

Rachel shrugged. "Perhaps I already have a good idea. Anyway there are still some intangibles in your idea Mandy even if you did act in good faith. I presume you are expecting me to come along too. I happen to have a job remember so how can I be expected to take leave at the drop of a hat?"

"You have forgotten sister. It is Christmas time and I presume even Whitakers' must condescend to allow their employees time off at this time of the year. And your other so called intangible?"

"How do you propose to get any kind of booking at this time of the year especially at such short notice?"

"I already have. I have already got our tickets to fly out on the 22nd of the month. Not, I repeat that I have mentioned anything to Jake yet because we have to live through the Nativity play first!"

"You have already got tickets? In that case where are we supposed to be staying once we get out there?"

"Why where else but a the hotel you have already described so brilliantly. After all there is now no danger at that place, not now that all your baddies have been dispersed and according to all the reports the place ought to be ideal for Jake. Besides after your description of the area I see no reason why you should be left to keep the merits of that hotel all to yourself."

"Let me get this straight. You have gone to all this trouble because you still believe Lance will be taken in by a certain message on one Christmas card?"

"Well I suppose that curiosity has been know to play tricks on the mind. At least I considered worth giving it a go!"

Rachel shook her head, still quite unconvinced by Mandy's aspirations. Even so she supposed that under the circumstances her sister required some consideration this year for after all this was her first Christmas without Doug and she supposed upon reflection there was also Jake to consider. There was no doubt in her mind that the boy would love it out on the Island especially around Caletta where there were few rocks to interfere with his bathing experience.

"I am still totally unconvinced with your argument I am afraid Mandy. But as you have set your heart on taking Jake away this year, which on the surface is something I can appreciate, then I suppose I ought to tag along that is if I want to spend Christmas with my family instead of on my own!"

Mandy nodded as she watched Rachel move away. Yet the bland expression she had worn in front of the other rapidly changed to one of contrivance as soon as the other girl disappeared and without further ado she moved towards the telephone!

"You are saying that in spite of all this you still have complete faith in the girl?" Curt Broad slammed his pen down on the table in his office after listening to Lance's deliberations and eyed his underling with something that could be said to denote complete displeasure.

"In all truth I must say that I have. Rachel may at one time have been misguided over Brad Stevens or whatever he liked to call himself but she is certainly not at present!"

"Then perhaps you can explain why I have received a phone call informing me that your Miss Aldred is presently making plans to fly out to Fuerteventura again?"

"As a matter of fact I am already aware of such intentions. You see I happened to have received a Christmas card from her sister stating that they are planning to spend Christmas on that Island because as Mandy explained she had a yen to see the Island for herself!"

"You say that you have received a Christmas card and you believe it was merely a seasonal greeting? Really you are slipping Turner!"

"What exactly are you getting at Curt? I know that you have not called me in here without some due reflection therefore might one take the liberty to enquire what you expect me to do about it? And saying that might I also add a rejoinder and enquire whether you consider you have already interfered enough in my private affairs?"

"I am afraid that in you current employ you are failing to be aware of the fact that there is little time for you to live a so called private life. Indeed in the past it has been noted that agents who took advantage of such outlets normally became a liability to the Service!"

"So I am right in presuming that is the reason why you found some excuse to separate Mandy and Michael yet again?"

"Of course. In truth I considered it to be a kindness on my part to be able to act now rather than when they became even more involved. But I am afraid that in your case Mr Turner you quite frankly cause me to worry!"

"Then perhaps I can rectify that situation and save you the trouble of worrying for much longer. How much notice do you require?"

"If that is the case then perhaps it would be wiser if I employed someone else to follow the happy holidaymakers to Fuerteventura. For in fact, in spite of your obvious confidence in Miss Aldred I still hold my own suspicions concerning the girl more especially now it has been reported that certain members from the Al Queda cell have recently been spotted on that Island as well!"

Lance gritted his teeth. "If that is the situation then I suppose I am duty bound to be on hand to finish what I initially started!"

"Under the circumstances perhaps we ought to offer you some assistance in this task then?"

"Thank you but no. In this matter I prefer to work on my own that is always providing you still trust me!"

"You have always had our complete trust Turner. Perhaps that is why in the past you have always been regarded as being the best in your field!"

"Whilst that might be gratifying to hear, please still bear in mind that I intend this to be my last assignment in the Service!"

"Supposing you leave, what else can you do? As far as I know you have had no training in any other field!"

"You can safely rest assured that I will be able to find something even if my only prospect is to convert my talents into that of being a security guard for some firm!"

"Then I expect you to give the same attention in this matter even if officially it is to be your last case. In this instance we will be watching your progress very carefully

Mr Turner therefore it might be just as well if you refuse to let any emotions colour you judgement!"

"Have I ever?"

"One presumes that there could always be a first time, so please prove us to be wrong in these assumptions. But to get back to cases I understand that our friends have secured a flight for the 22nd of this month. Therefore I am expecting you to be in position by that time!" The man nodded with no glimmer of emotion showing on his face as he signalled that the interview was now over and Lance was left to ponder in his thoughts as to whether Rachel and her sister had genuinely gone out to Fuerteventura to celebrate their Christmas or whether there was after all some underlying meaning to their visit as the department had suggested there might be.

The weather forecast in the U.K. had promised the folk back home a white Christmas. Now sitting on the promenade at Caletta, Rachel could not help but feel mesmerised by the sudden variation in temperature. Of course the locals had labelled the new day as being a cold morning and that only the English would be foolish enough to appear in shorts and tee shirts and they were after all well known for being slightly eccentric. But the sharp contrast in the temperature between here and home had met them at the airport when they had disembarked from the plane. Yet even if the locals deemed the English to be quite eccentric in the gear they chose to march around in at this time of the year, they themselves obviously did not see anything wrong with the Victorian tradition of Christmas decoration; for every year more and more of their dwellings were now decked out in Christmas finery with the occasional Father

Christmas attempting to do acrobatics in the most unusual places.

For a moment Rachel thought about the girls from the office where she worked who would by this time be well established in their traditional Christmas fayre and she questioned herself as to whether she was actually missing out on this. The answer when it came was a most definite no especially when it was possible for one to be able to relax in the sunshine at this festive time of the year.

She idly watched as a figure approached her from the direction of El Castillo. The man did not appear to be an Islander nor a European for that matter although she admitted that nowadays it was often difficult to be able to differentiate that difference. Not that any of this mattered for the person concerned meant nothing at all to her and therefore she closed her eyes wondering how Mandy was coping with the unpacking that she had been determined to do.

Well she had after all volunteered to help but her sister would have none of it. Perhaps Rachel suspected she was even glad to get rid of her and so after promising to keep an eye on Jake who couldn't wait to test the water, they had come here. Not that there weren't enough pools around the hotel but they had not been good enough for the youngster not when the real thing was so close and she supposed that the water in the bay was shallow enough for the boy to be able to test his prowess in jumping the waves in comparative safety. Funny really but when she had come here her eyes had skimmed the bay for sight of a surf board rider, but at this time of the day at least there were none in sight.

Opening her eyes she suddenly noticed that the stranger had dropped something as he had passed her by and hoping to attract him before he had gone too far Rachel stood and after scooping up what amounted to a screwed up slip of paper, she shouted after the retreating figure in an attempt to attract his attention.

Upon hearing her voice the stranger half paused and then turned towards her. For a moment Rachel thought he was about to come back to see what she was holding, until quite suddenly he paused and then as if sensing the presence of a third person he turned and moved away quite quickly leaving Rachel standing holding and waving the object she had rescued a few minutes earlier.

"So that is how he manages to contact you is it?" The voice of the third person seemed to be familiar and yet the tonality sounded quite ugly.

"Contact me? Lance what are you doing here?" The shock at seeing him caused her voice to explode.

"I don't expect you thought you would see me. Yet I have a question. Rachel have you currently any idea what you are now playing with?" His hand reached out to grasp the object she was still holding onto. His grasp was firm and determined and there was obviously no way in which he could have been deterred.

"Perhaps you would care to explain!" She set him with a glint in her eyes that promised no leniency towards his action.

"I believe you have just been contacted!" The accusation in his voice was there again as he nodded towards the piece of paper.

"You say I have been contacted? If it is not a silly question would you mind explaining by whom?"

Now he appeared almost single minded in his efforts to unwrap the folds in the paper, almost as if he wanted to find something and thrust the contents back into her face. It was only once the paper was finally straightened out that he paused with a look of bewilderment on his face as he finally deciphered the contents of that paper.

"It's a shopping list!" The expression he held finally gave way to one of incredulity as he gave vent to his feelings.

"I had no idea what it was, the man simply dropped it as he passed by me and I thought it could have been something important. Maybe one can consider that it was if he had been charged by his family to collect certain items before he returned home!"

"But it was all screwed up!" His face still echoed the tell tale signs of total disbelief.

"Perhaps he had already done all the shopping!" Now she was beginning to lose patience. "But you have not yet told me why you should take an interest in other people's litter?"

"Why was he carrying parcels or something that I missed? Oh maybe I should apologise but I was led to believe ----!"

"I suppose an apology could be considered to be a start. On the other hand exactly what were you given to believe and if I may be so bold as to add, by whom?"

At least she supposed she could take some comfort in the fact that he now had the manners to allow a look of contrition to pass across his face. "Do I really have to explain?" The groan that issued forth from his lips appeared to be almost agonising.

"Perhaps it would be an idea if you did just that!" She surprised herself at the firmness within the timbre of her voice.

"I was informed that it was suspected that certain members from the Al Queda cell currently stationed in

Morocco were present on the Island and one is forced to admit that considering the short distance involved that it was a feasible statement!"

"Perhaps in that case it is the Authorities you should have contacted instead of trying to molest innocent holiday makers in your quest to establish law and order!" She turned away determined that he would not see the tears that were currently stinging her eyes.

"Rachel I guess I am sorry!" His arms were on her shoulders steadying her less she was determined to move away.

"You are sorry, for what? Is it for putting your job first?" Somehow she still found the strength to sound cutting.

"What would you say if I told you I intend to leave the Service at the first opportunity and certainly in the near future?"

"I would ask what had promoted this sudden change of heart on your part!"

"Then maybe you ought to take a good look at yourself in the mirror-------!"

"I thought you were supposed to be watching me Rachel!" A young voice determined not to be ignored, succeeded in breaking the tension that now surrounded them. "Hi Lance, have you come to spend Christmas with us as well?"

"Well I haven't actually been asked yet!" Lance much to Rachel's annoyance, turned his attention onto the youngster.

"Well if you are waiting to be invited then I am asking you!" The child thrust his hand into Lance's own. "By the way Rachel told me that you were pretty good on a surf board Lance. Will you teach me please?"

"Well if your mother agrees I would be more than pleased to do just that!" The declaration at least to Rachel's ears, was one of firm intent but Jake who had already thrust his hand into that of Lance's was now urging him back towards the hotel. Rachel was left to follow now feeling that she was but a mere appendix to the situation.

Christmas Eve dawned with the promise of what portended to be another beautiful day and the girl was left to watch as the two males in her life attempted to exact their skills with the surfboards. In truth she had to admit that Jake appeared to be an avid learner in this new technique, no doubt storing up the memory of this new experience so that he could relate it to his agog friends once he was back in the classroom. Mandy herself came out to watch the proceedings resembling one who was now showing satisfied plumage in viewing her offspring. Indeed it was only Rachel who felt she was cut adrift for she had still not establish the context of Lance's final expression to her when he had told her to go and take a look in the mirror.

Not however that she had been granted very much opportunity to pursue the matter further for Mandy, upon seeing Lance, had seized the opportunity acting indeed as if she had almost expected to see him there!

So engrossed however were the others in their chosen pursuits that no one else apart from Rachel noticed the man from yesterday pass them by along the promenade yet again. This time however in Rachel's eyes the character appeared to be decidedly furtive. In all truth she would have called out to the others if they had been close enough to catch the tenet of her voice. Perhaps it was because of this or because they were all so seemingly occupied at the time that Rachel decided to take matters into her own hands and follow the character at a distance.

There were plenty of folk out enjoying the winter sunshine by the Castillo but the character she was trailing passed them by making instead towards the small harbour that had nestled there from time immemorial. It being so close to Christmas now most of the craft had already been secured and left behind for their owners to enjoy the festive season, although it appeared that one craft had not been even though the vessel appeared to be currently deserted. The man she was following seemed now to hesitate as the local bus that trundled around the resort approached from around the corner. This was the stop where most of the passengers alighted whilst others waited to climb on board and the vehicle was generally popular with the visitors especially with those who found some difficulty in walking.

One person who alighted however obviously found little difficulty in walking and he obviously had pre-conceived ideas as to what he intended to do. Rachel drew a sharp breath as she watched furtively as this character moved over in the direction of the one she had followed. Together the two of them then made towards the boat and now she wondered whether she dared follow or whether indeed the ideas currently in her mind were but a figment of her imagination. Being Rachel however she was still gripped with a stubbornness of will that even her own father had once said would be her undoing.

Cautiously she began to edge forward anxious to hear their conversation. In turn the men now had their backs towards her so she believed she would not be noticed. Besides by this time her mind was clearly fantasying. Was it possible that these people were carrying some cargo on that boat that was illegal? The devil currently inside of her drove her on to take a better look.

Maybe indeed she would have climbed aboard onto that craft if she had not suddenly heard those whistles and a moment later she found herself gripped by a pair of strong arms.

"What the hell do you think you are trying to do now?" The voice was familiar in its exasperation.

"I just wanted to find out ----!" She broke off in mid flow as she saw the police already boarding the vessel.

"I believe you told me I ought to inform the Authorities if I had any suspicions remember? Well I took your advice and did exactly that and now what do I find? You appear to be determined to get yourself arrested as well!"

"But you were on the beach with Jake. Where is he now?" Rachel looked around her almost wildly half expecting to see the boy left in some sort of difficulty because Lance had apparently deserted him.

"I was on the beach yes when I noticed you had decided to play a game of Sherlock Holmes along the promenade. You needn't worry about Jake because he is currently safe with Mandy since you succeeded in breaking up our man thing. But then Jake is the least of my worries right now. Did it never occur to you that these men could have been dangerous?"

He was still hold of her when one of the Guardia moved across in their direction. "Senorita Aldred I am led to believe?" His English was good much better than her Spanish Rachel bemoaned. Nevertheless she nodded her head in acknowledgement. "I must ask you if you will accompany me back to our headquarters. There are several items that we would like to clear with you!"

"This is ridiculous, the girl knows nothing!" Now it was Lance's turn to protest.

"I'm afraid we must tend to disagree with you on that point Senor. You see we have it on very good authority that the girl perhaps knows far more about the current situation than what she would care to admit!"

"With that I suppose you are inferring that Curt Broad has been blowing off wind in your direction?"

"And should that be the case Senor perhaps you would specify how you yourself fit into the equation?"

"For want of a better word I suppose you could term him as being my boss. At least he is at this moment in time!"

"The Senor did lead us to believe that you yourself was emotionally involved in the matter!"

"He did? Now how like him that appears to be. But then Curt Broad can never be described as being a foot soldier!"

"Perhaps I consider we are wasting time now Senor. Therefore Senorita if you would step to the car maybe we can conclude our investigations before Christmas!"

"In that case I will be coming too. You needn't look like that Senor, after all it was I who summoned the police to the scene in the first instance!"

"But what about Jake?" She still had her nephew in mind.

"I've already told you he is back with Mandy. No doubt she will wonder what has become of us but all the same ------!"

"Perhaps then it would be better if you returned to the hotel Senor and attended to your friends. At least you can set the Senora's mind right in that I do not think we will be keeping the Senorita for too long."

"Perhaps under the circumstances I do not feel obliged to leave my fiancé in such circumstances!"

"Your fiancé? That I am not!" Rachel had almost forgotten the arm of the law as she turned to glare at him.

"Not I admit until midnight tonight!" A wry smile had crossed his lips the sort extracted from a person who did not feel very much like smiling in the present circumstances.

Once at the police station she was escorted to a room and Lance followed standing at the back of the place almost as if he was now in judgement of the whole proceedings. At least she supposed she had the satisfaction of seeing the two suspects also escorted inside and she was grateful when they were taken to another part of the building.

Her interrogator made himself comfortable on a chair at the other side of a large table and Rachel watched as he made some effort to clear his throat and wondered if this was intended to give him inspiration for the task ahead. To her mind he would have to be mighty clever for as far as she was concerned as she considered that she had nothing to answer for and then of course she remembered what Lance had said about Curt Broad and it caused her to shiver a little.

"And now Senorita, perhaps you would tell us exactly why you decided to follow this character in the first place. Indeed what do you consider first alerted your suspicion on the matter?"

Rachel watched as the stenographer handled his pen. Well she supposed her tale would make interesting reading. "Because he actually dropped a shopping list!" Lance groaned possibly gauging the other man's reaction.

"Did you say a shopping list Senorita?"

"Yes. That was why, bearing in mind recent events on the world news channel I considered that perhaps one or two items on the list could be regarded as being suspicious!"

Lance visibly groaned again, visualising this to be her imagination at work yet again. "If that was the case, why did you not inform Senor Turner of your suspicions?"

"Because I was afraid that he might possibly jump to the wrong conclusion concerning my own involvement!"

"Then Senor Turner did hold some suspicions concerning your actions?"

"I thought so at the time but obviously I was later proved wrong. It appears it was his boss who was suspicious of my motives, not Lance, although I suppose one can be forgiven for believing he could have shown a little more backbone at the time!" Perhaps it was as well that there were others present in that office, at least it did her good to give vent to her feelings even if it did make the other man feel uncomfortable. Still the policeman was not obviously satisfied.

"I have the list here Senorita. Would you be good enough to point out the items on the list that you considered to be suspicious?"

She had always wondered why she had taken Chemistry whilst she had been at school. It wasn't even that she had been particularly good at it. But certain things she did remember and now it appeared she had a use for this knowledge. "These two items when mixed together in the right quantity provides enough power to cause an explosion especially if ignited in a small space!"

The police officer scratched his head thoughtfully. "But on the other hand I suppose one could concede Senorita that they could be used for other purposes; domestic cleansing for example?" Was it her imagination or did she now hear a snort coming from behind her. Still the interview was to be abruptly halted with the advent of two further policemen, those whom she had seen escorted the two suspects earlier on. They immediately proceeded to her interrogator's chair and imbibed in a lengthy discussion. At last they apparently finished their rhetoric and stood back their arms folded as if in some triumphant gesture. The man in front of her cleared his throat before proceeding and she suddenly realised that his voice had changed.

"It appears that the chemicals you mentioned were indeed intended for a domestic pursuit. Maybe you are unfamiliar with our customs Senorita but in Spain we enjoy to celebrate the New Year during which time it is customary for displays of fireworks to celebrate the passage of time. Furthermore the two people whom you suspected Senorita were guilty of no more erroneous crime than that of collecting the necessary ingredients for a display that was intended as a surprise for their next of kin. As we have no further reason to detain them they have therefore been released to carry on with their supposed plan of action. Nevertheless despite the fact that you appear to have been misguided on this issue, your actions in the circumstances were none the less commendable. The only thing I beg of you is that in the future would you please consider leaving such investigations to those who are better equipped to deal with such matters for although we realised that the cell of Al Queda poses a threat to these Islands, we would much prefer to handle such matters ourselves. Therefore in future if you do happen to notice anything that you consider could be suspicious, perhaps you would condescend to inform us rather than to proceed in an attempt to take matters into your own hands!"

She left the department feeling she had been duly chastised. The fact that Lance said nothing at all about the incident only served to rile her even further.

"Well come on try and look a little more light hearted, after all it is Christmas Eve in case you have forgotten, a time when families ought to be together in a more congenial frame of mind!" He spoke at last as they were in the process of entering the hotel and Rachel still feeling in a less than congenial manner to him turned round.

"I would have expected that you would have found something better to do obeying your commander's instructions Mr Turner than to worry over such trivialities as Christmas?"

"I thought that I had already explained. I have passed on all my relevant information to the Authorities here, a matter that you yourself prescribed some time ago. And, after doing this, as I am no longer employed by the Service I think that puts me in a position to enjoy my Christmas. Did I mention that Mandy has invited me to join you tonight?"

Rachel felt her fists clench but as her sister timed her appearance to coincide in a quite succinct manner the occasion passed. "Lance, Rachel, I am so glad that you are both at liberty to join us tonight and I am sure that Jake feels the same. He appears to be very smitten with the new challenge you have given him Lance with the surfboard, he can talk of little else. Really it is most fortuitous that you were able to get away and come to join us here!" Rachel cast her sister a most suspicious look. "Perhaps you had better go and change Rachel and then you can tell us what all that was to do with the police earlier on!"

"Now you can hardly blame your sister for being vigilant Mandy. One could consider that her actions today were admirable even if some might consider them to be foolhardy!"

"I'll go and change!" By this time Rachel had heard quite enough. How could that man appear to be so condescending towards her? She moved away towards her room in a stalking rather than a walking mode, leaving Mandy to eye Lance in some expectation.

"Well have you asked her yet?"

"Asked her what?"

"Oh come off it Lance, I'm beginning to wonder which of the two of you is the more perverse. You haven't given in your notice and followed us out here for nothing I know that!"

"Then perhaps you will get an answer to your question when I am good and ready Mandy!" It was the other girl's turn to look abashed as she watched as he turned to make his own way towards his quarters. Indeed the only comfort for her speech came from the lips of one small child who pushed his hand into hers.

"Don't worry Mum, I'm sure they will sort it out for themselves. Anyway I'll tell you something for nothing. I have seen the ring!"

"You have seen what ring?"

"The ring that Lance once promised to buy for Rachel. I saw him looking at it in that box this morning!"

"Then perhaps we should give them lea way and keep well out of it ourselves!" The voice of experience now spoke with conviction.

"Did you play hard to get too when Dad bought you a ring?"

"I've forgotten, that was all a long time ago!" At least the boy saw his mother blush a little and concluded that he must be right. Still as far as he was concerned it seemed to be a very silly game that grown ups played.

The boy's eyes never shifted off the other two that evening. Perhaps he willed with all his might that Lance would ask his Aunt to dance. He even set the pair of them in his wide blue eyes, and maybe, just maybe he succeeded in having some influence. It had now got rather warm in the dining room and he eyed with satisfaction the point when the two of them slipped out through the open French windows. So this was it, pity he couldn't get in closer to the action but by that time his mother was practically forcing him to stay at the table.

Outside on the patio Rachel felt Lance's sweet breath touch the nape of her neck as his hands searched to find the finger he desired. "My Christmas present as promised!" He breathed the words as the ring was slipped onto her finger. "You see I have reached the conclusion that the only way I can keep my eye on you and prevent you from diverting into further mischief is to marry you!"

Rachel gazed down at the diamond now twinkling back at her from that finger. "I did say I would only marry for love!" She breathed although a smile was now tingeing her lips as she spoke.

"That as well, but then I thought that you already knew. You see I guess I fell in love with you the very first time I saw you here at the airport and now I cannot imagine life without you even if at times you can be infuriating! Do you think you could possibly manage to be ready for an Easter Wedding? Will that allow enough time for all the feminine things that appear to come before such occasions? You see I have heard that there are some opportunities coming up in the National Park once the season starts in that part of the world and that wouldn't be a bad place for you to be able to develop your creative powers!"

She made to reply but no words were actually issued from her lips, instead the nod of agreement she spontaneously gave resulted in these being firmly crushed by the pair of lips that belonged to the man with that floppy brown hair, who didn't resemble a surfboarder in the tuxedo he was currently wearing but could easily have been mistaken for a member of Her Majesty's Secret Service.

★ ★ ★ ★

I KNOW

Vocal Duet

COUNTRY SING A LONG
Tempo: 80

Words and Music by Jim Steele
Contact No.01253 591905

19 20 21
I'm a WO- MAN who wants a Part- ner to LOVE- - A MAN I Can TRUST
G F
22 23 24
with my HEART! KNOW what I want! I'll tell you what I want!
C F Bb
25 26 27
I've lots to give, my Treas- ures to im- part to a love sinc- ere.
C F
28 29 30
I'm read- y to start! That's what I want. That's what I want.
31 32
That's what I want. THAT'S WHAT I WANT!

Other Novels By Kathleen Steele

MARINA BAIXA
Romance and Intrigue leads from the security of the Lake District to uncertainty in Spain!

ARMS OF GOLD
Following September 11th, what connection does the Lake at Windermere have with the Mediterranean around Majorca?

RADIANT VIBES
Pollution in the Irish Sea leads to strange findings and unusual relationships!

OASIS IN TIME
The location of those illusive weapons of mass destruction provides surprises!

PUT AND TAKE
Casinos on the Fylde Coast? Would you like to take a chance?

THE UPPER CUT
Scurrilous behaviour on those Upper Reaches serves to create ripples that stir those once still waters!

THE PINK ROSE
The Border Folk's response to the proposed Regional

Assemblies brings mayhem!

TWO FACED
Buying a computer should require a Government Health Warning!

ROUND AND ROUND
Wind and Tide can make uneasy bedfellows in the struggle to find a new Power Source!

NEXT STOP PARADISE
Love and intrigue are stimulated on life's merry-go-round!

CHECK OUT
The development of the provincial Airport, heralds the development in human relationships

HIDE AND SEEK
Hidden treasures require attention to detail, or else----!

LOST AND FOUND
Where there's a will, there's a way!

FOOTLOOSE
When a positive charge meets a positive charge, then ------!

IN THE SHADOW OF THE STORM
Do the fish always behave like that or is this the calm before the storm?

DISTRACTION
A hidden cell in the Lake District leads to a tempest of

ferocity which contrasts sharply with the peace and tranquillity that place is noted for!

A LIGHTER SHADE OF PINK
A sequel as requested to THE PINK ROSE. Meet the various characters again as this time our friends attempt to extend their franchise into Cumbria!

THE HEART'S REFRAIN
The mists around those magical Islands reflect the mist that obscures Anton's vision.

THE TURN OF THE WHEEL
Romance and fortune can be linked!

VENGEFUL RETURN
Two men and yet there can only ever be one boat! A sequel to MARINA BAIXA and NEXTSTOP PARADISE

NOT HERE
What is the connection between that house fire and those windmills out at sea?

THE RUN OF THE RABBIT
Could the government really be conspiring to move that Nuclear Power Plant into the midst of the Langdale Valley?

STAR OF THE DAWN
Can the star of early morning point the way to life's fulfilment?

SKETCH ME LOVE
The shrouding mist of those tranquil Islands serves to

disguise a more sinister scheme to involve them in man's game!

SPLIT WIDE OPEN
Mischievous Pranks or mysterious happenings disturb the peace in the hamlet of FellBeck!

POWERFUL CIRCLES
What is the connection between those ancient customs and the future?

BISPHAM BROOK
Could this be the case where such water comes to create mayhem or is there something more sinister behind the apparently innocent flow?

CRAB ISLAND
The Atlantic Isles offer peace, tranquillity and dramatic scenery to the innocent holidaymaker yet one cannot but speculate that there is something more!

SHAP
The fells of North West England may provide a refuge but other things also transpire in a community that proves that they are not quite so isolated!

INNER TURMOIL
Recovering from a trauma in her life Krisha is soon to find that the past often has a habit of catching up on one!

CRISP LIES THE TRACK
Will the ashes of the past support the love of today?

THE VIPER'S BITE
Beware of reptiles with warm blood in their veins!

SOFTLY THE NIGHT
Rags to riches ------perhaps?

VEIL OF SECRETS
Can love survive the tide of deception?

WEB OF TORMENT
When the storm infiltrates, can peace survive?

If you have difficulty in obtaining any of the above copies contact 01253 591905